WHERE ALL THE LADDERS START

The Last P.I. Series

Book Three

Richard Bowker

Cover by Jim McManus

Book design by eBook Prep www.ebookprep.com

First Edition, January 2015
ISBN: 978-1-61417-710-4

ePublishing Works!
www.epublishingworks.com

DEDICATION

For John and Pam

"Oh, I think I'm turning into a god!"
—Emperor Vespasian, on his deathbed

CHAPTER 1

I got off my bike and stared at the guy in the brown robe. The guy in the brown robe stared at me. He was sitting at the front of a cart piled high with apples, pumpkins, squash, and other fall produce; half a dozen dead turkeys hung from hooks at the back of the cart. He was big and broad and scary, with small black eyes, long stringy hair, and a scraggly beard that was interrupted by a deep scar on his left cheek.

"Hiya," I said, trying to break the ice.

He stared at me for a second, and then his eyes moved to the horse, who ignored him.

"Looking for me?" I asked. "Walter Sands? Got a bit of a late start today. Sorry if I kept you waiting."

The guy didn't respond. I hadn't really expected him to be looking for me. But Lower Washington Street was an odd place to park a cart filled with food.

"The Food Market is a few blocks over," I tried.

"They'll love your stuff."

Nothing.

"Well, have a nice day."

He didn't look like he was interested in nice days. Fine. The world is filled with strange people, and he was just one more of them. I walked around the cart and entered the building that housed my spacious, well-appointed office.

Okay, those adjectives aren't entirely accurate, but the place fits my needs, which mainly consist of a stove to keep me warm and shelves to hold the books I read to pass the time while I wait for clients to show up. Also, a desk and a couple of chairs in case a client actually does show up. Not that this had been happening much lately. Or, well, ever.

I carried my bike inside and walked upstairs.

From the hallway, I noticed that the door to my office was open. I always close the door when I leave at night. Of course, the door doesn't lock, but that doesn't really matter. Nothing worth stealing in my office.

I took out my gun. I wasn't especially worried, but it pays to be careful. "Please don't do anything stupid," I announced, and then I went inside.

And there, sitting by my desk, was the most beautiful woman in the world. She was wearing a powder-blue robe, and she was staring at me.

"Mr. Sands," she said calmly, ignoring the gun. "Do you remember me?"

It was impossible to forget her. "Of course," I said. "Sister Marva. How are you? And please, call me Walter." We had met during one of the many disastrous episodes in my previous case. She was a disciple in the Church of the New Beginning up in Concord. Long black hair, creamy white skin, deep blue eyes. I found it hard to break my gaze away from those eyes.

I sat down behind my desk, and that's when I noticed that she was pregnant. Well, that was interesting. Beautiful pregnant woman shows up in the private eye's office, needing his help. That's the way it's supposed to happen.

"So, um, what can I do for you, Sister? The last time we met—"

"You almost killed Brother Flynn," she reminded me.

"Yes. I'm very sorry about that." Flynn Dobler was the leader of Sister Marva's Church. A very smart, charismatic fellow. I snuck into the Church in the middle of the night and pointed a gun at him while he lay in bed. I remembered Marva coming in and leaping on top of him, desperate to protect her master from the intruder. All because of a really stupid theory I'd come up with about a kidnapping I was investigating. This had not been my finest moment as a private eye.

"It's all right," she said with a sympathetic smile. "Everyone makes mistakes. But now we need your help."

"We? The Church?"

She nodded.

"Why?"

"Brother Flynn has disappeared," she said, and the smile faded, and her beautiful blue eyes filled with tears.

"Disappeared?" I repeated. "How? When?"

"A week ago. He was there one night in his room, and then—in the morning—he was gone." The tears started falling down her cheeks.

Again, this was the way it happened in the novels I'd read. And now it was happening to me. But this didn't feel like a novel—this was a real human being, shedding real tears. I wanted to comfort her, but I also needed to do my job.

"I'm sorry to hear that," I said. "Was there a note? Were there witnesses?"

She shook her head. She wiped her cheeks with the sleeve of her robe. I wished I had a handkerchief to offer her. In my novels, the private eye always had a handkerchief.

"You've checked around the Church's farm, I suppose? There are plenty of wild animals up there, I'm sure. Wolves. Wildcats. Feral dogs. Probably some crazies, too."

"Yes, of course. We've looked everywhere."

"Well, um, any theories? Do you suspect foul play?"

Sister Marva lowered her eyes. "Brother Joseph does," she murmured.

"Who's he?"

"He's the disciple who, who runs things. Brother Flynn's second-in-command, I guess you'd say."

"Who does he suspect?"

"You should ask Brother Joseph, I think. He asked me to come here and talk to you. Because I go to the Food Market every day, with Brother

Reggie. He'd like you to come up to Concord and investigate."

Brother Reggie was presumably the giant in the cart. "You said Brother Joseph suspects foul play," I said. "What do *you* suspect, Sister Marva?"

She blushed. "I think that perhaps God took him from us."

I struggled to figure out what she meant. "You mean, like, he died of natural causes?"

She shook her head. "I mean—God brought him up to heaven. While he was still alive. Because He loved Brother Flynn so much."

"Why do you think that?"

"Because Sister Lucy saw it happen."

"Sister Lucy saw God take Brother Flynn up to heaven," I said, making sure I had this straight.

"Yes. You should talk to her too, I think."

"I think you're right." Maybe a more experienced private eye would have decided right there that this case wasn't going to be worth the trouble. But I'm not very experienced. And, frankly, I had nothing better to do. I decided to change the subject. "By the way, congratulations on your pregnancy, Sister Marva."

She smiled and inclined her head. "It's a blessing." Her smile made you happy to be alive.

"Do you mind my asking: is Brother Flynn the father?"

Her face clouded and she looked down at her belly. "I don't think—I don't think that has anything to do with Brother Flynn's disappearance, Walter," she replied. And then she fell silent.

OK, one more mystery. I considered. My friend and occasional employer Bobby Gallagher had a van, but it was out of commission while his driver/mechanic Mickey tried to scrounge or repair or manufacture a gasket or a flange or a defibrillator or some-such item; I don't know much about vans. "I'll take the case," I said. "But if you want me to go up there today, I'm afraid I don't have—"

"You can ride with us in our cart," Marva suggested. "We return to the Church after we finish selling our food. We should be at the Market now, actually. I'm sure Brother Reggie is tired of waiting."

I considered some more. "That means I'd have to stay the night at the Church," I pointed out. "I need to be back in Boston tomorrow."

"We come to the Food Market every day. You can come back with us in the morning."

That was that, then. I had a case. "All right," I said. "I get two new dollars a day. Ten dollars in advance."

Sister Marva gave me another smile. She looked relieved and grateful. "That's wonderful. But would you prefer to be paid in food instead?"

That wasn't a bad idea. Inflation was getting to be a problem. Who knew what the Church's money would buy when I got around to spending it? "Food would be fine," I replied.

We went back down to the street, where Brother Reggie did not in fact seem to be tired of waiting. It wasn't clear that he had even moved since the last time I set eyes on him. But his face lit up when he saw Sister Marva, like a dog recognizing his master. Marva and I agreed to meet at the Food Market later. I filled a bag with produce from the cart and grabbed one of the turkeys. Looked like ten dollars' worth to me, and Marva didn't haggle. Then Brother Reggie helped her up onto the cart, and they headed off.

I watched them go. The Church of the New Beginning. *Leave the past behind*, it preached. Start fresh—no technology, no government, none of the baggage that still weighed so many of us down. Look at where all that stuff had led us—to the War, and the violence and chaos and despair that followed in its wake. Reasonable enough, I supposed.

But now, strangely, the Church had a missing-person case on its hands, and it had decided to call on that useless relic of the past, a private eye. Well, I had already seen some strange things in my brief career; no reason for this case to be any different.

I brought my bike out of the building and arranged the sack of food over the handlebars; I held onto the turkey. Then I pedaled home to the townhouse in Louisburg Square where I lived with Gwen, the most wonderful woman in this godforsaken world, and Stretch, the most wonderful dwarf in the world. Both of them were at work—Gwen at the Boston *Globe* and Stretch in the governor's office. I put the turkey in the icebox and the produce on the kitchen table, and I wrote them a brief note:

*Off on a case! Won't be back today, but I
will be back tomorrow. Enjoy the food.*
—*Walter*

There, that would intrigue them. I left the note
beside the produce, and I headed off to the Food
Market, munching one of Marva's apples.

CHAPTER 2

In good weather, the Food Market is held in a large, abandoned stretch of cracked and rutted asphalt near a large, mostly abandoned highway. Somebody told me the place used to be where the city towed cars that had been parked illegally on downtown streets. This is the kind of detail about the old, pre-War world that seems so bizarre you think someone must have made it up simply to confuse people like me who hadn't experienced that world. But of course there are lots of people still alive who did experience that world, and one of the things you quickly learn is not to get them started talking about the old days, dredging up their memories of tow trucks and parking tickets and whatever else they've got buried in the deep recesses of their brains. Before long they'll probably be weeping, and you might be, too.

Along with the Salvage Market, the Food Market is one of the centers of life in Boston. There are small food shops closer in to the downtown area that cater to people with more money and less time. But most of us visit the Food Market at least a couple of times a week, strolling through the stalls and carts of the farmers and the butchers and the fishermen, bartering and buying and sometimes just smelling the aroma of the fruit and the vegetables and the meat and everything else for sale there.

It's a nice place to be, but there's been a bit of an edge to the place lately, a hint of anxiety as the weather gets colder and the food gets a little scarcer and a little more expensive. It wasn't just the weather that was causing the anxiety. The political situation had become much more confusing since the defeat of the referendum that would have made New England formally part of the United States under the leadership of the Federal government in Atlanta. For better or worse, I had been part of the events that ended up disgracing the U.S. president on the eve of the vote, with predictable results. After the referendum failed, the Feds had removed their troops from New England, set up stricter border checkpoints, tightened their trade and immigration policies, and generally made it clear that New England was on its own.

Many New Englanders like the idea of being on their own, no longer attached to a government that was descended from the one that had gotten us into this mess in the first place. But there are plenty of disadvantages. For example, no emergency aid—of food or fuel or medicine. And, perhaps more important, no Federal troops to help keep order. Oh, Boston has a police department, and New England has a tiny military force. But it doesn't have sufficient tax revenue to raise an army that could really protect its citizens.

And you could see the results at the Food Market. There were a few police on hand, but not enough of them to handle a significant disturbance. So everyone at the market was armed—with guns if they could afford them, with fierce-looking knives if they couldn't. Nothing bad was happening when I arrived there—usually nothing bad did happen—but the display of weaponry didn't enhance the shopping experience.

"How's it going, Walter?" one of the cops standing by the entrance said to me.

"Hey, Pete," I responded. "It's going fine." Pete Callahan and I had been in a youth camp together once upon a time, and that's not a bond that breaks easily. He was a little older than me—maybe 25—and still painfully thin; he had never completely recovered from his post-War childhood. "How's Mary Beth?" I asked him.

"She's pregnant—did you know that?"

"No. That's terrific. How's she doing?"

Pete looked gloomy. "Well, not that great. She had to quit her job, and the medicine she's supposed to take is expensive. But staying at home and resting seems to help."

"I'm sorry she's having problems. Give her my love."

"I will."

"Do you know where the cart from the Church of the New Beginning is?" I asked.

"Why do you want to buy their stuff? It's good, but it's awfully expensive."

"I'm not shopping. They have a case for me."

"No kidding! Good to see you're still getting work. They're over there by the fence. Nice spot."

"Thanks, Pete."

I made my way over to the fence. Apparently people didn't mind the high prices—Marva's cart was already almost two-thirds empty. She handled the selling while Reggie looked on and occasionally helped load up someone's satchel. He didn't appear to be armed, but he was so huge and scary-looking that a weapon wasn't necessary. I wouldn't be inclined to steal an apple and risk getting stomped by him.

Marva gave me yet another smile when she spotted me, and then she continued doing business.

Unlike all the other vendors in the Food Market, Marva didn't bargain with customers. She would just smile at them and repeat her price. And then people would pay it. Partly, I think, this was because Marva was so sweet that they didn't want to make her feel bad by haggling with her. But it was also true that the food she was selling was worth the price. You find lots of stunted fruits and vegetables at the Food Market, especially this late in the season. But the Church's produce was all gorgeous—the pumpkins were plump and unspotted, the apples were so shiny that they looked fake. And just looking at one of their turkeys would make your stomach growl. They were a welcome addition to the market.

Along with Brother Reggie I helped load the food into customers' satchels, and soon there were just scraps left in the cart. Marva was pleased. "This means we'll be home before dark, even with the late start."

She and Reggie closed up shop and got up onto the cart. I joined them, and Reggie threaded his way out of the market.

I asked Marva about the Church selling its produce at the Food Market. "This is new, right? I don't recall seeing you here before."

"We've been doing it for a little while now."

"I thought the Church didn't believe in money—but you sure made a lot of it today."

"I don't know," she responded. "I just do what I'm told." And then she fell silent. She was good at that.

I thought about Mary Beth and brought up another subject. "Has your pregnancy been difficult, Sister Marva?" Having a baby is a lot riskier now than it was in the old days, everyone says.

This time she shook her head and smiled. "No problems at all. It's been wonderful."

"I'm glad."

Working for Bobby Gallagher, I have gotten used to driving to out-of-the-way places like Concord, so I quickly became impatient at the cart's slow progress. But Reggie and Marva seemed to find the pace soothing—Marva even dozed off a one point, her head bouncing pleasantly against my shoulder for a while. I wondered if either of them had ever ridden in an automobile. Reggie looked old enough to have lived before the War; Marva, like me, had probably missed it. Of course, there are still lots of cars around, if you can find fuel and spare parts to keep them running. But, like other remnants of the old days—except, apparently, money—the Church of the New Beginning obviously wanted nothing to do with them.

The horse plodded across the bridge over the Charles and into Cambridge, then along the old highway that took us north to Concord. We only saw a few other people on the way—a couple of men on horseback, a family trudging somewhere on foot; a single ancient car raced by, spooking the usually placid horse. We exchanged greetings with the passersby, but the greetings were always a bit wary. Strangers can be dangerous, especially on an otherwise deserted street. But neither Reggie nor Marva seemed frightened.

The sun was low in the sky when we finally turned off the highway and onto the packed-dirt road that led to the Church of the New Beginning. The horse perked up; even Reggie's tiny black eyes seemed to brighten. Before long we saw the Church's main building, topped by a cross tilted to the right with its arms bent down, so it looked a bit like an arrow pointing up into the sky.

One thing was different now from when I had

been there before: a high gate blocked the path up to the building. On either side of the gate a fence extended out into the woods as far as I could see. Guarding the gate were a couple of guys almost the size of Reggie. Before, you could walk right up to the main building and ask to see Brother Flynn. Or sneak into his bedroom at night with a gun. Maybe I was the reason for the security.

The guards greeted us and opened the gate. Reggie stopped the cart at the entrance to the main building. He helped Marva down, and I got off by myself.

By the entrance an old woman sat on her haunches, staring at us as we approached. She hugged a long shawl around her; beneath it, she wore the same sort of powder-blue robe that Marva was wearing. Her gray hair was splayed across her shoulders; her eyes were bright with excitement. She was talking to herself.

When I came up next to her, her hand shot out and grabbed my arm, and suddenly she was talking to *me*. "It's true," she said softly, in a rush, as if every second, every word, was precious. "It's all true, every word of it. The wonder! Oh, the wonder! Do you see? *Do you see?*"

She smiled at me, and she seemed to be willing me to agree with her—*yes, I see!* But before I could respond, Marva reached out and gently disengaged the woman's hand from my arm. "It's all right, Sister Lucy," she murmured. "Everything is all right."

Sister Lucy turned her gaze to Marva and

nodded slowly, happily. *Yes, everything is all right.*

Marva raised Sister Lucy's hard gnarled hand to her lips and gently kissed it. Sister Lucy's smile widened, and tears swam in her eyes. Then Marva lowered Lucy's hand and placed it back on her shawl. Lucy grasped the shawl and nodded. "All true," she whispered.

Marva nodded to her and turned to me. "Let's go," she said.

So I went inside to start my case.

CHAPTER 3

The building was warm, welcoming, and different. Different because it was utterly new—no faded, stained wallpaper, no useless electrical sockets, no furniture bought at the Salvage Market or scrounged from some long-abandoned house. Instead, rough-hewn beams supported the ceiling, brightly colored hooked rugs covered the wide pine boards of the floor; fresh paintings and quilts hung from the walls. A new beginning.

In the large main hall, blue-robed women and brown-robed men greeted Marva enthusiastically and stared warily at me. At the far end of the hall, burning logs crackled in a large fireplace. Children scampered underfoot. I smelled something meaty and delicious. *Where do I sign up?*

We walked up a wide staircase to the second floor, along a gallery that looked down on the main hall, then down a hallway decorated with children's drawings. Marva pointed to a door.

"Brother Joseph is in there," she murmured. She put her hand on my arm. "Thank you for coming, Walter," she added. And then she walked back down the hall.

I knocked on the door.

"Come in," a deep voice said from inside.

I opened the door. An oil lamp flickering on a table in the corner of the room revealed a large, gray-bearded man sitting behind a desk. He rose and extended a hand. "Mr. Sands," he said. "Good of you to come."

I nodded. "Call me Walter."

"And I am Joseph."

We shook hands—his grip was crushing—and he motioned me to what looked like a hand-made wooden chair. We both sat down and gazed at each other across the desk. Under bushy eyebrows, his brown eyes looked weary, like they had seen too much. His gray-brown hair was sparse; there was a sprinkling of dandruff on the shoulders of his robe. Little tufts of hair grew out of his ears. I wondered what he had been in the pre-War world—an accountant? An English teacher?

"I heard about that case of yours when the president was kidnapped," he began. "I was impressed. We could use your skills here." His voice was hoarse. I wondered if he had been a cigarette smoker, back when there had been cigarettes to smoke.

I assumed he knew about the part where I had been convinced Flynn Dobler was the kidnapper, but I didn't bring it up. "I'm sorry to hear about

Brother Flynn's disappearance," I said. "He seems like an exceptional man."

"Indeed. Did Sister Marva say much about Brother Flynn's disappearance?"

"Just enough to confuse me. What happened, exactly?"

"Brother Flynn went into his room one night, and in the morning he didn't come down to breakfast as he usually did. We entered eventually, and the room was empty. His bed didn't look like it had been slept in. We searched everywhere, and we didn't find him. He has disappeared."

"What about Sister Lucy's, er, vision?"

Brother Joseph nodded. "Marva told you about that?"

"She mentioned it. Sister Lucy was sitting by the front door when I came in."

"Yes, she does that a lot. Why, I have no idea. She is not the most...balanced person in the Church. Like all of us, she's had her share of losses in life, and they have clearly affected her mind."

"So you think she's mistaken?"

"Yes, I do. There was nothing miraculous about Brother Flynn's disappearance. And I'm sure you'll agree with me once you've started your investigation."

"All right," I said. "Do you have a theory? Sister Marva said you suspected foul play."

Brother Joseph sighed. "I believe Brother Flynn was murdered."

"Who murdered him? Someone in the Church?"

"Yes. His name is Harold Bastable. *Brother* Harold."

"So he's a, what do you call it, a disciple."

Brother Joseph nodded mournfully.

"What's his motive?"

"It's simple enough. He wants to take over the Church."

"Take over? How? Maybe you'd better talk me through it."

"Yes, of course. I'll have to start by giving you some background, I suppose." Brother Joseph abruptly stood up and started pacing behind his desk. "First, let me say that Flynn Dobler is—or I should say *was*—a great man. I owe my life to him. And everyone here feels the same way. When I met him I was half-mad, I think. I begged, I stole—I did many things I would prefer to forget. One day I stuck a gun in a man's ribs and threatened to kill him. That man was Flynn Dobler. He started talking to me, and after a while I understood everything about the world, about myself, about the past and the future. And I joined him. I have never regretted it."

I recalled my own brief encounters with Flynn Dobler. "He has that effect on people," I said.

"Yes," Joseph agreed. "But…" He paused in his pacing and grasped the back of his chair. "But he doesn't know how to run a Church. Or anything, for that matter. Look at this chair."

I looked. It was an elegant ladder-back wooden chair. New, like all the furniture here. "It's beautiful," I said.

"It is," Brother Joseph agreed. "But why are we

spending our time hand-crafting beautiful chairs? There are no end of perfectly good chairs to be had for free within walking distance of this room."

"But that's the idea, right? A new beginning. Don't use anything from the past."

"It's a *stupid* idea!" Brother Joseph growled, slapping the back of the chair. And then he calmed down. "No, it's a wonderful idea. But it's not working. The Church has been falling apart, Mr.—*Walter*. People are attracted by Brother Flynn's charisma, and they like the *theory* of starting over. But in practice—" he shrugged. "It's too hard for many. They have already suffered enough. This is just another form of suffering. They end up disillusioned. Worn out. They wander back to their old lives."

"I was surprised that you're selling produce from your farm at the Food Market," I said. "Using money isn't part of Brother Flynn's philosophy, right?"

"Yes, you're right. That was my idea. Brother Flynn didn't like it. He didn't like a lot of my ideas. But he acquiesced. He knew we had to make compromises in order to survive. For example, we needed to build a barbed-wire fence to keep out intruders. But we can't make barbed wire ourselves. Sometimes we can barter for things we need, but often we can't. Sometimes all that works is money. It's been my job to figure these things out, and take the blame from people who think I'm destroying Brother Flynn's vision."

Brother Joseph sat back down in his beautiful chair. I noticed that his hands had a slight tremor, as if he had been holding up a heavy weight for too long and was about to drop it.

"OK," I said. "So where does Brother Harold come in?"

"Brother Harold is one of our recent arrivals—less than a year. I don't know how Brother Flynn decides who should be admitted to the Church. But I can see why he chose Brother Harold—no one is a more ardent believer. He wants to write Brother Flynn's biography. He wants to spread his gospel to the ends of the earth."

"I don't get it. Why would he want to murder him, then?"

"I think Harold wants to turn Brother Flynn into a god, so that Harold himself can run the Church through Marva and her child."

I pondered that statement. "Um, huh?" was the best response I could come up with.

"Brother Harold would deny it, but he was becoming frustrated with Brother Flynn—the real Brother Flynn, not the myth he is interested in creating. He has plenty of ideas for solving our problems, and Brother Flynn wasn't interested in them. I believe Harold decided that the Church would be better off with Brother Flynn as a symbol than as a living human being."

"Does this tie in with what Sister Lucy saw?"

"Sister Lucy *imagined* that she saw something. Lucy imagines a lot of things. She is very suggestible. She gets confused easily."

"You're saying that Brother Harold planted this

idea about Brother Flynn going up to heaven in her brain?"

"Yes, I do. And it's worked. People here know perfectly well that Lucy imagines things, but still, many of them are inclined to believe that it really happened. Because the alternative is too awful to contemplate."

"You said Harold wants to run the Church through Sister Marva. How does she fit in?"

"Sister Marva doted on Brother Flynn," Brother Joseph said, "She is sweet but very naïve. And Brother Harold has her ear. He is making her believe that it's her duty to carry on Brother Flynn's work—in the way Harold thinks it should be carried on."

"Is Brother Flynn the father of her baby? I asked her, and she didn't exactly respond."

"I assume so, and so does everyone else. I think Brother Flynn told her not to say anything, and Marva is simply following his wishes. Brother Flynn would get angry if you even brought up the subject in his presence. My theory is that he took advantage of her in a moment of weakness. He prided himself on being above that sort of thing, but Sister Marva is quite attractive, as you can see, and was undoubtedly hard to resist."

"So your theory is that Brother Harold murdered Brother Flynn, disposed of the body somehow, then convinced Sister Lucy that she saw Brother Flynn ascend into heaven?"

"Yes, something like that."

"Would the murder have taken place in Brother Flynn's room?"

"I suppose so. I don't see how Brother Harold could have lured him outside in the middle of the night."

"Can I see the room?" I asked.

Brother Joseph stood up. "Certainly."

He picked up the oil lamp and led me back to the gallery, then down another long hallway. He pointed to a door on the right. "This is it," he said.

"No lock," I pointed out.

"There are no locks anywhere. Brother Flynn didn't believe in locks."

"So anyone could have gone in here at any time." Like me, I recalled.

"That's true. We searched the place the morning after he disappeared. I would have noticed if anything changed after that."

"Any signs of a struggle? Bloodstains? Overturned furniture?"

"Nothing. It all looked normal."

We entered, and he set the lamp on a table.

I looked around. It appeared much the same as when I had been in it before. A bed, a table, two chairs. A few papers and a lamp on the table. Behind the table, a door that led out to a small balcony where I had first met Dobler. A chamber pot sat in the corner. The bed was neatly made.

"Did anyone make the bed afterwards?" I asked.

"No. Nothing's been touched. Presumably he didn't sleep in it that night."

Next to the bed was a tiny closet. A couple of brown robes hung on hooks; a couple pairs of sandals lay in a jumble on the floor. I tried to remember what Brother Reggie and Sister Marva had worn on their feet on their trip to Boston. "You don't wear sandals outside in the cold weather, do you?" I asked Joseph.

"No, we generally have sturdier shoes this time of year. Many of them are left over from the old days, I'm afraid."

"Did Brother Flynn have shoes like that?"

"Yes, but he often wore those shoes indoors. As do I. They're warmer, more comfortable for some of us."

I looked down at Joseph's feet; he was wearing pre-War high-topped sneakers. I went over to the table and looked through the papers.

"Those are copies of our financial accounts," Joseph said. "We would always give them to him for review, but he rarely had anything to say about them."

"And you handle the finances?"

"I make the financial decisions. Brother Scott does the accounting and disbursements. Sister Marva would have given him the money from the Food Market, for example."

I glanced at the papers, but I couldn't make any sense of them; if they contained any clues, I wasn't likely to find them. And then, in the lamplight, I noticed a sheet of paper that had nothing to do with finances. There was only a single phrase printed on it:

Down where all the ladders start

I stared at the phrase.

"Mr. Sands? Walter? Does that meaning anything to you?"

"Maybe. What is it?"

"One of Brother Flynn's thoughts, I suppose. Not that I understand it. Perhaps an idea for a sermon. He gave wonderful sermons."

His thoughts. I recalled sneaking a look into the chapel on my first visit to the Church; Marva had called it the "meditation area." On the wall I had seen another one of Brother Flynn's thoughts: *Tomorrow is another day.*

For all his charisma, Brother Flynn apparently wasn't the world's most original thinker. "Do you have books here?" I asked. "Or doesn't Brother Flynn believe in them?"

"Books are vestiges of the old world," Joseph replied, as if he were reciting a creed. "Someday we will make our own literature, our own poetry. But first we must purify ourselves of the past."

No books. No Shakespeare, no Dickens, no Raymond Chandler. No William Butler Yeats. I wasn't going to be joining this Church.

I opened the doors to the balcony and walked out onto it. Brother Joseph followed with the lamp. Another chair, another table. I looked over the railing. It was twenty feet or so down to the grass below. We went back inside.

"Did you check the ground below the balcony?" I asked.

"You mean, the next morning?" Joseph responded. "I don't think so. For what?"

"Look," I said. "You think Brother Flynn was murdered in this room. But there's no sign of a struggle. There's no sign that Dobler's bed was slept in, so probably no one knocked him out while he was asleep. So how was he killed? And how did the murderer get rid of the body? Drag it along the corridor, down the stairs, and out the front door? That's a pretty noisy job. Other people sleep in the main building, right? Sister Marva, you? It'd wake them up. So maybe he threw the body off the balcony and dragged it somewhere to be buried. Or maybe he used a ladder. But in that case there'd be marks on the ground. Is Brother Harold a big guy?"

"No," Brother Joseph said. "He's not big at all. But maybe he had an accomplice."

"And who would that be?"

"I have no idea," he admitted.

"Ah. Well, I don't know if your theory is right, Brother Joseph. But I find it a bit puzzling. I guess I'm going to need to talk to everyone— Harold, Lucy, Marva—all the disciples."

"I can arrange that. We'll be eating supper soon in the refectory—you're welcome to join us. I'll make an announcement there."

"Thanks. One more question—what happens to the Church if I discover that Brother Harold murdered Brother Flynn?"

Brother Joseph shrugged and assumed his mournful look once again. "It's possible that we're doomed no matter what happens. But we need to know the truth."

"Finding out the truth is my job," I informed him.

CHAPTER 4

We left Brother Flynn's room, and then I noticed Sister Marva, sitting in near darkness in a small room across the hall. As I recalled, most disciples lived in small cabins on the Church's grounds. But Marva apparently needed to be close to Brother Flynn.

"Sister Marva," I said. "Do you mind if I ask you a few questions?"

She looked up at Brother Joseph.

"It's all right, Marva," he said gently.

"Of course you can ask me questions, Walter," she replied.

"I'll leave you then," Brother Joseph said. "A gong will announce dinner."

He walked away, and I went into Sister Marva's room. As my eyes adjusted to the dim light, I saw a plain, windowless room, much smaller than Brother Flynn's. It contained a table, a chair, and a chest of drawers on which sat a small mirror, a hair brush, and a few other items. And the narrow bed on which Marva was sitting, with her hands folded over her belly. Was she resting? Or, perhaps, praying?

"I'm sorry to bother you," I said.

She smiled softly. "It's quite all right," she said. "As you can see, I'm not exactly busy." She pointed to the chair. "Please have a seat."

I sat. "Do you really believe Brother Flynn ascended into heaven? Brother Joseph thinks Sister Lucy—"

"Yes, Brother Joseph believes Sister Lucy is a bit crazy. But don't you think sometimes people like her have experiences that aren't, well, available to the rest of us?"

"I suppose. But that doesn't necessarily mean the experiences are real."

She inclined her head, granting my point.

"You probably also know that Brother Joseph suspects Brother Harold of murdering Brother Flynn."

Marva inclined her head again. "I know that. But—have you met Brother Harold yet, Walter?"

"Not yet, no."

"No one could be more loyal to Brother Flynn than Brother Harold. No one is less likely to murder him. It's just impossible for me to even imagine that. I respect Brother Joseph and all he's done for the Church, but—" She sighed. "It's all so distressing."

"Brother Joseph says he's afraid the Church is falling apart. People are drifting away."

At this Marva teared up, as she had at my office. She was particularly beautiful when she cried. "Yes, and it's awful," she said. "Don't they understand how important the Church is? The world needs us."

"Did Brother Flynn say anything out of the ordinary to you before he disappeared? Was he unhappy? Worried?"

"Not at all. Not that I noticed, anyway. If anything, he seemed excited. Things have been difficult at the Church, but lately that didn't really bother him. He seemed…ready."

"Ready to ascend into heaven?"

"Of course I didn't understand that at the time. But looking back…I don't know."

"At my office, when I asked you if Brother Flynn was the father of your baby, you didn't answer me. Why is that?"

Marva twisted her hands in her lap. "Because it's not right," she replied.

"What's not right?"

"I don't want to be looked on as someone special. I'm just another person Brother Flynn saved. I was twelve years old then and doing things that were—well, crazier than anything Sister Lucy is accused of. Can you understand that, Walter?"

"Of course. I could say the same thing about myself."

"Well, I don't know how you were saved, but Brother Flynn found me and he took me into his Church and he fed and clothed and protected me. Without him I would have died long ago."

More beautiful tears.

"Brother Joseph says Brother Harold wants to

run the Church through you—you and your baby."

Marva shook her head. "No, no, I don't want that. I just want to be here. To help. To be a good mother for my child."

Fair enough. "The night Brother Flynn disappeared," I said, "did you hear anything? See anything?"

"No, and that's strange, because I sleep lightly—in case Brother Flynn needs anything. I think maybe—" She paused.

"Maybe what?"

"I suppose you'll laugh at me, but maybe God didn't want me to notice anything. So I wouldn't try to stop Brother Flynn. Because He knew I'd try."

"I don't have any idea how God operates, Sister Marva, so no, I'm not going to laugh at you. But can I ask you something else? Does the phrase 'down where all the ladders start' mean anything to you?"

She looked puzzled. "No. Should it?"

"It was written on a sheet of paper on Brother Flynn's desk. I just saw it there."

"I have no idea why he would write that, Walter. Or what it means."

I heard the distant sound of a gong. I was hungry, and I was running out of questions, so I decided to end the interview. "Are you going to supper?" I asked.

Marva smiled. "Yes, but you go ahead. I'll be down shortly. I hope you find out the truth, Walter."

Richard Bowker

"That's exactly what Brother Joseph asked me to do. And I'm going to try."

I left her in her room, still sitting on the edge of her bed, as if waiting for something to happen. Or someone to return.

CHAPTER 5

━━━◆ ◆ ◆ ◆ ◆━━━

I made my way back downstairs, following the smell of dinner. The refectory was a large room off the main hall. It was bright and cheerful, unlike most other dining halls I'd frequented during my stints in youth camps and the army. On the far wall was another large arrow-like cross, like the one I had seen on top of the building. I supposed it represented progress or something. Let's start over—and do it right this time.

There were forty or fifty people in the room, old and young, sitting at long benches. They were all wearing the Church's robes, blue for the women, brown for the men. They fell silent as they noticed me.

Brother Joseph motioned to me to sit next to him. I complied.

"How was your talk with Sister Marva?" he asked.

"Not especially illuminating, I guess. She

seems to be taking Brother Flynn's disappearance hard."

"We all are. But she more than most, I'm sure."

Brother Joseph signaled to someone, and servers started bringing out the food and setting it on the tables. When the food had been served, Joseph stood up. He cleared his throat, and the conversation and clatter died down. "I would like you all to welcome Mr. Walter Sands," he said when the room was quiet. He gestured at me, and I gave the crowd a nod. "I have asked him to investigate Brother Flynn's disappearance. We need to explore every avenue in finding out what happened to our beloved leader. We will arrange for people to speak with him after supper."

"The wonder!" someone called out from the other side of the room. "Praise be!"

It was Sister Lucy, of course. She was beaming with delight.

Brother Joseph looked annoyed, but he didn't respond. Instead he bowed his head and closed his eyes. "Let us pray," he intoned. Everyone bowed their heads, including Sister Lucy, so I did too. "Dear God, we ask you to help us find Brother Flynn. And if we cannot find him, we ask for the courage and the wisdom to carry on along the path he has set for us. This world is a harsh and unforgiving place, and we cannot survive it, we cannot improve it, on our own. But with you, and with Brother Flynn, we can accomplish anything."

He paused for a moment in the silent room, and then he sat down and picked up his spoon. It was time to eat.

And then I noticed Sister Marva walking quietly into the refectory. Conversation died once again. Everyone turned to stare at this beautiful woman carrying Brother Flynn's baby. She walked past us and sat next to Sister Lucy.

Beside them was an intense, slender young man with Hispanic features. He wore glasses, which seemed out of place at the Church, like Brother Joseph's sneakers. Was this Brother Harold? He met my gaze and nodded; I nodded back.

Slowly the conversation picked up again. The meal began.

The food was fabulous—fresh bread and butter, and a stew made from the meat and vegetables they were selling at the Food Market. It wasn't good enough to make me join a Church that had no books, but I would enjoy it while I was here.

I thought of Brother Joseph's prayer and all the talk about Flynn Dobler's ascension into heaven. I realized that I didn't know exactly what kind of religion this was. Did they believe in Jesus? Did they read the Bible? How could they, if there weren't any books?

The world has its share of religious people. I have a friend who is convinced he is Jesus Christ; he drags a cross around downtown Boston all day warning people to repent, for the end is nigh. This doesn't seem to me to be a good way to earn a living, but who am I to talk? He gets by. But most of us, I think, are like my father. He didn't say much; the struggle to keep the both of us alive after the War on our little farm in Maine seemed to take up whatever energy he possessed. But I was an inquisitive kid, and once I pestered him about God. Is He real? Does He exist? And all my father would say was: "If there is a God, He's got a lot of explaining to do."

I had come across people here and there who tried to do His explaining for Him, but none of them made much sense to me.

"I've heard of you."

I looked at the man on the other side of me from Brother Joseph; he was eyeing me as he hunched over his stew.

"Pleased to meet you," I said. "My name's Walter."

He nodded. "Brother Scott," he muttered. And then he looked down at his stew. He was short and pasty-skinned, and his hand was trembling so much he could scarcely bring a spoonful of stew to his mouth without spilling it. I recalled that Brother Joseph's hands shook, too. Was everyone around here this tense?

I smiled at him. "Scott," I repeated. "You take care of the money, right?"

His eyes darted to the right, to the left, then back down to the stew. He muttered something into the stew.

"Excuse me?"

"Later," he whispered.

"Sure thing," I replied. "I'm going to talk to everyone, I hope."

He nodded the briefest of nods, and then returned to his stew.

I turned back to Brother Joseph. "Is this the

entire Church?" I asked, gesturing at the people eating supper in the refectory.

"Pretty much," he replied. "There are a few folks in the kitchen, of course. And the guards at the front gate. And perhaps a couple of people in the infirmary."

"Have a lot of people left?"

"We used to be twice this size. And I worry that some who have stayed just want to ride out the winter here before they leave."

It was going to be a tough winter, I knew. Prices were rising; food shortages were likely. With the Federal government pulling back much of its support for New England, we were on our own. And unless Governor Bolton managed to convince the Feds to change their minds, things weren't going to be pretty. "Why don't you just recruit more disciples?" I asked. "Great food, shelter—I'd think lots of people would want to join up. I know you said some people get disillusioned, but still."

"People who are just interested in food and shelter aren't what we need. We exist in order to change the world. To show the world that you don't need electricity, and telephones, and automobiles, and all those things that people still long for from the old days. You just need each other, and what you can create with your own hands."

"A lot of people are just going to be looking for a way to survive," I pointed out.

"That's what the guards are for. And the barbed wire. To keep those people away."

"So how will you find the right sort of people, now that Brother Flynn is gone?"

Brother Joseph shook his head. "I don't know," he replied. "I don't know."

I ate the stew and the bread until I was ready to burst. And then it was time to go solve my case.

CHAPTER 6

Brother Joseph set me up in a small room near his, and I began interviewing the members of the Church of the New Beginning.

Somewhat surprisingly, Brother Harold volunteered to be first. Up close, the Hispanic features seemed to be blended with a hint of Asian. He spoke quietly and quickly; he seemed very sure of himself. "I suppose I'm what you'd call your 'prime suspect,'" he said, "so we might as well get this out of the way."

"OK, but really, it's too early for me to have suspects. So I take it you didn't kill Brother Flynn?"

"Of course not. This is a fantasy of Brother Joseph's. It's understandable, of course. But I didn't kill Brother Flynn—no one killed him."

"Because he ascended into heaven?"

"I think that term is technically incorrect," he responded. "He didn't *ascend*, he was *assumed*. Do you understand the distinction?"

"I don't have a clue."

"*Ascension* implies that he left this plane of existence on his own power," he explained, as if this was the most obvious theological point imaginable. "*Assumption* implies that a higher power took him from us."

"Okay. So he didn't, like, become a god. That's the word Brother Joseph used."

"Brother Joseph simply doesn't understand— possibly because he doesn't want to understand. The distinction between ascension and assumption is subtle but important."

"Why?"

"Because it affects how we think about Brother Flynn and our future as a Church. It's absurd to think of him as a god. We have all lived with him. We know that he was a human being, with a human being's faults. But we also know how special he was. How important he was. How much God must have loved him."

"So, you believe that Sister Lucy's vision was true—that Brother Flynn's body just went up into the sky or something?"

"It's the only explanation of Brother Flynn's disappearance that makes any sense. You will investigate—as you should—and you'll find nothing. No body, no blood, no clues of any kind. I realize that Sister Lucy doesn't seem like the most reliable witness, but I do believe her, yes."

I decided to change the subject. "Brother Joseph says you're writing Flynn Dobler's biography."

Brother Harold inclined his head. "I'm

unworthy of the task, but I have presumed to undertake it. Someday it will be vitally important."

"Tell me what you know about him. Where did he come from? What happened to him after the War? How did he get his ideas?"

"You're asking a great deal," Harold pointed out. "First, let me say that I have not been a disciple as long as many others. I came when the Church was already well-established here in Concord. I had wandered long in the wilderness before I arrived here."

Brother Harold seemed to enjoy lofty prose. I decided I wasn't likely to enjoy his biography. "OK," I said. "I'll take what I can get. Where was he born? Where did he grow up? How old is he?"

He shook his head. "Those are things Brother Flynn never spoke of. For him, life began when he started preaching on the streets of Boston."

"This was after the Frenzy?"

"Yes, the Feds had arrived, and life was starting to get back to normal. His message was difficult for many to hear, but for some—"

"Yeah, I know. But surely he said something about his family, his home, what college he went to—didn't he?"

"If he did, no one I have talked to recalls it. But why does this matter? It didn't matter to Brother Flynn. Obviously he was shaped by the War—we all were, even if we were born after it ended, or we aren't old enough to remember it. It's what he did afterward, it's what he drew out of his experiences, that matters."

I didn't buy this, actually. The more you don't talk about something, the more important that something becomes—at least, from a private eye's point of view. But I wasn't going to convince Brother Harold of that. "Do you know what the phrase 'down where all the ladders start' means?" I asked him.

Like Sister Marva, he looked baffled by the question. "I have no idea. Why?"

I shrugged. "Don't worry about it. Let me ask you something else. Was Brother Flynn religious?"

He continued to look baffled. "I don't understand. What do you mean?"

"I assume he was, but I don't quite get it. Why is this place a Church? What's with the robes and the tilted cross? I mean, as far as I can make out, Brother Flynn's message is political, or sociological, or economic, or something. What does it have to do with God? Or religion?"

Instead of baffled, Brother Harold now looked deeply offended. "It has everything to do with God," he insisted. "What do you think caused the War?"

I recalled the explanations I'd heard, mainly from my friend Henry Fisher, the Angriest Man in America. "There was this bunch of renegade Chinese generals who decided to—"

"Don't be ridiculous," Brother Harold interrupted. "Of course there were human decisions that led to the War. Someone pushed a button. Then someone else pushed another button in retaliation. Lots of people pushed lots of buttons. That's all unimportant. What's important is that they were carrying out God's plan. And His plan was to show us the error of our ways. We worshipped technology instead of Him. We thought we could conquer life and death. We forgot to live our lives according to His laws. And we have paid for our sins."

"They weren't my sins," I pointed out. "So why am I paying?"

"You've been blessed, as have I. We have experienced the consequences of God's wrath. And we have heard Brother Flynn explain its meaning so that we can understand and find our way to the truth."

Brother Harold's eyes were glittering. His face was alight with the rapture of certainty. I'm sure my face was not. "I don't feel blessed," I said.

"Someday you will," he reassured me. "Someday you will."

"Without Brother Flynn?"

"We will find a way."

"What way is that? Brother Joseph said you were getting impatient with Brother Flynn, and that's why you wanted to take over the Church."

"Again, that's absurd. I suppose that, having seen the truth, I have become a bit frustrated that we haven't been able to bring the good news to more people. But frankly, I'm more frustrated with Brother Joseph's approach of compromise and surrender. The more we become like the institutions we're trying to change, the less capable we'll become of actually changing them."

"Um, OK. He also said you're manipulating Sister Marva so that you can run the Church through her."

For the first time Brother Harold seemed to get genuinely angry. "That's utterly false," he protested. "Everyone here loves Sister Marva, and we're all trying to help her as best we can. This can't be easy for her. No one was more devoted to Brother Flynn than she was. And now he's gone. It may have been God's will, but sometimes God's will is hard to accept."

And that was Brother Harold. I probed a bit about the night of Flynn Dobler's disappearance, but he had nothing interesting to say. He had no alibi, but I hadn't expected one. He claimed he was alone in his cabin, asleep, when Brother Flynn disappeared. He had heard nothing; he had seen nothing. He had sensed nothing out of the ordinary in the days leading up to the disappearance.

Fine. Then I talked to so many others—the rank and file of the Church, the ones who built the chairs and baked the bread and milked the cows and spun the wool. Sister Cindy, small and blonde, bewildered by the disappearance and the acrimony, wanting only for things to be the way they used to be. Why can't we all just get along? And Brother Duane, not the brightest disciple in the Church. He looked almost as strong as Brother Reggie but had even less to say.

And then there was Brother Reggie himself, who seemed offended that I was asking questions and he was expected to answer them. "Why are you here?" he demanded. "We know what happened to Brother Flynn. Sister Lucy saw him go up to heaven."

"I'm here because it's my job."

"Then get a better job."

"Do you think it's possible that Sister Lucy could be mistaken?"

"Sister Marva believes her," Reggie pointed out, as if that clinched the case.

"What do you think of Brother Harold?"

"Sister Marva likes him."

And that was Reggie's point of view on everything.

I wanted very much to talk to Sister Lucy, but I was told she went to sleep right after supper and couldn't be disturbed. Tomorrow morning, I was told.

So I got nowhere. No one could imagine Brother Flynn being murdered, especially not by Brother Harold. No one wanted to disbelieve Sister Lucy. And no one could imagine any other explanation. Everyone wanted to tell me the story of how Brother Flynn had saved their lives, pulling them out of despair and hopelessness. Now things were not going well at the Church, and no one knew what to do.

And then Brother Scott slid into my small, chilly room, and the case finally got interesting.

CHAPTER 7

Brother Scott looked every bit as nervous as he'd appeared at supper. He sat down. He twitched. He trembled. He looked guilty—of something, anyway. But he immediately took the offensive in our interview. "So Brother Joseph hired you to find Brother Flynn," he began.

"That's right."

"Don't you see what he's up to?"

"What do you mean?"

"It's so obvious. And I suppose you're in on it. Make people think he's honestly interested in finding out what happened. When he was the one who murdered Brother Flynn so he could run the Church by himself."

"I'm not in on anything, Brother Scott. I'm just doing my job. Which is to get at the truth."

Brother Scott stared at me. His left eye twitched. He was starting to make *me* feel nervous. Then, abruptly, he blurted out his secret. "The Church's money—it's all gone. And

Brother Joseph is going to blame me. But it wasn't me. It was him."

Then he fell silent and looked away, as if that was all he could bear to say.

"Why don't you give me some details?" I suggested.

"Well, what do you need to know? I'm in charge of the money here, like I told you. When money comes in, like from the Food Market, people give it to me. When we need money for some expense, I hand it out on Brother Joseph's say-so. I keep it all in a drawer in my desk."

"And the drawer isn't locked, right? Your room isn't locked."

"Yes, precisely. No locks in our Church. Brother Flynn was clear about that."

"And all the money disappeared around the same time Brother Flynn did."

"That's right. Joseph must have stolen it. Who else would have done it? Almost a thousand dollars—that's a lot of money, even with the inflation we've been having lately. And then Brother Flynn must have found out and confronted him about it, so Joseph killed him and got rid of the body. Now Joseph has all our money, and he's running the Church. Everything that Brother Flynn worked for, destroyed by a greedy—"

"If Joseph stole the money," I interrupted, "what would he do with it? No one needs money here, right? And where would he hide it? Again, no locks, right?"

"He goes to the city sometimes. He could have

put it in a bank while he was there. Maybe he's going to wait for a while and then disappear."

Brother Scott's theory was worse than some of the ones I've come up with. "Why didn't he just disappear right away—as soon as he stole the money?" I asked. "He could bribe someone to get a visa and be out of New England in no time. No one's going to bring him back here to stand trial. So what's the point of waiting? He must have known you'd notice the money was missing and accuse him."

"I think he's going to kill me the way he killed Brother Flynn," Brother Scott responded, his left eye twitching even more rapidly. "Or he'll claim that *I* stole the money. And how could I prove he was wrong?"

"But again, why is he waiting?" I persisted. "Why would he hire me, and give you a chance to talk to me?"

Brother Scott was near tears at this point. He looked like he was about to keel over from distress. "I—I don't know," he admitted. "I didn't do anything wrong," he whined. "I don't deserve to be put into this position. All I've ever tried to do is help. Now Brother Joseph is going to find out the money's missing and he'll blame me, and probably throw me out of the Church. And then what will be left?"

"What do you mean, he's 'going to find out'?" I asked. "If he stole the money, he's not going to find out anything that he doesn't already know."

Brother Scott seemed not to notice my perceptive comment—or maybe he purposely ignored it. Instead he launched into the story of how Brother Flynn had saved his life. Another heartbreaking story of the Frenzy and its aftermath, of a man lost in a wilderness of confusion and despair, living in a rented room on Clarendon Street in Boston, trying his best to survive while civilization struggled to reassert itself after coming close to utter collapse. And one day he met a man who could explain it all, who could give him purpose and meaning and hope. Brother Scott never looked back.

The story wasn't much different from Brother Joseph's or many of the other people I'd talked to. I felt sorry for Brother Scott, but not as sorry as he felt for himself. At the end of his tale he buried his head in his hands, and his body shook with sobs. "There's nothing left," he said finally. "Nothing."

I tried to come up with something that might make him feel better. "What about the idea that Brother Flynn ascended, um, was assumed into heaven?" I asked. "A lot of people here seem to think that's what happened."

He raised his head and glared at me. "It's bullshit," he hissed. "Complete bullshit. Maybe Joseph didn't kill Brother Flynn, but he sure didn't end up in heaven." Then, abruptly, he stood up. "I can't stand this anymore," he said. On his way out the door, he added: "There's more going on here than you'll ever know." Then he slammed the door behind him and stormed off down the hall.

Well, that was interesting. What was going on

here? What hadn't I figured out yet? Or did Brother Scott have some other crazy theory he didn't want to share with me?

I sat there for a while, and then I decided I was really tired. I had talked to too many people; I had learned too little. And Brother Scott had worn me out. I went to find Brother Joseph in his room.

"What did you find out?" he asked me.

I decided not to tell him about Brother Scott just yet; I needed to think about him a little more. "Nobody confessed," I said. "And nobody offered much in the way of evidence. So, not a lot of progress."

He didn't look surprised. "Perhaps tomorrow."

"I'd like to examine the grounds in daylight. And I certainly need to talk to Sister Lucy."

"Good luck getting anything sensible out of her," he remarked.

"I do have to get back to Boston tomorrow," I added. "It's important."

"We'll get you home. Just don't give up." He looked as tired as I felt.

Back in my room, I turned down the lamp, lay down on the thin mattress, put the thin blanket over me, and stared up into the darkness.

And now what? Now it was time to sleep. But this quiet little room in Concord turned out to be no different from everywhere else I had spent the night, and sleep was hard to come by. *The Sandman*, a friend had once ironically dubbed me: the one who brings sleep to good little children. Fat chance. Usually my restless brain drifts through memories it is better off forgetting; tonight, at least, it stayed focused on the case. On Brother Joseph and Sister Marva and Brother Scott and all the rest. I remembered Scott's final remark to me. What was going on here that I'd never know?

Finally I focused on Flynn Dobler. Brother Harold had been uninterested in his past, in what had made him the person he was. That was an odd attitude for someone supposedly writing the man's biography. And it wasn't an attitude a private eye could take. Who was Flynn Dobler?

That, I figured, was the key to solving my case.

He had to be more than what I'd heard so far, from people who thought he was some kind of latter-day prophet who was going to save the world. But what?

The minutes passed and then, possibly, hours. At home I'd be reading a book to make it through the night. But there were no books in the Church of the New Beginning.

Finally I couldn't stand it anymore, and I got out of bed. The full moon had risen, and it was easy enough to find my way out into the hallway. From other rooms I heard the sound of gentle snoring. I walked down the hall. Was this the time of night when Brother Flynn had disappeared? I imagined Flynn Dobler and Brother Joseph arguing about the missing money. I imagined Brother Harold somehow flinging Flynn Dobler's body off the balcony. I imagined God summoning Flynn Dobler to His side. *You have done well, My son. Now it is time to join*

Me.

I imagined Flynn Dobler sitting in his silent room, writing those words:

Down where all the ladders start

I made my way to the gallery overlooking the Church's main hall. The fire burned low in the massive fireplace.

And then I heard something off to my left—the sound of a door opening. I turned, and I could dimly make out a figure walking quickly away from me along the gallery. I realized that I was standing between the person and the staircase. The person wasn't heading for the staircase. Where was he—or she—going? To someone else's room?

I followed, as quietly as I could. The figure disappeared down a hallway. I followed.

At the end of the hallway I heard a door open and then quickly close. I hurried up to the door and put an ear up against it. I heard the sound of someone racing down a set of stairs.

Why hadn't anyone told me there was a back staircase?

I looked down at my bare feet. No shoes, no coat, no gun. The experienced private investigator, always ready for anything. I opened the door in time to hear a door slam shut below me. I felt my way in the pitch black down the steps. At the bottom I stubbed my toe against the door. I stifled an "Ouch!". Then I opened the door, and I was outside.

I looked around. By the light of the moon I saw

a stand of trees and some buildings looming in the distance. But no shadowy human figure racing through the night. Should I go left? Right? Should I go back inside and put on some shoes and a damn coat? It was cold out.

I went to the left. I was on some kind of path. Not a very good path, though, because almost immediately I stubbed another toe on a rock. I kept going, though. I figured I was at the rear of the main building; the path seemed to loop around towards the front. I sped up as my eyes adjusted to the darkness. Who was I following? And where was….

I heard a sound behind me and, before I could turn, I felt something smash down on my head. And that was that.

When I awoke, Sister Marva was staring down at me. "Are you all right?" she whispered. "Walter? Are you all right? What are you doing here?"

I managed a groan in reply.

She helped me to my feet. The world was spinning. I leaned against her. And then my vision steadied, and I saw another figure, standing motionless in the moonlight.

I could clearly make out the blue robe and the long gray hair. It was Sister Lucy. She was looking up, with her arms raised, as if she were waiting to catch something dropped from the sky. I could only dimly make out her face, but I had no doubt that it was filled with wonder.

I looked at Marva. She raised a finger to her

lips. We watched Sister Lucy for a few moments, and then Marva pulled me towards the front door of the Church.

The last remnants of the fire flickered in the fireplace as we walked across the main hall. Marva picked up a candle and lit it. "What happened?" she asked. "Did you fall?"

"Someone whacked me with a rock or something. Was it you?"

Sister Marva looked puzzled. "Of course not, Walter. I would never do a thing like that."

We went into the refectory, then beyond it into the kitchen, where a fire burned in another fireplace. "Was it Sister Lucy?" I asked.

"No, no. You're not thinking straight, Walter. I don't know who it was." Marva found a towel and soaked it in hot water from a kettle on the fire. Then she gently bathed my wound. It felt great, although my head was starting to throb. "I hope you don't have a concussion," she murmured. "I should take you to the infirmary."

"That's OK. I'll be fine."

"But really, you're not fine. And if someone is outside knocking you unconscious, we should find out who it is."

"There was someone upstairs, in the gallery, and I—" Marva was right; I couldn't think straight. "Is it always this busy here in the middle of the night?" I asked her.

"No, but Sister Lucy sleeps erratically. I like to guard her when I can."

"The way you guarded Brother Flynn."

"Yes," she said sadly. "I suppose."

"What's she doing out there?" I asked.

"Watching."

"For Brother Flynn?"

"Of course."

"Does she expect him to return?"

"I don't really know. That…vision, or whatever it was, was the most important event in her life. She may just be trying to relive it. Anyway, if you won't let me take you to the infirmary, you should at least get some rest."

She was right about that. She finished washing my wound, and then helped me mount the main staircase. We found my room and she deposited me there before, presumably, going back downstairs to watch over Sister Lucy.

Then I crawled into bed, and this time I had no difficulty falling asleep.

CHAPTER 8

When I awoke and staggered downstairs with a colossal headache, breakfast was already over and the refectory was empty. I wandered into the kitchen and got a hunk of bread from a kindly disciple who was washing the dishes. I ate it as I found the door from the main hall to the back staircase, went outside, and tried to retrace my steps from the night before. An ugly rock lying on the ground seemed to be the most likely suspect as the weapon that had conked me on the head. I knelt down and inspected it—sure enough, there was what looked like dried blood on one side of it. I searched for other clues but didn't notice any.

I walked around to the front of the building, and there was Sister Lucy, squatting next to the entrance, just as I had first seen her when I had arrived.

"Good morning, Sister Lucy," I said.

Lucy looked up at me, and her eyes gleamed.

"I saw you standing in the moonlight last night," I went on. "Would you like to talk about that?"

She reached out her hands for me, and I helped her to her feet. "There," she said, "there," pointing to where she had been standing, down the path in the direction of the barn. She led me quickly towards the spot, clutching my arm with both her hands.

When we reached it, Lucy stopped abruptly. She looked around, smiling, as if she had finally arrived home. I didn't notice anything in particular. The morning was chilly: there was frost on the grass, and our breath made vapor clouds. A few last leaves were falling from an almost-bare maple tree. There was horse manure everywhere on the rutted path. A crow cawed in the distance.

"Night," Lucy whispered abruptly. "Silence. I was alone. I'm often alone. Do you know why I'm alone?"

"No, Sister Lucy," I replied. "I don't."

"Because I frighten people. Because—" She let go of my arm then and gestured at the sky, at the trees, at everything. "Because I *understand*. And sometimes that's too much."

"What is it that you understand?"

"I don't know. I mean, I know, but I have no words."

Well, that was helpful. "Night," I repeated. "Silence. Are we talking about Brother Flynn? The night he left?"

She looked past me, down the path, towards the

Church. "Blessed be his name. He came. Out of the light. Into the darkness. Towards me. Towards *me*."

"What happened then?"

"Then—then the darkness too became light. And the light became blinding. It was like nothing you have ever seen, or imagined. And then he touched me. And his touch filled me with love. It filled everything with love."

Sister Lucy waved her arms to encompass the universe. She smiled, and her eyes filled with tears. "And what happened next, Sister Lucy?" I prodded.

"And then he rose." Sister Lucy's gaze rose with the word. She looked up into the sky, as she had last night, and she reached out her arms. And now I saw that she hadn't been trying to catch something last night—she was trying to embrace something. Something too big for any one person to embrace.

"He rose," she went on, "into the heavens. So that he could be with us, and around us, and in us. For ever and ever. The wonder!"

I stood there looking at Sister Lucy as she gazed up into the cloudy autumn sky, and it occurred to me that I had never seen anyone so happy. This was beyond joy; it was ecstasy.

"Was anyone else with you when this happened?" I asked. "Did anyone else witness it?"

Sister Lucy shook her head. "I was blessed," she admitted. "I don't know why he chose me to witness it. I am not worthy."

"And this is what you told people here at the Church?"

She lowered her gaze from the heavens. "Yes, of course. But the whole world must be told. And you must help me!"

"Thank you, Sister Lucy," I replied. "I'll do my best."

As I had seen Sister Marva do, I tried to gently disengage Lucy's hand from my arm. She resisted for a moment, and then, smiling, she took her hand away. She wrapped her shawl tightly around her. The ecstasy had passed, and Lucy looked like a tired old woman. A little confused. A little crazy. "The wonder," she whispered. I smiled and helped her back to her post by the front door.

I walked around the main building. I stopped under Brother Flynn's balcony and looked for signs of a body being dragged through the grass, or a ladder being planted in the ground. There were none. Any other clues? No.

I explored the large barn and other outbuildings, all newly built, all filled with life as the day's work began. There were cows to be milked, chickens and pigs to be fed, furniture and clothing to be made, wool to be spun...Beyond the buildings were the fields and the orchards, all in good order after the harvest, and the cabins that housed the disciples who didn't reside in the main building.

As a child, I had spent my share of time helping my father on his little farm in Maine. I had hated that farm, even as I desperately wanted to make my father happy (and desperately wanted enough food to eat). What I was yearning for, I now realized, was the chance to do something really useless with my life, and it took me a long time to figure out what that was.

I went into a few of the buildings and chatted with some people I had missed the previous night. I learned nothing new. Then I made my way back through thin woods to the barbed-wire fence that the Church had built. I wanted to see how easy it was to get onto (or out of) the Church's land without going past the guards and through the front gate. I followed the fence east from the gate until, abruptly, the fence stopped.

I looked around: any clues? Scraps of clothing? Footprints? A message hurriedly scrawled on a scrap of paper? No such luck.

So I walked past the fence, through more woods. Eventually I came upon a little neighborhood: a dead-end street with a few abandoned houses on it, collapsing under the weight of time and neglect. I followed the street away from its dead end, and then turned onto another, longer street, and in ten minutes or so I found myself out on the old Route 2.

I stood on the highway. After a while an ancient truck rattled slowly past; its driver nodded warily to me. I gave him a cheery wave in return. Civilization, of a sort. I walked back along the highway and in a few minutes found the path that led to the Church's front gate. The guards looked surprised to see me. I had interviewed them the previous night, so no introductions were necessary. "Just taking a morning walk," I said. "This fence doesn't do much to keep out people who aren't in a car."

One of them, a bearded fellow named Brother Willis, nodded. "We're supposed to fence in the entire farm. Don't know if that'll ever happen now."

"Lot of work," his companion, the tall, not very bright Brother Duane, said.

"No one patrols the farm at night, do they?" I asked.

Both men shook their heads. Brother Willis said, "If you're asking—could someone have just sneaked onto the farm in the middle of the night, gone into the main building, and kidnapped Brother Flynn or killed him or something, I suppose the answer is yes."

"Bastards," Duane muttered, as if Brother Willis had convinced him this had actually happened.

We were interrupted at that point by Sister Marva coming down the path in the cart, which was loaded with food for the Food Market. This time she was accompanied by Brother Harold.

"How are you feeling, Walter?" she asked.

"I have a bit of a headache, but otherwise I'm OK. Where's Brother Reggie?"

"Things are a bit…confused this morning," she replied. "Brother Reggie will take you back to Boston later."

"You're wanted at the Church," Brother Harold said. He looked upset.

"Why? What's going on?"

"Just go, would you?" he responded impatiently.

Willis and Duane had opened the gate. Harold flicked the reins for the horse to start moving down the road to the highway.

I hurried back to the main building. People were congregated in the entrance hall, whispering to each other. They, too, looked worried. "Where's Brother Joseph?" I asked.

"I'll take you," Sister Cindy replied. She led me upstairs. "I don't know what's happening to us," she said. "Everything used to be so wonderful. And now…"

We stopped in front of a small room. The door was open. Inside, Brother Joseph was sitting behind a desk. The top of the desk was littered with papers. He looked worn out, defeated. "Where have you been?" he asked when he noticed me.

"Investigating," I said. "What happened?"

"It seems that Brother Scott left the Church last night," Joseph said. "And he took all our money with him."

CHAPTER 9

Brother Joseph dismissed Sister Cindy. I sat down on the opposite side of the desk. The room, like the top of the desk, was a mess—the bed unmade, the drawers in the dresser open and their contents dumped on the floor.

"This is Brother Scott's room?" I asked.

Joseph nodded.

"Are you searching for him?"

"Of course. But we won't find him. We didn't realize he was missing until well after breakfast. He could have reached Boston by now, even if he walked the entire way."

I patted the back of my head, which was still throbbing. It occurred to me that I could have gotten the searching started a lot sooner, if I'd been thinking straight. "I can give you some background here," I said. And I told him about my interview with Brother Scott, followed by my late-night adventure.

Not surprisingly, Joseph was more upset by

Scott's accusation that he had stolen the Church's money than by my bashed head. "That's absurd!" he exploded. "What a contemptible little man. Why didn't you tell me right away?"

I shrugged. "I guess I should have. But I thought it was pretty clear what was going on."

"But you gave him a chance to disappear with all the money!"

"He doesn't have the money," I said.

"What do you mean? Do you believe his accusation? You think *I* have the money?"

"Of course not. You didn't steal the money—that doesn't make any sense, and Brother Scott knows it. No, Flynn Dobler took the money."

"What do you mean?" he demanded. "*That* makes no sense."

"It's not a theory you want to hear, but it's the only one that fits the facts."

"What theory?"

"Brother Flynn wasn't murdered—I don't see how anyone could have pulled it off without making any noise or leaving any clues behind. And he didn't ascend into heaven—Sister Lucy is a nice old lady, but she's not what I'd call a compelling witness. Besides, private eyes don't believe in miracles; they're not part of our worldview. Theoretically he could have been kidnapped, but again—no noise, no clues. And no motive for anyone to kidnap him. No, Flynn Dobler stole the Church's money and left here in the dead of night."

"But why? Why would he do that?"

"The Church has been falling apart," I pointed

out. "Everyone's been worried about that. No matter how appealing, Brother Flynn's ideas just weren't working. To survive, you need to make money, build barbed-wire fences—make compromises. He didn't want to do that. Sister Marva said he seemed excited in the days before he left. She thought he was getting ready to go to heaven. But that wasn't it; he was excited because he had made the decision to get out of here."

"I refuse to believe it," Brother Joseph responded. "If that's the case—if Brother Flynn took the money—then why did Brother Scott leave?"

"Precisely because everyone else in the Church is going to react the same way you just did. The money's gone, so they'll blame Brother Scott. He was the one in charge of the money. They're not going to blame Brother Flynn."

Brother Joseph pondered my argument, and then shook his head. "If Brother Flynn wasn't murdered, then Sister Lucy is right: he went to heaven. He wouldn't just steal all our money and leave us."

We were silent for a moment. Then I said, "Even if you don't believe my theory, you've got to admit that it fits the facts. So if you want my professional advice, the next step in this case is to follow up on it, see if we can figure out where Flynn Dobler went after he disappeared. That may not be easy, but it's not impossible."

Brother Joseph shook his head. "The next step," he said, "is to find Brother Scott and get our money back."

"You're the boss," I replied. "Finding Brother Scott should be easier than finding Flynn Dobler. But he's not going to have your money—at least, not all of it. If there's nothing left in the desk, then he took everything that came in since Dobler disappeared."

"Then I want that money back, at least."

"All right. Any idea where he might be?"

"How would I know?" he asked impatiently.

"Um, OK. So can I get a ride back to Boston? Sister Marva said—"

He waved me silent. "Brother Reggie and some of the others are out searching the grounds. He can take you when he gets back."

"That'd be great."

He turned his attention back to the papers on Scott's desk.

Brother Joseph was not in a good mood. Neither was anyone else, as I discovered when I talked to some of the disciples while waiting for my ride back to the city. No one had any additional information to offer about Scott and his disappearance. He was not well liked, but he was faithful to Brother Flynn. A few people tried to spin a hopeful story out of what had happened: *God is testing us. We will come out of this stronger than ever.* But they didn't sound especially convincing.

A few of them decided to blame me. Which, I suppose, was not unreasonable. The last thing anyone had seen him do was to talk to me. A few hours later, he was gone. What had I said to him?

What had I done? I had my own theory about what Scott was thinking after our interview, and why it convinced him to leave the Church, but after my conversation with Brother Joseph, I didn't bother offering it to anyone else.

Finally Brother Reggie returned. Brother Scott was nowhere to be found on the farm, or on the highway nearby. Not that anyone really expected to find him. As Brother Joseph pointed out, even on foot he could have made it to Boston before they started searching. Or he could have flagged down a passing vehicle and paid for a ride with the money he'd stolen. Or he could simply be hiding out in an abandoned house in the wilds of Arlington or Belmont.

Brother Reggie was not happy when he found out he had to take me into the city. "Not my job," he told Brother Joseph. "My job is to be with Sister Marva."

"She's already gone to the city with Brother Harold," Joseph told him. "Don't blame me for that—she's just doing her job."

Brother Reggie looked stricken. He glared at me as if it was all my fault. But he got a fresh horse, hitched her up to a spare cart, and we headed back to the city.

"Sorry you have to do this," I said to him.

He just grunted.

"And I'm sorry you didn't get to go to the Food Market. I know how loyal you are to Sister Marva."

"Sister Marva is the best person in the world," he asserted.

"She's great," I said. And then: "I'm going to try to find Brother Scott."

"I'll find him first," Reggie growled. "And when I do, I'll kill him."

And that was pretty much the end of our conversation.

I was glad to be going home to Gwen and Stretch. I wondered how many other little communities like the Church of the New Beginning had sprung up since the War, trying to put into practice a different way of living, now that the old way had failed so completely. And how many of those communities had disappeared without a trace after someone killed someone, or stole someone's money, or fucked someone's woman? And what would the disciples up in Concord do when their community disappeared?

I'm a lucky man, I thought, not for the first time.

It seemed to take forever for Brother Reggie to get me home. When we finally arrived at Louisburg Square, darkness was falling. Even though I wanted nothing more than to get rid of him, I felt obliged to invite Reggie to stay the night, or at least to eat supper with us. He grunted his refusal. He would water and feed his horse at a nearby stable, and then make his way back to the Church by moonlight. He wasn't afraid. He, too, wanted to get home.

I hurried inside, only to be met by Stretch in the front hall. "Where have you been?" he demanded.

"On a case," I said. "Didn't you—"

"Sure I read your note, but I didn't think it'd

take you this long to get back. We've gotta go."

"Go where?"

"To a meeting with Governor Bolton."

"Bolton? About what?"

"About the future of our country. Come on, Walter. We're already late."

"You know Gwen and I—"

"I know about that, but Gwen won't mind. This is important."

To Stretch, pretty much everything is important. And, despite being an extremely short person (well, maybe because of it), he is extremely difficult to argue with. He allowed me to pee and grab a leftover turkey leg and an apple to eat on the way. Gwen wasn't home yet, so I scrawled another note to let her know that Stretch had kidnapped me, and we would both be back after we had taken care of the future of our country.

CHAPTER 10

I was dying to tell Stretch and Gwen about my case, but clearly this would have to wait; Stretch had more important things on his mind. We walked down Beacon Hill toward Government Center while I ate my supper, and he filled me in on what he thought was so important. "You know that the delegation from the Federal government is in town, right?" he began.

"Um, I guess so."

"You need to *pay attention*, Walter," Stretch said, continuing to be exasperated with me. "Don't you read the newspaper? They're in Boston to negotiate with us about relations between the two countries. Assuming they recognize that New England is a country. Assuming they want relations with us. Nothing is more important to the people of New England than the outcome of these negotiations."

"OK. Sure. I couldn't agree more." Once the referendum about being part of the United States failed, Governor Bolton had put together an Executive Council that purported to represent all the New England states, but most of the jaded, suspicious inhabitants of those states didn't recognize the council as legitimate. Did we have a constitution? Did we have laws? If so, where were the troops and courts to enforce them? So tax revenue was down, prices were up, and the Church of the New Beginning was building a fence around itself, just in case. And what about the Federal government in Atlanta? We had thumbed our noses at it, but the rest of the United States had the food and the medicine and the technology we needed, and we didn't have a whole lot to offer them in return. Would the Feds let us descend into anarchy once again? If they decided to help us, what would they demand in return?

So, that's where we were: in a mess. And the Feds were here to talk to us about the mess.

Looking on the bright side, Stretch had gotten a promotion. Before the referendum debacle, Stretch had been a lowly bureaucrat working for the Sewer Commission. But sewers weren't something we were worrying about right now (although Stretch still felt very strongly about their importance). And he had played a key role in uncovering the funny business that had taken place during the president's visit. So Governor Bolton had made him one of his advisors, a role Stretch took very seriously indeed. Nothing was more important than advising our governor.

"So, um, what's this got to do with me,

Stretch?" I asked him.

"We need your skills, Walter. We need your help."

"Why me? What's going on?"

Stretch looked annoyed. "That's what this meeting is *about*."

"Have I mentioned that my head hurts? I got whacked with a rock last night."

He glared at me. What was a little headache, compared to the future of our country? "You'll be all right," he said. "You always end up all right."

"Thanks for the sympathy."

Bolton had his office in one of the big old office buildings that reminded us just how important government used to be, back before government managed to destroy just about everything. Some of the buildings still had electricity and telephones and other reminders of what most of us had lost. They had their own dedicated power plant somewhere or other, which was a matter of much grumbling in certain quarters—one more problem the governor had to contend with.

"I thought that Governor Bolton didn't have a very high opinion of me," I said as we crossed the broad open plaza of Government Center.

"That's not true," Stretch replied. "Look at how you cracked that case with President Kramer."

"Well, you know, that case didn't go as smoothly as I might have liked." In addition to incorrectly fingering Flynn Dobler as a suspect in the president's kidnapping, I had also managed to decide at one point that Bolton was the culprit.

Which landed me in jail for a not very pleasant night and presumably made Bolton my enemy.

At the entrance to Bolton's building we approached two armed guards, who took my gun and let us enter. "Don't worry about that," Stretch said to me. "These things happen. He knows you're the right man for the job."

We got into the elevator. Elevators always amazed and scared me. In my brief career as a private eye I have flown in an airplane, I have used a telephone, I have even watched a movie. But I can't say I have ever gotten used to these wonders that people once thought of as ordinary parts of their ordinary lives.

We got safely off the elevator and walked into Bolton's outer office, where his secretary was lounging at her desk, reading a pre-War novel by electric light. She was an attractive, plumpish blonde named Lisa, and I had been praying very hard that she wouldn't be there. She glared at me. I managed a weak smile in return. In my previous case, what had really landed me in jail was when I managed to intrude on her and the governor in what those pre-War novels called *an intimate setting*, and it was clear that she still wasn't happy about it, or me. I couldn't blame her.

"We're here to see the governor," Stretch announced importantly.

Lisa turned her glare onto Stretch, then returned it to me. But she picked up the phone and let the governor know we were here, after which she waved us dismissively into his office.

Stretch marched in. I followed. Governor

Bolton was sitting behind his desk. He glared at me. Lots of glaring going on. "I don't know why I'm doing this," he said. "You're a terrible private eye."

"Nice to see you again," I said to the governor.

Bolton had short gray hair and a scar next to his right eye. He was rubbing the scar while he glared. He used to be a real estate agent—one of many pre-War professions that no longer made any sense. By the end of my previous case I had decided that he was smarter than he looked. "This is all Chuck's idea," he grumbled.

Stretch's real name is Charles Moseby. Other people seem to call him *Chuck*, but Gwen and I couldn't bring ourselves to do it. I gave it a shot, though. "I have the utmost respect for Chuck's ideas," I replied. "But he hasn't told me yet what this particular one is."

"I thought the three of us should go over it together," Stretch explained. "Make sure we all agree."

Bolton gestured to Stretch to continue.

He complied. "So, like I was saying, Walter, the Federal negotiators are in Boston. They're staying over at Charles River Park. You've been there, right, Walter?"

"Yup." I'd had a very strange meeting with President Kramer when she was staying in the building.

"OK. So we have meetings during the day, over at the State House. Trying to figure out how we should work together. And this is where we get to the confidential stuff. Would you like to talk about that, sir?"

"As long as Sands doesn't say anything about this to that roommate of yours who works for the *Globe*," Bolton grumbled.

"Right," I said. "Not a problem." I like to think I'm pretty good at keeping things from Gwen. On the other hand, she's *really* good at getting things out of me. And Stretch knows that. So he was running a bit of a risk here.

"All right, then," the governor said. "The meetings are not going well. No, that's not right—they're going terribly. Fenwick isn't offering us anything."

"Who's Fenwick?"

"Roger Fenwick," Stretch explained. "The leader of the delegation."

"A cold bastard," Bolton added.

"Got it."

"Fenwick says everything is open to negotiation," Bolton continued, "but on most issues he's refusing to budge. Or he's asking for concessions he knows we can't make. We're beginning to think the meetings may just be a sham. Fenwick may have some other purpose altogether for coming to New England."

Bolton looked at me expectantly, as if I should know what that other purpose was. But I didn't have a clue.

"He's been sneaking out at night," Stretch explained. "We think he may be talking to Richardson or Velazquez or someone like them."

This was not going well. "Um, who are they?"

Bolton threw up his hands. Stretch looked

profoundly disappointed in me. "Listen, Walter," he said. "We are trying very hard to keep New England together. But it's not easy without Federal troops to help keep order. Everywhere you look, some town or island or county is declaring its independence. Or some gangster or warlord or whatever has taken someplace over and is running it for himself—like the way Jim O'Malley has basically been ruling Charlestown as his own private empire for years. So maybe Fenwick is also negotiating with one of those guys—or a bunch of them."

"The Feds still don't want New England to be a separate country," Bolton continued. "What's in it for them?"

"They could just invade us," I suggested. "We can't stop them."

"Why bother? They'd risk another Frenzy. Maybe they'd rather put a figurehead in charge of New England—someone who'd preserve the illusion of independence while secretly doing America's bidding."

"They know that Governor Bolton is not that person," Stretch said proudly. Stretch used to be a staunch American patriot. Now he's a true-blue New Englander and has no use for the Feds. It has been an impressive transformation.

"OK," I said, "but if you think this guy Fenwick is going out to secret meetings at night, why not just stop him? Tell him he has to stay inside. Tell him it's too dangerous or something. Which would certainly be true."

"We have made known our security concerns,"

Bolton growled. "He is ignoring those concerns."

"So you want me to—what? Follow him? That's not going to work."

"Why wouldn't it?"

"Too obvious. There's not enough traffic to—"

"Wherever Fenwick is going, he goes there on foot," Stretch said. "Alone. He walks away from Charles River Park at night, disappears, and then comes back a few hours later. You're perfect for this job, Walter. You know the city. You're not associated with the government. If he spots you, he'll probably just assume you're a mugger, or a crazy."

"And probably just shoot me."

"You've got a gun. You know how to protect yourself."

"Sure, but—"

"Isn't that the sort of risk a private eye takes?" Bolton demanded.

I rubbed my aching head. Yeah, private eyes take risks. And we pay the price. "So what exactly do you want me to do?" I asked. "See where he goes? Report back to you in the morning?"

"That's right," Stretch said. "Just find out what he's up to. We can take it from there."

I liked the way Stretch said *we*. He was proud of his promotion. Maybe someday he could be the governor of New England. I'd vote for him. "Well, can you tell me what he looks like?"

Stretch grinned. "I'll go over there with you and point him out when he leaves the building. Then you tail him and let us know what you find out.

Simple!"

I was in no mood for this. Gwen was waiting for me at home. But I wasn't getting enough cases to turn one down. "Two dollars a night," I said. "Also, I'm going to raise my rates if prices keep increasing around here."

"Two dollars will be fine," Stretch replied, with a quick glance at Bolton to make sure he hadn't overstepped his authority.

Bolton glowered at Stretch but didn't overrule him. "You're not in the employ of the New England government, do you understand?" he said to me. "If you get into any trouble with Fenwick or anyone else, we'll deny everything. And people will believe us. Why would we hire such a terrible private eye?"

"OK, sure. Good point."

"And don't try to be a hero. Like Chuck said, no interference. Don't follow him into any buildings. Don't try to find out who he's talking to. Don't do anything stupid. Got it?"

"Nothing stupid. Got it."

Bolton dismissed us with a wave. Stretch and I left his office. Outside, Lisa resumed glaring at us. I decided not to ask if I could get my two dollars in advance from petty cash.

"That went pretty well, don't you think?" Stretch asked as we went out into the corridor and waited for the magical elevator to arrive.

"It certainly did," I replied. "And I'm going to do everything in my power to reward the governor's confidence in me."

Stretch looked at me dubiously. He often finds

my sense of humor somewhat obscure. "Governor Bolton can be a bit gruff, but he does think you can help," he said.

"I'm sure you're right. Do you really believe this guy Fenwick is meeting with rebels from New Hampshire or wherever?"

The elevator arrived, and we took it back down to the lobby.

"Why else would he be sneaking out at night?" Stretch said. "To see the sights? I can tell you the governor is very worried. His job is on the line. More than that: New England's survival is on the line."

I got my gun back from the guards and we walked out of the building. Charles River Park was just a few blocks away. "Why does Bolton care about this stuff?" I asked Stretch. "Why doesn't he just quit and let someone else try to solve the problems? He and that secretary of his could go somewhere warm and leave this all behind."

Stretch gave me yet another disappointed look. "Walter, would you drop a case if it got too hard?" he asked.

"Well, probably not," I admitted.

"So why would he? You're both trying to help people, right? It's not easy nowadays. Nothing is easy nowadays. But we've got to keep trying."

Stretch is an inspiration to us all. He can be very annoying. We made our way through the city streets to the tall apartment building where Fenwick and other guests of the government stayed. Like the building in Government Center where Bolton had his office, it too had electric lights shining from many of its windows, and soldiers guarding its doors.

"He comes out the front," Stretch said. "And he's hard to miss. Nobody else leaves the building after dark without a military escort." We stood in the shadows of an abandoned pizza shop across the street.

"When?"

"Usually after eight. And he comes back sometime after midnight."

"Any idea what time it is now?" I asked.

"The clock outside Bolton's office said 7:10 when we left."

"Be prepared to get cold, then."

"It's always good to spend time with you, Walter."

It's hard to stay annoyed with Stretch for very long. "Why thank you," I replied. We were silent for a few minutes, and then I said, "Do you think Gwen is going to be mad at me?"

"Don't be silly. You're the best thing that ever happened to Gwen. And she's the best thing that ever happened to you."

"Well, that's certainly true." We fell silent again. Somewhere in the distance a dog howled; at least, I hoped it was a dog. A police car drove by; that was always an encouraging sign. There were few pedestrians. That wasn't such a good sign. "What'll happen if the negotiations with the Feds fail?" I asked Stretch.

"They can't fail."

"Don't see why. We're more trouble to the Feds

than we're worth. We have been ever since the War. The Brits bailed us out to begin with, then they got tired of us and went home. Then the Feds stepped in and kept us going for a while longer. What if we've run out of people to bail us out?"

"Then we'll have to solve our own problems. Don't you think we can, Walter?"

"Beats me, Stretch." Then I told him about my case at the Church of the New Beginning, and how that whole endeavor was at risk. "Life is pretty fragile, don't you think?" I said. "Somebody presses a button he shouldn't have pressed, and the world explodes. This Church has some disagreements about policy, and its leader disappears, and the whole thing starts to collapse. Not much room for error."

"That's why it was smart of the Church to get you to help," Stretch responded. "And I'm sorry about your head."

"Thanks, Stretch. It's feeling much better." It wasn't, but I didn't want to make him feel bad. I had already been too depressing for his taste.

"What's your next step on that case, Walter?"

"I have to find Brother Scott. I have an idea or two about that. And I'm pretty sure he know more about Brother Flynn's disappearance than he's told us so far."

"That's exciting."

"All my cases are exciting, Stretch."

Except when I stood out in the cold and the dark with a headache waiting to tail some guy who (it was becoming apparent) was going to stay in his apartment and enjoy its soft bed and central heat and electric lights instead of risking frostbite and the crazies lurking on the streets of Boston.

Except that, finally, he did appear. The door to the apartment building opened, and a solitary figure stepped out. He nodded to the guards, and then walked quickly across the plaza and down to street level. Stretch pulled me back into the shadows of the pizza shop's doorway. "That's him," he whispered. "Good luck!"

Fenwick didn't bother looking around. He just set off with long strides down the deserted street—like a man who was late for a meeting with rebels and warlords. Time for me to go to work. "Give Gwen a hug for me," I ordered Stretch.

"Sure will, Walter!"

And then I took off after Roger Fenwick.

CHAPTER 11

Fenwick made his way quickly through the night-time streets, and it was all I could do to keep up, never mind keep myself from being noticed. Tailing someone was one of those private-eye skills that I hadn't practiced much. But my quarry didn't seem nervous about possibly being followed. He never looked behind, never hesitated. At least the exercise warmed me up.

The first stage of the journey took us past a jumble of dismal, deserted high-rise buildings and refuse-strewn parking lots. Fenwick kept going, as I figured he would; there were better places to meet with rebels, if that's what he was up to. Then I saw the lights of Mass. General ahead, and I thought—is he sick? Is he going to the hospital? But why would he go there every night? And why would he want our lousy medical care, when he could go to a hospital down in Atlanta? Medical care was exactly the sort of thing we needed the Feds to help us with.

So I wasn't surprised when he strode past the hospital, heading towards the Charles River, and Cambridge. He made his way up onto the Longfellow Bridge. I held back, letting him extend the distance between us. There were no other pedestrians, although an occasional car or carriage went past. I thought of Brother Reggie heading back to Concord in his cart. Would he be home by now? What was the mood in the Church tonight?

Then Fenwick stopped abruptly in the middle of the bridge and leaned against the railing, looking out at the river. The river was pretty in the moonlight, but not pretty enough to be worth a long, dangerous walk. It occurred to me that he was thinking about jumping, and that made me nervous. Was I supposed to jump in and rescue him? Jumping into the Charles River on a cold night was not my idea of private-eye excitement.

Eventually Fenwick started walking again, a little more slowly this time. More cars passed; another carriage went by, a lantern lighting its way through the darkness. Most were headed toward Cambridge. And as we approached the end of the bridge I suddenly understood where he was going. So obvious! So…unexciting.

The Longfellow Bridge brought you to Kendall Square on the Cambridge side of the river. I'm told that Kendall Square was once the home of companies that employed thousands of highly educated people who spent their days inventing computer software and medicines and other such wonders. The companies are all gone now, of course; MIT, the university that educated those people, is gone as well.

In their place, Kendall Square is now the home of One-Eyed Joe's.

One-Eyed Joe is a large man—almost the size of Brother Reggie—with a bald head and big black patch over his left eye. Some say he lost the eye fighting off half a dozen crazies during the Frenzy. Others say he lost it during a raucous brawl after a card game with some British soldiers. I've also heard that he lost it falling off his bicycle when he was a kid, back before the War. People's pasts are often rather hazy nowadays. What we do know for sure about One-Eyed Joe is that he runs the biggest brothel in the Boston area.

If you've got to have brothels, I suppose you could do worse than One-Eyed Joe's. I've talked to some of the girls, and they say they are treated reasonably well, and of course they make more money there than they could in most other fields of endeavor. But I find the whole idea of brothels very depressing. After I got out of the army Joe tried to convince me to work security at his place. He was a genial enough fellow, with a soft voice that belied his ominous appearance. From his perspective, he was just providing a needed public service. What was wrong with that? But I turned him down. My field of endeavor doesn't pay well, but I have my standards.

So as Fenwick made his way into Kendall Square, I was convinced that he was looking for entertainment at One-Eyed Joe's. But then I started to get confused. As part of Joe's public service, I knew that he offered transportation for customers who didn't want to brave the city streets. Or he would send a girl to you. Why not take advantage of his many fine entertainment options? Was Fenwick afraid of blackmail? Were the Feds that strait-laced?

The brothel was in a long repurposed brick building on Main Street in the square. Joe had installed old-fashioned gas streetlamps along the sidewalk in front—to give prostitution a quaint nostalgic feel, I guess. A few security guys were standing by the entrance. From inside I could hear music playing—again, something old-timey, with brass and a piano. Ah, the good old days! A mixture of ancient cars and horse-drawn carriages were parked on the street.

I stopped short of the place and watched Fenwick.

He talked to one of the security guys, who went inside. And then Fenwick waited, leaning against a lamppost, his collar raised against the cold. Why? Was a girl being summoned? Where would he take her?

Several minutes later the security guy returned, holding a satchel. He handed the satchel to Fenwick. In return, Fenwick took something out of his pocket and handed it to the security guy. Paying him, apparently. And then he strode off across Main Street, carrying the satchel, still heading north.

Had he stopped off at One-Eyed Joe's simply to

buy supper? Was he bringing food to his meeting with the rebels?

Now tailing Fenwick became harder, as he entered an area of narrow, deserted streets. If I stayed too close, he was bound to notice me. If I stayed too far back, he could make a sudden turn and I'd lose him. And I sure didn't want to lose Fenwick now, after wasting a few miles of my life in pursuit of him.

At first the streets were lined with tall empty buildings where those technology companies had once thrived; they were now just so many monuments to futility. Then the buildings became smaller—medical offices, restaurants, gas stations, a sprinkling of apartments. And then we encountered pockets of close-packed three-deckers in the midst of the commerce. And it was all a wasteland. Many blocks were blackened ruins, the result of fires that no one had been around to fight. The houses that were still standing had sagging roofs and shattered windows, victims of slow-motion destruction that had now lasted for more than two decades.

Life in downtown Boston is reasonably safe nowadays (although the departure of Federal troops might be starting to change that). Life is happening in Boston; law and order have been, more or less, restored. And rural areas are pretty safe as well. The people on the farms are hardy, self-sufficient, and hospitable; they'll offer a traveler a meal and a bed, although they'll keep their shotgun handy just in case.

It's the suburbs and the deserted areas of the

city where you have to be careful. There's no particular reason to be in these places—there are no communities, there's not enough land to grow your own food, and anything worth scavenging has probably already been scavenged. The only people you're likely to find are the crazies—the people who, for whatever reason, have decided to live their lives in the shadows of our post-War world. There are fewer of these folks nowadays, but if you're going to find them, that's where you'd look.

So I wasn't happy that this was where Fenwick was leading me. I would much rather have spent the evening hanging around outside One-Eyed Joe's, having solved the case to what I'm sure would have been everyone's satisfaction. Wouldn't it be nice if Fenwick wasn't meetings with rebels; he had no secret plan to destroy New England's government; he was just looking to satisfy a primal need? Let's get back to the negotiations.

Too bad.

And eventually I lost him. He crossed a main street, and then turned down a side street. By the time I reached the side street, he was gone. I reached the next cross street and looked in every direction. Nobody. I listened. Nothing.

Now what?

I stayed where I was. He couldn't have gotten away from me unless he had started running, I reasoned. And I would have heard his footsteps in the silence if he'd been running. So…

So I waited, and listened, and looked around,

and finally I saw a glimmer of light appear. To the left. In the second-floor window of a two-family house.

I approached slowly. If Fenwick was meeting Richardson or Velasquez or whoever, there'd be guards outside, right? There'd be activity. There'd be noise. No reason to keep quiet. There was no one to disturb.

But I heard nothing, I saw nothing, except for that single light.

I stopped across the street from the house. The light in the window had the soft glow of an oil lamp. It appeared to be behind a curtain. I couldn't see any activity, any silhouettes moving back and forth. There was nothing out of the ordinary about the place. It was separated from its neighbors by narrow driveways overrun by weeds. Its second-floor porch sagged in the middle, waiting for one final snowstorm to put it out of its misery. The chain-link fence surrounding its tiny front yard had already given up the fight against time and weather and collapsed.

Why would the rebels—why would anyone—choose this place to meet?

I waited a while longer, and then I crossed the street to get a closer look. The front door was slightly ajar. Most of the first-floor windows were broken. I made my way carefully along the driveway into the back yard. The light on the second floor wasn't visible from behind the house. I looked around. The door to the small garage was open. If there had once been a car inside, it had long ago been carted off; cars and car parts were valuable, even if houses weren't. In the yard, a rusted metal swing set lay on its side, looking like some dead mutant creature in the moonlight.

This sort of thing is just part of the landscape nowadays, but that doesn't make it easy to get used to. The government has occasionally made noises about clearing out these deserted, dangerous neighborhoods and turning them into farmland or finding some other useful purpose for them. But there's never been the money or the will. So these places are likely to continue to burn and rot and rust, and remind us of the past.

I headed back out front and resumed my post across the street, sitting on the front steps of another house. The light was still glowing in the second-floor window. What the heck was going on? Was Fenwick the first one to arrive? Had the rebels and warlords failed to show up? Had Stretch and Bolton gotten this all completely wrong?

Time passed and the light still shone and I got colder and colder and my head started to pound. I needed to pee; at least I was able to do something about that. I was itching to march back across the street, go into the damn place, and find out just what Fenwick was up to in there. But Bolton had forbidden me to do that, and he was paying me two dollars a day for the privilege of ordering me around. So I continued the stakeout, cursing this stupid profession I had chosen. Maybe I had been too hasty in rejecting One-Eyed Joe's offer.

Damn scruples.

I tried thinking about my other case, but that didn't help. What kind of stupid case was it where God was one of the suspects?

I decided to think about Gwen instead. Sooner or later I'd be back home, and Gwen would be waiting for me. And she wouldn't be mad. I was pretty sure.

And then, finally, the light went out. Or, rather, it faded, and after a moment reappeared on the stairs. I crouched down in the front-yard weeds across the street. Then the light went out for good, and the front door swung open, and there was Fenwick once again, still holding the satchel.

He stood on the front steps for a moment, surveying his surroundings. He failed to spot me, and then he strode off into the night without a glance behind.

I took off after him, doing my private-eye duty once again. I was starting to hate the guy. Didn't he have anything better to do with his nights? Because I sure did.

He stopped at One-Eyed Joe's and handed the satchel back to one of the security guys. Then he crossed back over the Charles and once again paused in the middle of the Longfellow Bridge to look out at the serene, changeless river.

And that's when I had my sudden flash of inspiration, and I decided I didn't hate the guy anymore.

I also decided I had cracked the case.

This made me forget the cold and the headache and the general bone-weariness I was feeling.

Good for me!

It did not escape my notice that I'd had that I've-cracked-the-case feeling before, and later found out I'd been sorely mistaken. Governor Bolton and his attractive secretary would be happy to remind me of that. Sister Marva could also remind me, if she wasn't so nice. But, hey, I wasn't wrong this time—I just knew it!

Fenwick hurried back into Boston, up Cambridge Street, past Mass. General. I wasn't especially concerned if I lost him now, but I wanted to be able to say I followed him all the way to the apartment building and watched him go inside. No loose ends.

And I did it. I was back in the doorway of the pizza shop looking on as Fenwick strode past the guards and back into Charles River Park. I took a deep breath. There. Hadn't been so bad.

I headed back to Louisburg Square, aware that I had to stay vigilant. My neighborhood was safer than the wilds of Cambridge and Somerville, but danger still lurked late at night. Fortunately, no one sprang out of the darkness at me, and I made it back home without a problem.

A candle burned in the window of our once-elegant townhouse. Gwen had stayed up for me, as I had known she would.

CHAPTER 12

◆ ◆ ◆

Gwen will reject any notion that she is beautiful, but she is. Not in a Sister Marva sort of way, I suppose. Her skin isn't flawless; her cheekbones are too pronounced; her eyes sometimes seem too hollow. Deprivation and despair have taken their toll, as they have on most of us. But when she looks at you—when she offers you her smile—life just doesn't seem quite so hard, and you understand why it's worth the struggle.

She was sitting on our patched brown Victorian sofa wearing her patched blue robe. Two glasses of cider and a plate of bread and cheese and apple slices sat on a side table. She had lit a fire in the fireplace, so the front parlor wasn't as cold as it usually was. She patted the sofa next to her, and I sat down gratefully. She snuggled up against me. "Happy anniversary," she whispered.

"Happy anniversary," I replied, kissing the top of her head. The clock on the fireplace mantel told me it was after one in the morning. "Although I guess it was yesterday. Sorry."

"Doesn't matter in the slightest."

This was why I'd had to get home from the Church. It was the anniversary of the day Gwen and I had met, in an abandoned house where we had both taken shelter, back when we were very young and very scared. Or, rather, it was the date on which we later decided to celebrate our anniversary—we weren't paying much attention to calendars back when we met. Anyway, she had come pretty close to blowing my head off at our first meeting, but she had thought better of it, and decided to fall in love with me instead. Lucky me.

"Stretch gone to bed?" I asked after a while.

"Of course." Stretch was an early-to-bed, early-to-rise kind of guy. "He told me what you've been up to at the Church of the New Beginning. But he was sketchy about tonight. Care to fill in the details?"

I considered. I wanted to hear Gwen's opinions about a lot of things, but I was too tired. And this wasn't the time. "Not really. Not now. And I'm not supposed to tell you about what I was up to tonight. Stretch's orders."

"That's fine," she said. If I wanted to talk, Gwen was always happy to listen. If I didn't, that was fine too. "Stretch told me about your head. Are you OK?"

"I'm OK. Occupational hazard."

"Stupid occupation," she replied. "Are you sure you don't have a concussion?"

"Yes," I lied. I drank the cider, ate a hunk of bread and cheese, and closed my eyes, feeling Gwen's familiar warmth pressing into my side. She must have been really tired, staying up this late. I was tired too, despite my aversion to sleep.

"We should go to bed," I said.

"Soon," Gwen replied, snuggling closer.

I listened to the clock on the mantel ticking away the seconds of our lives. Another year together. Another year of fighting off the darkness. Someday the darkness will overwhelm us, I suppose. But so far it hadn't.

After a few minutes I looked down at Gwen. She was asleep. I disentangled myself from her and went over to blow out the candle. Then I went back to the sofa and picked her up. She awoke and sighed with pleasure, putting her arms around my neck and burying her face in my chest. The weight of her felt good in my arms. I carried her upstairs in the flickering shadows of the firelight. At the top of the stairs I made my way in the darkness to our bedroom and laid her gently down on the bed.

"This was worth waiting for," she murmured.

"I'm not done yet," I whispered.

I extracted her from her ratty old robe and got her under the covers. Then I quickly disrobed and joined her.

"Do we need foreplay?" Gwen asked.

"Don't see why."

She giggled. I tunneled beneath the covers and pulled her pajama bottoms off as she ran her hand through my hair. Then I made my way back to the surface and took my position on top of her. She spread her legs and guided me into her. "How many times have we made love?" she whispered into my ear as I began.

"Nowhere near enough," I replied, and we proceeded to add to our lifetime total.

Afterward we lay in each other's arms, as we always did. "Someday sleep will come easy," she murmured.

"And someday dreams will come true."

We had said those words many times before, but somewhere along the line we had come to realize that this was the dream that had come true, and all the other ones didn't really matter.

And then, finally, sleep came for both of us in the silent city.

Stretch barged in on us the next morning, as he sometimes does. He is generally respectful of our privacy, but of course the survival of the nation was more important than anything. At least to Stretch.

"Sorry to wake you up," he said, "but I'm going to work, Walter, and I need to know what happened last night."

"We're both naked," I pointed out.

"Right. Sure. I'll turn around." He turned around. "Gwen isn't supposed to know anything about this," he noted. "You remember what Governor Bolton said."

Gwen smiled. She adored Stretch. "Don't worry about me," she said. "I'll go downstairs." She found her pajamas and robe, put them on, and left the room.

I put on my pants, and Stretch turned back to me. "Well?" he said. "Did you find out where Fenwick was going?"

"I did. He went to the second floor of a two-family house at 34 Rosewell Street. I think that's in Somerville, but it might be Cambridge. I don't really know where the boundary is, not that anyone cares."

"Somerville? What was he doing in Somerville? Did you see anyone else there? Was he meeting with the rebels? We should send troops over and check it out."

I got a fresh shirt and socks out of my dresser. "Send troops if you like," I said, "but there wasn't any meeting. He was there by himself. He brought dinner from One-Eyed Joe's. He took a lamp up to the second floor, he stayed there a couple of hours, and then he left. There wasn't another soul around. The place was dark before he entered, and it was dark after he left."

"Then what was he up to? Besides eating dinner."

I sat on the bed and pulled on my socks. "I don't know for sure, Stretch, but I have a theory."

That got Stretch excited. "What is it, Walter?"

"I think he was going home."

"Home?"

"Check Fenwick's background. Find census records, property deeds, old phonebooks, whatever information the government's got lying around about the old days. You must have some way of figuring out who used to live at that address. I'll bet that's where he grew up."

"But he goes out every night. Why would he want to go back there night after night?"

Stretch's imagination is a bit limited, seems to me. He was born after the War and he was born too short; his parents gave him away as soon as they could get rid of him, and he has fended for himself ever since he's been able to fend. For him, the past isn't worth thinking about. Why waste time on all that old stuff? What's done is done. The future is all that matters.

He would not make a good private eye.

I found my shoes where I had tossed them aside last night, and I put them on. "He keeps going there because he's homesick, is my theory. For lots of people, the old days are hard to leave behind, Stretch. Back then was probably the last time they were really happy. Why shouldn't they want to return to where they were happy?"

Stretch looked dubious. "We have records, I guess."

"Check them. Maybe I'm wrong. But if I'm right, you don't have anything to worry about. Fenwick isn't talking to rebels—he's communing with his childhood. Now if you'll excuse me, I have to perform my morning ablutions."

I don't think I convinced Stretch, but I'd given him something to think about. "Okay, Walter. Thanks," he said. "I'll talk to the governor. That'll be great news—if it's true." He turned and bustled out of the bedroom.

"You guys still owe me two dollars!" I called after him.

"You're worth every penny, Walter!" he called back from the hall.

By the time I got downstairs Stretch had left for work. He was a busy man. Gwen was in the kitchen, waiting to eat breakfast with me. "Want eggs?" she asked.

"I do, very much."

She took eggs and milk out of the icebox, and we set about preparing the meal. "Care to tell me what Stretch's case is all about?" she asked me. "It sounds very interesting."

"I want desperately to tell you, but I'm under orders not to."

"The *Globe*'s readership is keenly interested in the status of the negotiations with the delegation from Atlanta," she observed as she scrambled the eggs. "If one of its reporters were to get a scoop about those negotiations, or the people involved in them, that reporter's reputation and career prospects would be greatly enhanced."

"They can't run that place without you and they know it," I replied, pouring two glasses of milk and cutting off some hunks of bread. "Anyway, let me tell you about my other case. I could use your advice."

"I can't wait. I love giving you advice."

When breakfast was ready, we sat down at the kitchen table to eat, and I told the story of the missing charismatic religious leader with my usual flair and panache.

Well, that's a lie. I was thrown off my stride early on when I described Sister Marva, and I saw the shadow that passed swift as a dream across Gwen's face. I immediately understood my mistake, but what could I have done about it? Marva was a big part of the case.

Gwen wasn't jealous of Marva's beauty, I knew, although she had good reason to be suspicious of my ability to resist female temptation. No, it was the description of Marva's bulging belly that caught her off guard and let that shadow slip by her many defenses. Gwen would gladly have produced a half dozen babies to help populate the future that Stretch was so enamored of, but after years of frequent and energetic and joyously unprotected lovemaking with yours truly, there hadn't been a hint of a pregnancy. Was it her? Was it me? It didn't matter which of us was the problem. She didn't want just any old babies; she wanted *my* babies. And that didn't look like it was going to happen.

Gwen didn't say a word about this, of course. Her focus, as always, was on me: my case, my problems. At the end of my recitation she said, "I suspect everyone."

"Okay. That's helpful."

"Well, they certainly seem like quite a crew. Do you think Brother Scott's up to something with Brother Flynn?"

"I don't see how that would work. But I could be wrong."

"And you think Flynn just...left the place? Walked away in the middle of the night?"

"Nothing else fits the facts. Unless we want to believe Sister Lucy that he ascended into heaven."

"And you don't think that's possible?"

"I think I should rule out the mundane before I consider the miraculous."

She tilted her head in that adorable way of hers and considered. "It's odd that Flynn Dobler is so secretive about his past," she said.

"Some people can't stop talking about the old days," I pointed out. "Other people can't forget about the old days fast enough. Both approaches seem reasonable to me."

"You should talk to Ken Hendrikson," Gwen said. "He's written a couple of stories about the Church, I think. Maybe he knows something about Dobler."

I vaguely recalled Hendrikson, one of Gwen's colleagues at the *Globe*. A dour, bald guy who liked to wear ancient tweed jackets. "I'd love to," I said. "But you can't tell him about the case. It's not my story."

Gwen pouted. "You and your ethics."

"There's one other thing I wanted to tell you," I said. I was worried about this one. "You know Mary Beth Callahan—Pete's wife?"

"Of course, Walter," she replied gently. "Mary Beth's pregnant, too. I know."

"How come you didn't tell me?"

"*My* ethics this time. She didn't want the news to spread until she was sure the baby was OK. Last I heard she was still pretty worried."

"Pete seems worried, too. I ran into him guarding the Food Market—I think he's taking on extra shifts since she quit her job."

"Good for him."

We fell silent, both of us probably thinking about Mary Beth and Sister Marva. The world repopulating itself. Good for the world.

"Anyway, how's your head?" Gwen asked.

"Better."

"Got a few minutes before you go off looking for Brother Scott?"

Her foot began rubbing against my leg. Gwen has very sexy feet. "I believe I do," I replied.

She smiled. I smiled back. "Back upstairs?" I asked.

"Right here," she murmured.

My smile widened. I would make love to Gwen in the middle of the Food Market if that's what she wanted me to do.

So we stripped off our clothes and shoved aside the dirty dishes on the kitchen table, and I took her right there, amid the breadcrumbs. And then we laughed and put our clothes back on and cleaned up the mess, just another couple getting ready for another busy day.

CHAPTER 13

And a busy day it was.

The first task: try to find Brother Scott.

If he hadn't headed straight to Boston, this would be hopeless. I had no chance if he decided to disappear into the wilderness—heading west on Route 2 to look for work in a shop or on a farm somewhere in rural Massachusetts. But I didn't think he'd do this. My theory was that he'd either find a job in the city, or try to make his way south from Boston, into the United States proper. Into warmth, into civilization. He wasn't a laborer; he wasn't an adventurer; he was an accountant.

I figured the fastest way to verify that he was in Boston would be to head on over to the Salvage Market.

The Salvage Market is located in a dreary commercial area called Downtown Crossing. Like the Food Market, it consists of many small vendors. Anyone can set up shop outdoors and try to sell whatever they think someone might buy. There's a rough organization to the place—over here for household goods, over there for tools, down this street for auto parts, down that one for clothing. The permanent merchants have indoor shops in the former malls and department stores. The big ones have their own trucks that they send out to bring back saleable goods. Others work with wholesalers like my friend Bobby Gallagher, who doesn't want to be a salesman but loves to go out with his associates in search of treasures; I join him when I don't have anything better to do, which is more often than I'd like.

The forward thinkers among us are not thrilled about the Salvage Market. "We should be creating our future, not just scavenging our past," I've heard Stretch say. Fair enough. But most of us don't care about creating the future; we're just trying to cope with the present. And it's not like anyone's going to open an auto parts manufacturing plant around here anytime soon. So we try to make do with all the stuff that got left behind when the War came and things fell apart. I like to think of it as the past's gift to us. It's the least the past could do.

So I biked over to the outdoor clothing stalls to start my day. There aren't as many of them as there used to be, I think. A shirt is a more perishable commodity than a hammer; besides, we actually do have a bit of a cottage industry making clothes. But there are still attics and closets to be explored, filled with jeans and jerseys and boxers with heart patterns on them and t-shirts celebrating long-forgotten rock bands. So there are still a lot of stalls where you can furnish yourself with a cheap wardrobe. And that's what Brother Scott was going to need, if he didn't want everyone to notice that he was from the Church.

I went over to Janice Kohl, a friendly gray-haired lady with whom I was acquainted. "Hey, Janice," I said.

She gave me a bright smile. "Good morning, Walter. Still hanging out with that no-good deadbeat piece-of-shit loser Bobby Gallagher?"

Bobby and Janice had had a fling once upon a time. It had ended badly. Bobby claimed that he was entirely without fault in the matter; I have my doubts. "Off and on, Janice. Purely a business relationship."

"Tell him I hope he gets a painful disease that makes his tiny little needle-nose dick shrivel up and fall off. Would you do that for me?"

"I'd be delighted."

"Appreciate it, Walter. Now, how can I help you?"

"I don't need any clothes at the moment, thanks. I'm just looking for a guy who may have stopped by here yesterday. He would have been wearing a brown robe—like a monk? I'm thinking he came here to buy some clothes so he could change out of that robe."

"Scrawny, nervous little guy?"

"That's the one."

"Yeah, he stopped by—sometime in the late morning, I think."

"Did he buy anything from you?"

"No, apparently my selection of apparel didn't appeal to his sophisticated fashion sensibility. Also, he was a cheapskate. Check with Rosie across the way—I think he stopped there next."

"Thanks, Janice." So, that part was easy. Scott must have come to the Salvage Market soon after he arrived in the city.

I went to talk to Rosie across the way. I didn't know her. She wasn't much taller than Stretch and had one less eye. But she didn't look unhappy to be out in the sunshine on a fine fall day. "Hi Rosie, my name is Walter Sands," I said. "I'm sorry to bother you, but my friend Janice over there tells me that a guy in a brown robe stopped by your stall yesterday."

She rolled her eye. "Him. Toughest two dollars I ever made. Complained about the price of everything. My prices are as fair as anyone's in town. Take a look, if you don't think so."

"I have no doubt that they are, Rosie. Do you remember what he ended up buying?"

She considered. "Black pea coat," she said. "There was a rip in one pocket, but so what? That's easily mended. No reason to give someone thirty percent off my already low price. The condition is built into the price. I'm not trying to cheat people here. Ask Janice. Ask anyone."

"I couldn't agree more. Your prices look more than reasonable. Did he buy anything else, Rosie?"

"Blue corduroy pants. Two t-shirts. One had a couple paint stains on it. Big deal. The other was a Bud Light shirt. You're too young to remember Bud Light, but I'm not. Horrible stuff. Tasted like cat piss. Cold cat piss. Plus a gray turtleneck jersey. Okay, there was a little rip in the shoulder. I gave him twenty cents off for the rip—just to get rid of him, really. What a pain."

"That's terrible. Sounds like he was really annoying. He didn't happen to mention where he was going after he bought the clothes, did he?"

Rosie shook her head. "No, and I hope I never have to talk to him again. You wouldn't be interested in a nice pair of pants, would you? Yours are a bit ragged."

I looked down at my pants; she was right, of course. "Maybe some other time, Rosie. I need to find this guy. He stole money from some folks I know."

"Doesn't surprise me one bit. People nowadays."

We both shook our heads at the depth to which humanity had sunk, and then I headed off on my quest for Brother Scott, now presumably wearing a black pea coat, blue corduroy pants, and a gray turtleneck with a rip in the shoulder.

This was going to be the hard part. Once he was no longer wearing his brown robe, Brother Scott could melt away into the city. There were plenty of abandoned buildings where you could find a place to stay, alone and unnoticed and impossible to find. But I didn't think he would do that. Because those places wouldn't have locks, wouldn't have beds or blankets, wouldn't have running water, wouldn't have fireplaces or stoves or oil lamps…Squatting in those places is hard and frightening; it isn't for the faint of heart. And I believed that Scott had a faint heart. I figured he would end up in one of the many rooming houses that dot the city. The owners of these places had once been squatters themselves, but now they pay their taxes, so their water is hooked up and the fire trucks come when needed and the cops on patrol pay attention to them. They have locks on their doors and food in their pantries and sheets on their beds. They are a part of the city that works.

I couldn't visit all those rooming houses, but I had one clue: Brother Scott had mentioned that he'd been living on Clarendon Street when Brother Flynn had come into his life. Would he return to the same place he'd lived back then?

Well, why not? The only problem was that Clarendon Street stretched all the way through the Back Bay and into the South End. Couldn't he at least have mentioned a cross street?

I didn't have a better idea of where to search, so I biked to where Clarendon Street started, in the Back Bay near the river, and I began knocking on doors. And in return I got blank stares, shakes of the head, and angry warnings to quit bothering people; also several barking dogs, and more than one rifle barrel aimed at me through the narrow opening of a chained door. Okay, then. Like staking out the apartment building at Charles River Park and then trailing Roger Fenwick for miles in the cold and dark, I was once again enjoying the real life of a private eye.

This went on for a couple of hours. When I reached Copley Square I bought a couple of apples from a street vendor and took a break in the shadow of the Boston Public Library, heartbreakingly deserted ever since the Frenzy. I figured I should have pressed harder at the Church for information about Scott's past. Maybe someone there remembered his address. Not likely, though, if they didn't even know where Flynn Dobler came from.

When I finished my apples I forced myself to keep going—past Trinity Church and into the South End.

And finally I knocked on the door of yet another rooming house, and the door was opened by an old black guy wearing a flannel shirt and jeans who actually looked happy to see me.

"Hi," I began, "my name is Walter Sands and—"

"Walter! Pleased to meet you. Can I call you 'Wally'?"

"Um, sure."

"My name's Cleanthony. That's 'Anthony' with a C-L-E in front of it."

"Hello, Cleanthony."

"How are you, son? You know, it's tough goin' through life with a name like mine you have to spell out. 'Wally' now, no one's gonna have a problem spelling that."

It occurred to me that he may have encountered worse problems in the course of his life than the spelling of his first name, but I didn't raise the issue. "So Cleanthony, I'm sorry to bother you but—"

"No bother, Wally. None at all."

"That's great. I'm looking for someone, Cleanthony. A guy wearing a black pea coat, blue corduroy pants, gray turtleneck jersey. He's short and thin, with wispy—"

"Scott! You're lookin' for Scott!" The news appeared to delight Cleanthony.

"That's right—Scott. See, he's—"

"It's so great to have him back," Cleanthony gushed. "I don't know why he thought he should join up with that fool Church. Why you wanna go and do that, I asked him. Bunch of crazy people, dressin' up in them funny clothes and whatnot. Shoulda stayed here, with his friends. Looks like he's learned his lesson."

"I couldn't agree more. I wonder if Scott is, um, home?"

"'Course he's home! Gonna look for a job as soon as he can, but I told him, don't you worry about nothin', it's all gonna turn out fine, and you can stay here just as long as you like."

"That's very generous of you, Cleanthony. I wonder if I could speak to Scott."

"'Course you can! Right on up those stairs, last door on the left."

"Thank you so much. Scott is very lucky to have you for a friend."

Cleanthony grinned and nodded vigorously in agreement. "What did God put us on this earth for, if not to be friendly?"

This seemed so wise that I had nothing to offer in return. So instead I nodded vigorously back at him and entered.

The place had seen better days, of course. There were the usual water stains on the wallpaper in the hallway, and many of the panes of glass in the bay window facing the street were cracked. But the place also showed signs of attention—the floor in the hallway had been re-sanded recently, the furniture was polished, there were artificial flowers in a blue vase on a mahogany table by the stairs. And the walls were filled with family photographs—too many to take in. I paused in front of one that held pride of place above the mahogany table—a family portrait with Cleanthony in an army uniform, a serious young woman in a sleeveless dress next to him, and two small boys on their laps grinning mischievous gap-toothed grins at the camera.

"Ain't they beautiful, Wally?" Cleanthony asked softly from behind me. "I've been a lucky man."

Again, I could only nod.

"You go on upstairs now and say hi to Scott."

I did as I was told. The second floor hallway displayed more framed family photographs—how had Cleanthony managed to hold onto them all? A couple of doors were open along the hall. In one sunny room an old woman sat in a rocking chair, knitting. She looked as delighted to see me as Cleanthony. "Hello," she said.

"Hello."

"Are you coming with us tonight?"

"Um, I don't think so. Where are you going?"

"To that place—you know the one. In Copley

Square. It's Cleanthony's birthday!"

"Oh. I don't think I can make it. But I'll be sure to wish Cleanthony a happy birthday."

She nodded. "You do that. Everybody loves Cleanthony."

That didn't surprise me. I went on down the hall. I knocked softly on the door on the left.

"It's open, Cleanthony," Brother Scott called out.

I took out my gun, just to be on the safe side, and then I opened the door. Scott was sitting at a small desk in the corner of the room, reading a book. His back was to me. "Afraid I'm not Cleanthony," I said. "He's much nicer than I am."

Scott whirled around. "What—? How did you—?"

I shut the door behind me. Scott had taken off his gray turtleneck with the rip in the shoulder and was wearing the paint-stained t-shirt. "I think the Bud Light shirt would have been a better choice," I said. "But not my call, obviously."

His eyes darted around the room. Looking for an escape route? A weapon? I didn't see either. The room was small. The twin bed was made, and books were piled up on the nightstand next to it. The top of the dresser was empty. A window looked out onto Clarendon Street. On the opposite wall hung a painting of cute puppies.

Now what?

"I didn't mean to hit you with that rock," he said quickly. "I didn't even know it was you. I just knew someone was following me. I was scared. I had to get away from the Church. I shouldn't have said anything to you about all this. I should've just kept my mouth shut. Like I explained to you: Joseph and the rest of them were going to blame me—for stealing the money, maybe even for killing Brother Flynn. I gave the Church my life, but there was nothing left for me there. Do you believe me?"

"I have this theory," I said.

Scott stared at me. His eye was twitching. "I didn't steal that money," he insisted. "Search me. Search the room. I haven't got it. I admit I took some money we got from the past few trips to the Food Market when I decided to leave the Church, but that's it. If they're mad about that, I'll pay them back as soon as I get a job."

"I know you didn't steal that money," I said. "See, my theory is that Brother Flynn stole it when he left the Church, and you're covering up for him."

"That's crazy, Brother Flynn would never—"

"Of course he stole the money. Or maybe that's not the right word. Maybe you gave it to him."

"No, that's not true, he took—"

Scott stopped abruptly, but it was too late. Now we were making some progress.

"What happened?" I asked. "Did you go to him when you noticed it was missing? Did you suspect that it was Brother Joseph? Were you hoping Brother Flynn would throw Brother Joseph out of the Church and give you his job? Or did you actually catch Brother Flynn stealing the money?"

"I—I don't have to answer these questions."

"Of course you don't," I said, "except I'm still holding the gun." I sat down on the edge of the bed. "Look," I went on, "I'm just trying to do my job and find Flynn Dobler. I don't care about you. Tell me the truth and I'll leave you alone—except I have to take back the money you stole. If you don't tell me the truth, well, things could get ugly."

I didn't know what I meant by that, but it seemed like the sort of thing I was supposed to say.

Brother Scott didn't know what I meant either, but he remembered whacking me over the head with a rock. Which could make the guy who got whacked pretty cranky. Which I was, come to think of it. My head still hurt a bit. And cranky people can do nasty things.

"I woke up and saw him opening the desk drawer where the money was," Scott said. Quietly, reflectively, like he was still trying to make sense of what happened. "It was the middle of the night. It took me a while to understand what was happening, what he was doing."

"This was the night he disappeared?"

"Yes, that night."

"Did you ask him what he was up to?"

"No, not really. You didn't question Brother Flynn."

"Did he say anything?"

"He—he just said he needed some money."

"What for?"

"He didn't explain that. He seemed to be in a hurry."

"Didn't that seem strange to you?"

"Of course it did. Like I said, it was the middle of the night. But I didn't really see how much money he took. It was only the next morning that I realized he had taken all of it. *All of it*."

Brother Scott's eye started twitching furiously.

"Why didn't you tell someone when you found out he'd disappeared?" I asked. "You know, when they started talking about him ascending into heaven. People don't generally need a lot of cash when they go to heaven. At least, that's my guess."

"You talked to people at the Church yesterday—you think they'd believe me?" Scott demanded. "They want to believe Sister Lucy. Brother Joseph may not believe her, but he hates me. He'd be happy to blame me for the missing money. Brother Flynn knew I'd be blamed, but he didn't care. You know what I think? I think he took the money just to make sure I got into trouble."

"Why would he do that?"

"Because—" Brother Scott paused, and then he said: "Ask Sister Marva."

"Ask her why Brother Flynn wanted to get you in trouble? What does she have to do with anything?"

"Ask her," Brother Scott repeated.

On the street outside a car went by. It needed a muffler. "I'm sitting here pointing a gun at you," I noted. "It would be way more convenient if you told me."

Brother Scott seemed to be gaining confidence.

His twitch had subsided; he folded his arms. "Shoot me, I don't care," he said.

I sighed. I wasn't going to shoot him. "I'm going to search the room," I said, "just to be sure you don't have the money."

"Go ahead. Everything I have is in the top drawer of the dresser. Probably about fifty dollars."

I went to the dresser and took out the money. I searched quickly through the rest of the drawers and around the room, but that was it. I put most of the money in my pocket.

"I'm leaving you five dollars," I said, "because I'm a terrible private eye."

He didn't thank me. He just turned and looked out the window. "You should've shot me," he murmured.

There wasn't anything more to say after that statement, so I turned and left the room. Downstairs, Cleanthony said a cheery farewell to me. "Come back again soon, Wally!"

"Thanks, Cleanthony. And happy birthday!"

Cleanthony looked delighted. "Thanks, Wally! Why don't you come out with us tonight to celebrate!"

"I wish I could, Cleanthony. I wish I could. But duty calls."

CHAPTER 14

———— ● ◆ ● ————

I got on my bike and headed home, thinking about the case. Poor Brother Scott. His information fit with my theory, of course, although it was unlikely to change Brother Joseph's mind. I would have to get back up to Concord, to return the money to him and find out what he wanted me to do next. And have another chat with Sister Marva, I supposed. I wondered if Mickey had found another manifold or carburetor or whatever it was he needed in order to fix Bobby Gallagher's van. It was too late to go up there today, I figured; maybe he could take me tomorrow.

Back in Louisburg Square, I was surprised to see Ken Hendrikson waiting for me on the front steps of our house.

"Walter Sands!" he said, advancing towards me as I got off my bike. "I was hoping you'd show up before long."

"Hiya."

We shook hands and reminisced briefly about the two or three times we had met, at parties of *Globe* folks that Gwen had dragged me to. He was not one of the more memorable people at those events. But he was bubbling with excitement today. "First thing, Walter, Gwen wanted me to make sure I let you know that she didn't tell me anything about your case. My contacts already let me know about Brother Flynn disappearing. This is a big story."

"Really?" I was obviously not a good judge of what made for a big story. "You want a glass of cider or something?"

"No, no, I'm fine." Hendrikson took out a pencil and a notebook. "Do you mind if I ask you a few questions?"

I considered. "I guess that's OK," I said, "but I have a favor to ask in return."

"What's that?"

"Do you think the *Globe* has a photo of Brother Flynn?"

"Sure. We have one in our files, from a story I wrote about the Church."

"Can I get a copy?"

"Of course. But it may run with this story, too."

"OK. And—do you happen to know anything about Dobler's background? Where he came from, and so on?"

Hendrikson considered. "No, not really. When I interviewed him, he didn't want to talk about that sort of thing. Just wanted to focus on his ideas."

"Figures. So why is this such a big story?" I asked. "People disappear all the time."

"True. They aren't assumed into heaven, though."

"Oh." *Assumed.* "You've been talking to Brother Harold."

Hendrikson raised an eyebrow, obviously impressed by my powers of deduction. "Yes, indeed. I've talked to several people from the Church."

"Including Brother Joseph?"

"Sure."

"What does he say about the 'assumption'?"

"He's keeping an open mind."

"Good for him."

"What about you?" Hendrikson asked. "You're the famous private eye. What do *you* think?"

"Well, I'm not at liberty to discuss the details of the investigation."

"Sure, but your high-level thoughts. Do you think it's possible God assumed Brother Flynn into heaven?"

"It's possible, I suppose. Anything is possible. But I don't think it's the sort of thing a private eye can say much about."

Hendrikson wrote something in his notebook. "But you talked to Sister Lucy, right? The witness."

"Of course."

"Do you believe her?"

"Sister Lucy seems like a very sincere person. I don't think she's lying about what she thought she saw. Whether she actually saw it—well, I'm not so sure about that."

"Do you have another theory about what happened to Brother Flynn?"

"I'll just say that there are any number of theories that don't involve the supernatural."

And then Hendrikson started pointing out the flaws in those other theories. Who would have murdered Brother Flynn? Why would he have left the Church that he founded in the dead of night? Perfectly reasonable objections, but sort of beside the point. If you have to choose between murder and a miracle, you choose the murder. At least, that's the way a private eye would think about it. Hendrikson seemed like a smart enough guy, but clearly he wanted to believe in the miracle. I considered telling him about Brother Scott, but decided against it. My private eye ethics again: it wasn't my story to tell.

Finally the interview staggered to a halt. "Thanks so much, Walter," Hendrikson said, putting his notebook away. "You've been a big help."

"I doubt that, but you're welcome. And don't forget the photo."

"I won't!"

Hendrikson got on his bike and hurried off to finish his story. I carried my bike up the front steps and went inside.

Stretch, it turned out, had already arrived home, and he was busy making supper. He looked relieved to see me. "There you are," he said. "I was afraid you'd gone back up to that Church."

"Nope. That turkey smells great."

"This is the last of it, I'm afraid. That was a

great call about Fenwick, Walter. We looked up the address you gave us, and before the War that house was owned by James and Marjorie Fenwick. Roger was their son. So he was going home, just like you said."

"Good for me." I was actually pretty impressed with myself. "So you're not worried about secret meetings with the rebels and such?"

"Not about the rebels, I guess. But we're still worried, Walter. Fenwick's taking a big risk walking over there night after night."

"He's an idiot. I can see going back there once, for old time's sake—but even then I'd take an escort. And a weapon. Going there every night is asking for trouble."

"That's why we want you to keep following him, Walter."

That took me by surprise; I was ready for a quiet evening with Gwen. "Huh? What for? I solved your case for you, Stretch. Have a cop tail him. Or a soldier. You don't need me."

"Yes, we do. The governor wants *you* to do it. His opinion of you went way up today. That's a good thing, Walter."

"Why is that a good thing? I work for, you know, the good of humanity. Damsels in distress. Not the government."

"You work for money," Stretch pointed out. "Governor Bolton has agreed to pay you ten dollars a day. I tried to get him to go higher, but ten dollars is pretty good, Walter."

Ten dollars a day wasn't pretty good; it was great. "Well, you make a strong case," I admitted.

"Okay, I'll do it. But I have to eat supper first. Fenwick isn't leaving for a while."

"Sure, we've got time. Gwen will be home soon."

And she was, returning from the *Globe* just as supper was ready. Gwen was full of apologies about Hendrikson. "Someone else gave him the story, Walter. It wasn't me."

"Sure, I understand. I think probably Brother Harold got hold of him—he was in town at the Food Market yesterday. I'm sure he pushed the idea that Flynn Dobler's disappearance was a miracle. It sounds like Hendrikson is buying into it."

"It's a much better story that way."

"If you say so."

We rehashed our days while eating the remains of the turkey, along with bread and autumn vegetables. Gwen had been at Mass. General working on a story about medicine shortages. Stretch had attended the negotiating session with the Federal delegation; he wouldn't say whether any progress had been made, but I got the sense that there hadn't been. And I told them about finding Brother Scott, which impressed them both a good deal. "Now what?" Gwen asked.

"Well, I have to bring the money Brother Scott stole back to the Church, and find out if Brother Joseph still wants me to track down Dobler."

"Why wouldn't he?"

"I'm not sure. He's really invested in his theory that Brother Harold murdered the guy. He'll probably tell me Brother Scott is lying. Or that

Scott was in on the murder plot."

"You don't believe that?"

"No," I said. "Brother Scott isn't someone who makes things happen. He's someone that things happen to."

After we finished supper I had to inform Gwen that I was heading out again, to my night-time case that I couldn't tell her about because Stretch would kill me. She wasn't happy.

"Please be careful, Walter," she said.

"I'm always careful," I protested.

"Of course you are. How's your head, by the way?"

"Fine. And I was careful then. It was dark out, and he snuck up on me."

"Well, it's dark out now. So don't let anyone sneak up on you."

"Will do."

And then it was back to Charles River Park, waiting in the darkness for Fenwick to appear yet again, not anticipating how the night's events were going to change my life.

CHAPTER 15

As I waited I pondered my cases, thinking about ladders starting and oil lamps flickering behind curtains in second-floor windows, and poor Brother Scott, sitting scared and defiant in his little room.

And finally I spotted Fenwick leaving the apartment building. He started walking briskly in the same direction as he had the night before. I let him get a head start, and then I took off after him.

It's a lot easier trailing someone when you know where he's headed; you're not worried about the unexpected turn that leaves you stranded. Of course, there was no guarantee that Fenwick was returning to his home in Somerville. But why would he have a different destination? Once again he made his way north to the Longfellow Bridge; once again he stopped in the middle to gaze out at the Charles River and then continued on to Cambridge. Once again he stopped at One-Eyed Joe's and talked to the security guys hanging out on the sidewalk, and waited while one of them went inside. The guy returned with a satchel a few minutes later, and Fenwick headed off towards Somerville, past the abandoned high-rises, the ruined doctors' offices, the charred remains of gas stations and Chinese restaurants and three-deckers. Just like last night.

...until three people appeared out of a side street and also started following Fenwick.

I kept my distance. I couldn't make out their age or sex or clothing. Did they know Fenwick? Were they going to meet him? Or attack him? They started closing in on him. Someone shouted something. Fenwick stopped and turned.

I stopped, too.

They surrounded him. "No!" Fenwick shouted.

They pushed him to the ground.

Well, that was pretty clear.

They were crazies, the creatures who still haunt places like this, survivors of the Frenzy, back when everyone was a little crazy. People hate and fear the crazies, not least because we recognize a bit of ourselves in them. The government has talked about putting a bounty on them   they're not really human after all, it's argued. Most people don't need a bounty to kill a crazy; after all, if you don't kill them, they're usually more than happy to kill you.

I took out my gun and ran towards them. I took aim, but I was afraid I'd hit Fenwick in the writhing mass of people. Besides...well, it turns out I'm not that good at killing. I'd had to kill a couple of thugs in my last case, and the memory still bothered me. Too many people have died.

So I shot the gun into the air over their heads.

The noise was enough to wake the dead. The three figures stopped their attack and looked up. Long hair, long beards, glittering animal eyes. One of them had what looked like black and red war paint on his face.

They stared at me, calculating. Should they attack me? Or should they run for it? "I've got plenty of bullets," I let them know. "But I won't shoot you if you disappear by the count of three." They didn't move. "One...two...two and a half..."

They got to their feet and scurried away. I let them go.

Fenwick was still on the ground. I approached him, and he looked up at me. "Hiya," I said.

This was the first time I had seen him up close. He was younger than I had imagined him, with dark hair and chiseled features. He didn't look badly hurt, just frightened.

"You OK?" I asked.

"I—" he croaked. "I—yes, I suppose so."

"You really ought to have a gun on you," I observed. "This isn't the safest neighborhood for a night-time stroll, Mr. Fenwick."

That got his attention. "How do you know my name?" And then: "Are you from the government?"

"Not exactly. But some folks asked me to look after you during these nocturnal peregrinations of yours. You're free to do what you want in your spare time, I suppose, but New England doesn't want to take the blame if you end up beaten to death by a bunch of crazies."

Fenwick looked around, maybe checking to see if the crazies were waiting for another chance to attack. I looked around, too. We were alone. He grabbed the satchel from One-Eyed Joe's and scrambled to his feet. He looked a little unsteady. "Well, thank you, Mr.—"

"Sands. Walter Sands."

"Mr. Sands. You've done your duty, and I'm grateful for your assistance. I'm all right now."

"You're not all right. And call me Walter. Let's go to your house and let you catch your breath."

"My house? What do you—"

"Over on Rosewell Street. The one you grew up in. We know you've been hanging out there every night, communing with the past. Perfectly understandable, but very risky."

He looked hard at me. "You know nothing, Mr. Sands," he informed me.

"Call me Walter," I repeated. Was that so hard? "If you're not communing with the past, that's fine with me. I'll just wait outside until you've finished doing whatever it is you're doing in there and then escort you home."

"This isn't necessary. I can take care of—" he stopped, realizing that we'd just had a graphic demonstration of how he couldn't take of himself.

"Look," I said. "They're paying me good money to make sure you're safe, and I need that money, what with rising prices and all due to the uncertain political situation. Just let me do my job, okay?"

That seemed to soften him. "All right," he said. "I suppose—yes. That would be fine. Walter."

I gave him a smile. "Great. Let's go, if you're ready."

We started walking. Up close, it was easy to tell what was in the bag from One-Eyed Joe's: the smell of roast chicken was unmistakable. He was buying dinner at the brothel so he could eat it at his childhood home? I decided not to ask. Fenwick didn't seem especially chatty, and I was just here to do my job.

But then, unexpectedly, he did start chatting. "Are you from Boston, Walter?" he asked.

"Not originally. I grew up with my father in Maine after the War. Then he died and another couple took me in. There wasn't much of a future in Maine, so they decided to come down to Boston. Turned out the Frenzy was at its height right about then—not a good time to arrive in Boston. First thing that happened was some bad guys stole me. Then I escaped from the bad guys and lived on the streets until I got swept up into the youth camps. Which wasn't much fun, either."

Fenwick nodded, as if this were a pretty standard life history. And I suppose it is. "This used to be a wonderful place," he said.

"So I've heard."

"I was in college when the War started," he said. "Out in California. I couldn't get back here. And it didn't seem like there was much point. My parents were with my sister in Washington when the bombs fell—looking at colleges. Abby wanted to go to Georgetown and study international relations."

Another standard life history. *International relations*. They used to study that? Well then, they should have studied harder. I thought about this for a second, and then continued the conversation. "I was stationed in Washington when I was in the army. It's still kind of a mess."

"Yes," Fenwick agreed. "We'd like nothing better than to move the Federal government back there. But that's not happening anytime soon."

"Boston is also kind of a mess," I pointed out. "It could use some help."

"It is a mess," he agreed again. "But it's *here*. It exists. In my mind I sort of thought it had disappeared. But nothing has disappeared, really."

That hadn't been my point, but I didn't press the issue. We had turned onto Rosewell Street. Silent, dark, empty Rosewell Street. We stopped in front of his house.

"It's cold out," Fenwick said.

He was right about that.

"You—you could come inside, if you like. I should warn you, though, that—"

"It's okay," I reassured him. "I've seen the insides of these old houses before. I know what they can be like after they've been abandoned for a couple of decades."

Fenwick shook his head. "No," he murmured. "You don't know—well, you'll see."

We went up the front steps. I saw rusted

mailboxes by the door. No mail had been delivered here in a long time. On the porch were a few empty flowerpots and an upended tricycle. "Watch out for the missing board," he said, pointing to a gap.

He opened the front door; it had been smashed in at some point, I noticed, and the lock was missing. He picked up the lantern he had left in the small entrance hall and lit it. The light flickered over two inner doors, both with their glass panels broken. A faded sign tacked to the door on the right said:

Crystal
Running late. Come on in.
XOXOXO

"Upstairs," Fenwick said. He opened the door straight ahead of us. Inside was a steep stairway. At the bottom of the stairs was an empty umbrella stand. The place smelled of mold and piss. We walked up the stairs; at the top was a small area with empty coat hooks. We went through another door, into a hallway lined with bookshelves; I would have liked to take a minute to read the titles of the books on those shelves. I saw a mirror and a still-life painting: apples in a bowl. We moved from there into what looked like a living room. In the flickering lamplight I saw an upright piano with sheet music stacked on top. A sofa. A coffee table. A floor lamp. A rocking chair. A fireplace. A TV cabinet.

And there, in the far corner of the room, sat a ghost.

CHAPTER 16

The ghost was seated deep in a wing chair, her face impossibly pale, her eyes impossibly dark. Her body was quivering, and her eyes stared at me as if I were the ghost. She looked ready to spring at me and devour my soul. She looked ready to jump out the window and fly off into the night.

But wait: private eyes don't believe in ghosts, any more than they believe in miracles. Her hair was gray and stringy. Her gnarled hands clutched and unclutched a filthy comforter wrapped around her. On her feet were ancient, ragged boots. She was as real as I was.

I made a deduction. "Hello, Abby," I said.

She didn't reply. She didn't stop quivering. She wrapped the comforter more tightly around her. Her eyes moved to Fenwick.

"Abigail, this is my friend Walter," he said softly. "Walter, this is my sister Abigail."

"Pleased to meet you," I said.

Again, she didn't say anything. Instead, her eyes moved to the satchel from One-Eyed Joe's. She looked like she was ready to devour it as well as my soul.

Fenwick handed me the oil lamp. Then he put the satchel down on the coffee table and took out the contents. A container of food: chicken, mashed potatoes, squash. A knife and fork. A napkin. A bottle of milk. Her eyes followed his every move, and when he was done she looked up at him, like a dog waiting for a signal from its master. Fenwick pushed the table over to her. "It's OK, Abby," he said. "You can eat now."

Instantly she attacked the food, ignoring the knife and fork, devouring the chicken first, then moving on to the potatoes and vegetable. Fenwick sat down on the sofa and buried his head in his hands.

I put the lamp on the table and sat down too.

Eventually Fenwick straightened up. I could see a resemblance between the two of them—the high cheekbones, the thin eyebrows, the deep gray eyes. She might have been beautiful, long ago.

"She's been here all along?" I asked.

He looked at me, and his eyes begged forgiveness—from me, from his sister, from the world. "I came back here the first night after I arrived in Boston," he said. "I just wanted to visit the place where I grew up. I expected it to be trashed or burned to the ground, like most of these places. I knew it would upset me—the memories, the loss, the stupidity of the War. But I had to come. And here she was. All these years, I just assumed she was dead. And if by some miracle she survived the War and escaped from Washington, why would she come back to this place?"

"Things were okay for a while in Boston after the War," I said.

"Yes, and that's the ultimate stupidity, isn't it? The bombs didn't fall on Boston. They didn't fall on Berkeley, where I was going to school. America wasn't invaded or occupied—we didn't *lose*. We should have been able to put things back together again. But somehow we couldn't. When I first came up those front stairs, Abby tried to kill me. If her gun hadn't misfired, she would have succeeded."

I nodded and remembered. We were a lot more fragile than anyone imagined. The government collapsed, the military collapsed, the economy collapsed, civil order collapsed. The diseases came, the crazy people took over, or the normal people became crazy, and Boston turned from a successful prosperous post-industrial city into an anarchic tribal wasteland. So much for civilization. I remembered my father saying to me: *We need to rely on each other, son. We're all we've got.* He said that a lot. And then he started dying, and that took a long time, and when he was gone, who was there left to rely on? Who was "each other" then?

"I'm not entirely sure when the anarchy started," I said. "But I've been here for over a decade, and I don't believe this neighborhood has been safe in all that time, or probably for years before. At some point the people who were still trying to live normal lives moved in closer to the center of the city. There just weren't enough people left to keep places like this safe."

"How has she survived?" Fenwick said. "That's what I'd like to understand. Where does she find food? How does she stay warm? How has she managed to avoid getting killed by those crazy people out there?"

"She hasn't said anything?"

Fenwick shook his head. We both looked at her. She was drinking the milk in long greedy gulps. Some of it dribbled down her chin and onto the comforter. "She hasn't tried to shoot me again," he said. "I guess that's progress. That first night—when I realized it was her—that was so wonderful. A miracle. Two decades have passed, and then some, and so much had happened to America, to the world, and here we were, together at last. I was part of a family again. But then…nothing. I talked, and sometimes she seemed to listen, but then her eyes would wander away from me, and I began to wonder if words even meant anything to her after all these years."

"They say that people out here have gone feral," I said. "I don't buy it. They're still human. They're just trying to survive. It's a different world for them, is all."

"I hope you're right. But when I first came here, this place was…not pleasant. It looked more like an animal's den than a human being's home. I've been gradually cleaning it up. Abby hasn't stopped me, but she hasn't looked happy about it."

"How many nights have you been coming?"

"This is the sixth. Every night is the same, more or less. Bringing her food from that brothel, cleaning up, talking to her, reminiscing, trying to bring her back."

I considered. Probably I should have kept my mouth shut, but I was feeling sociable. And I decided that I liked Fenwick. I liked how he was trying to take care of his sister. "You've been causing Governor Bolton and friends no end of worry," I said. "It's not just that they were afraid you'd get killed walking around by yourself at night. They thought you were meeting with rebels from New Hampshire or someplace, maybe arranging a coup that would replace Bolton with someone more friendly to the Feds."

Fenwick smiled ruefully. "That's not a bad idea, actually."

"Okay, but please don't do it," I said. "I have a friend who'd lose his job."

That made Fenwick laugh. "Well, that's as good a reason as any for deciding what to do about New England."

I made another deduction. "You've been stretching out the negotiations to spend more time with your sister," I said. "I suppose that's as good a reason as any for *not* deciding what to do about New England."

That made him think. "I suppose you're right," he murmured. We both looked at his sister. She had finished her supper and was wiping her face with the back of her hand. "Abby, I'm going to get a cloth for your face," he said to his sister. "Sit with Walter for just a minute, OK?"

Fenwick left the room. Abby stared at me and started to quiver once again.

"That chicken looked delicious," I said. "Your brother is a good guy."

She didn't respond. She just stared. What was she thinking? *Was* she thinking?

Fenwick returned with a wet cloth. "The plumbing still works," he said. "I hadn't expected that."

He leaned over his sister and tenderly wiped her face with the cloth. She resisted for a moment, and then let him clean her up, closing her eyes and raising her chin to make it easier for her brother. For a moment she looked almost content.

He nodded and turned back to his sister. "Enough about politics," he murmured. "Usually I just sit here and talk to Abby about the past. Trying to make a connection."

"Don't mind me," I said. "I'll go somewhere else, if you like."

"No, stay. It's fine."

And Fenwick started to reminisce, leaning forward, grasping Abby's right hand with both of his. "Abby, do you remember the first time we flew in an airplane—down to Orlando, to go to Disney World? And then, coming back, there was a thunderstorm, and the plane was hit by lightning? Dad said it was no big deal, happened all the time, but even the flight attendants looked a little scared, and you hid your face in Mom's lap until we landed in Boston, and then all the passengers broke into applause. You were always scared to fly after that. So that's why next summer Dad decided we should drive all the way up to Niagara Falls. Remember Niagara Falls? That thin plastic rain slicker they gave you on the Maid of the Mist? You brought it home with you and hung it up in your closet. I wonder if it's still there. And then on the way back Dad and I wanted to take a detour to Cooperstown and see the Hall of Fame, but you and Mom thought that was the stupidest idea ever, and we didn't bother. I remember how angry I was. I never got to Cooperstown. I wonder if the Hall of Fame is still there. I wonder if anyone cares. I don't. I shouldn't have complained so much. I should never have complained. Remember the Christmas Eve it was so cold, and we had to go to midnight Mass?"

That sort of thing. Fenwick was shedding tears by the time he got to Niagara Falls. Abby didn't respond, but she was listening, I was pretty sure. Eventually I decided to take a look at the rest of the house while he reminisced. There was a small candle on the coffee table. I lit it from the oil lamp and stood up. Abby stared at me suspiciously.

I went out to the hall and glanced at the books on those shelves, but for once books didn't interest me. I wanted to see how Abigail Fenwick lived.

I looked into the bedrooms. They were dismal. *An animal's den.* There were no beds, just blankets heaped up on the floor. The windows were boarded up or stuffed with towels. Chunks of ceiling plaster littered the floors. Piles of papers and ancient magazines were stacked in corners. I took a look—I saw a term paper on top. An essay on *Great Expectations.* The kitchen and bathroom looked a little better—Fenwick had obviously put some effort into cleaning them, but they still stank of rot and shit.

Where did she find her food? How did she stay warm in the winter? How did she fend off the crazies? I tried to imagine her trapping squirrels or rats and roasting them in the fireplace. Ransacking abandoned houses for ancient canned goods, as I had once done. Sneaking back to civilization and pawing through the garbage at One-Eyed Joe's for something edible. Year after year.

I searched the closets in the bedrooms. I found what I was looking for hanging up in the third one—the thin plastic rain slicker Fenwick had described to his sister. It didn't look like much of anything; it wouldn't have found a buyer at the Salvage Market. But it was a memory, and memories matter. I brought it back out to the living room, sat down, and blew out my candle.

Abby's gaze moved from Fenwick to the slicker.

And then she pounced, so fast I had no time to react. In an instant the slicker was out of my hands and in hers, and she was back in her chair, glaring at me, prepared to fight me to the death for her memory.

"It's OK, Abby," I said, gasping for breath. "I was just bringing it out here for you. Not a problem."

I tried to smile non-threateningly. Fenwick started to sob. "You still have the slicker," he said. Abby's gaze moved to her brother, and then back to me—wary, vigilant. What was I going to try next?

This is how you survive, I thought.

And eventually Fenwick resumed. More memories, endless memories, of times almost impossible for me to imagine—memories of TV shows and movies, of rock concerts and web sites, of birthday parties and sleepovers and Easter egg hunts, of long carefree days spent at the beach and in the woods. Riding their bikes, riding their skateboards, riding the subway. Studying hard in school because that's how you achieved a better future for yourself.

And finally, exhausted, he stopped. Abby remained vigilant. I waited.

"We should go," Fenwick murmured to me.

"Whenever you're ready."

He stood up and filled the satchel with the remains of the meal. He stared down at Abby. Abby stared at the satchel. "This is the hard part," he said to me. "What does she do all night, all day? Is she frightened? Have I made things better for her? Or worse?"

Abby looked at him warily. She clasped the slicker in her gnarled hands.

"Better," I replied. "It's got to be better—seeing you, hearing you, after all these years. Do you see how much she cares about that slicker?"

He nodded, and then bent over and kissed the top of her head. I thought I saw a fleeting glimpse of some kind of emotion pass over her—was it love for her brother? Or just some primal response to the touch of another person's lips? And then it was gone. "Goodbye, my darling," he murmured. "I'll be back tomorrow night. I'll take care of you."

Then he picked up the lamp. "Let's go," he said to me.

We hurried out of the room and down the stairs. At the bottom, we looked back up. Abby was there, in the shadows at the top of the stairs, for the briefest of moments, and then she stepped back into the darkness and disappeared.

Fenwick turned out the oil lamp and left it on the stairs. He opened the front door, and we stood on the front porch.

It was cold. We had a long way to walk. I waited. There was no sound from inside. There was no sound anywhere. "Enough," Fenwick said finally, and we headed down the steps.

Back through Cambridge to One-Eyed Joe's, where we dropped off the satchel. Then onto the Longfellow Bridge, where Fenwick again stopped in the middle. "My family wasn't well-off," he said as we stood there. "I can remember standing on this bridge on a warm night sometime in high school, just gazing out at the lights of the city, and feeling this burning desire to be successful, to make something of myself, to become a person my parents could be proud of. And here's the strange thing—I did it. Look at me—one of the most powerful men in the American government. I hold the fate of New England in my hands. But what does it matter? What does it all matter?"

"It matters to the folks living in New England," I pointed out.

"Yes, of course."

"What are you going to do?" I asked.

"About what?"

"About Abby. Will you bring her back to Atlanta with you?"

"I don't know," he admitted. "I suppose I'll have to. But I'm afraid. This is her home. This is her life. Take her away from it, and maybe she'll just—fade away. Or become uncontrollably wild. You saw the way she jumped at you."

"It's amazing that she's survived as long as she has," I said. "But you saw those crazies who attacked you. Sooner or later they'll get her, or some other crazies will. Or she'll freeze to death, or starve to death, or come down with a disease. This may be her life, but it's no way to live."

"I know that," Fenwick replied softly.

"You can't stall the negotiations forever," I pointed out.

"Of course. But these negotiations haven't dragged on just because of Abby. We need to get Governor Bolton to budge on some issues."

"You know that Bolton doesn't have a lot of room to maneuver, right? If he gives you too much, he'll probably lose his job, and you'll have to negotiate with someone even worse."

"We're offering to help," Fenwick pointed out. "He needs to offer something in return."

"Why? He's just trying to keep people like your sister safe. Make sure they don't starve, they have medicine when they get sick."

"You people were the ones who rejected the referendum to officially join the United States."

"Mostly thanks to your ex-president and her crazy scheme to get the referendum to pass."

Fenwick stared at me, and suddenly he grinned. "I know who you are!" he said. "You're the guy who figured it all out, who brought down President Kramer."

"Seems like there ought to be easier ways to win a referendum than the one she came up with," I replied.

"The politics of it were difficult."

I thought about that. "I hate politics," I said.

"And politicians?"

I thought some more. I didn't really hate President Kramer. "I don't know. I like people who take care of their family."

He glanced at me but didn't reply. We finished the trek back to Charles River Park in silence. But I was pretty sure what he was thinking: his sister was what mattered. And he had left his sister behind yet again, in darkness and squalor.

"You're going back tomorrow night?" I asked Fenwick outside the apartment building.

"Yes," he said. "Of course."

"Well, I still have to make sure you're safe. It occurs to me that the whole thing will be faster and safer if we drive."

"Drive? I don't have access to a car. And I'm not prepared to tell Bolton—"

"I'm pretty sure I can get a vehicle. And no one will know except a couple of friends of mine."

Fenwick looked dubious, but finally he nodded. "Then yes, that would be a big help."

"Great. We'll pick you up at eight."

"Thank you. Thank you for saving me," he said. "And thank you for finding the slicker."

"The first one was my job," I replied. "The second one was my pleasure. See you tomorrow night."

"Yes. Tomorrow."

Fenwick went inside the building, and I returned to Louisburg Square, satisfied with my day's labor.

CHAPTER 17

The next morning I gave a brief, truthful, and completely misleading summary of my night to Stretch: I followed Fenwick again. He went to the house again. He stayed upstairs for a couple of hours. He went back to Charles River Park.

No mention of the crazies. No mention of Fenwick's sister. No mention of the way I disobeyed Bolton's express instructions to keep the New England government out of it.

No sense getting everyone all upset.

Stretch told me to keep up the good work and went off happy.

When it came to Gwen, on the other hand…

I told Gwen the truth about Fenwick, the whole story, once again disobeying Bolton's instructions.

I didn't feel guilty about this. I needed to get her reaction to my story. I knew she wouldn't write up the scoop for the *Globe*. The story had become personal, not political.

Her eyes filled with tears as I told her about Fenwick's sister. "Oh, that poor woman," she said. "You can't leave her there, Walter. It's not safe."

"Well, yeah, that occurred to me."

"What are you going to do?"

"I'm not sure. It's not my decision, obviously."

Gwen hugged herself, and I could tell she was trying to find protection from her own bad memories. Not easy. "You can't leave her there," she repeated.

Gwen had spent her own time in the wilderness, wandering through abandoned neighborhoods, a teenage girl desperately searching for food and shelter and safety in places that offered little of any of these things. That's where we had found each other, an absurd miracle for which we would be forever grateful.

"I'll do my best," I promised. "But what if she doesn't want to go? It's scary leaving behind everything you know."

Gwen shook her head. "Doesn't matter. You have to help her, even if she doesn't want to be helped."

"Well OK, then."

Gwen likes being a reporter, likes simply reporting the facts and letting other people form their own opinions about them. But don't stand in her way when she forms an opinion herself.

But she didn't press the issue—I like to think that she knew I would do my best. So after breakfast I began the day by bicycling over to South Boston, where I visited the world headquarters of Bobby Gallagher Enterprises.

This was a warehouse that also doubled as the living quarters for Bobby and his two permanent employees—Mickey, a short guy with a shriveled arm who knows everything there is to know about engines, and Doctor J, a black kid who knows everything about everything. Neither of them bothered much with a last name. Bobby is middle-aged and garrulous and overweight; that last adjective doesn't get applied to many folks nowadays. When I got to the warehouse, Doctor J was sitting outside, reading a tattered book, a shotgun by his side.

"Hey, Wally," he greeted me as I got off my bicycle.

"Hey, Doctor J. Whatcha reading?"

He held up the book. It was called *Civilization and Its Discontents*. I have managed to get Doctor J interested in reading, but it turns out his taste is radically different from mine. He thinks the novels I read are mindless pap, and I think the stuff he likes is just strange and boring. "Any good?" I asked.

"Somewhat irrelevant to our present condition," he allowed. "Lookin' for The Man?"

I nodded.

"Upstairs in his office, pretendin' to work. I'll let you in."

"Thanks, Doctor J."

He got up and knocked the special knock I'd never bothered to learn on the warehouse door. After a minute the door opened and Mickey greeted me. "Hey, Walter," he said.

"Hey, Mickey." I went inside the warehouse, which was filled with random useless salvage like lawnmowers and TV sets, all of which were just for show. The hood of Bobby's van was open, and Mickey went back to work on the engine. Brutus, Bobby's large and irritable German Shepherd, signaled his displeasure with my presence by barking loudly.

"How's the van?" I asked Mickey, ignoring Brutus.

"Gettin' there," he replied. "Should be OK in a few hours, I think."

"That's great." That wasn't so great. I'd been hoping he could drive me back up to Concord with the money I'd recovered from Brother Scott.

I made my way past Brutus and up the metal staircase to the second floor. This was where Bobby and friends lived, and also where he kept the stuff that his clientele was really interested in—computer parts and guns and ammunition and fine jewelry. Bobby was in a dangerous business, but he was good at it.

The door to Bobby's office was open. The office was decorated with smutty pre-War calendars and tacky pre-War plaques with what I assumed were humorous sayings on them. Like "Schlitz—Breakfast of Champions." What in the world did that mean? Bobby was reading the *Globe*, his feet up on his metal desk. The workday had apparently not yet begun for him. "Good morning, Mr. Gallagher," I said.

"Huh," he said, looking up from the newspaper. "What a coincidence. I was just readin' about you in the *Globe*."

"Really?"

He passed me the paper. "Front page," he said.

I took a look. It was Hendrikson's article: "Miracle in Concord?" was its tantalizing title.

I scanned it quickly. As I had expected, it took a decidedly pro-miracle stance. And when Hendrikson got around to talking about me, he said this: "Walter Sands, the Boston private investigator, has been brought in to investigate Dobler's disappearance. He admitted that he has been unable to disprove the theory that Dobler was miraculously assumed into heaven, and he calls the main witness, Sister Lucy, 'very sincere.' He remains unsure about what happened that night but plans to continue his investigation."

He also worked in a reference to the lovely, pregnant Sister Marva, missing Dobler desperately but comforted by the idea that God had called him to heaven.

"Idiot," I muttered. I wasn't sure if I was talking about Hendrikson or me. At least the *Globe* had included that photo of Dobler I wanted, looking soulful and charismatic as he stared into the camera's lens.

"What's the problem?" Bobby asked. "That's great publicity for you."

"Can I keep this paper?" I asked.

"For your scrapbook?"

"That's right."

"Be my guest."

"Thanks. In return, I've got a business proposition for you."

Bobby eyed me suspiciously. "You don't have business propositions, Walter. You have favors to ask. Why don't you learn how to drive, like normal people?"

Bobby can be very perceptive. One of my many deficiencies as a private eye and human being is that I don't know how to drive.

"It really is a business proposition," I said. "I have a bodyguard job tonight—nothing to do with this Church thing. The guy I'm guarding has to go to a bad section of Somerville. No big deal, but it will be easier all around if we drive him there. I get paid ten dollars. I'll give you half for the use of your van."

"Sure. Mickey can take you, if he's got the damn thing running. Give him the five bucks."

"That's fine, but I'd like you to come along."

Bobby gave me a what-are-you-up-to look. "Why? I won't add anything to the party."

"Because this guy is important. You'll want to be on his good side. You'll want him to know the name Bobby Gallagher."

Bobby's gaze got even more suspicious. "Who is he?"

"Pick me up a little before eight. Find out for yourself."

I grabbed the newspaper and stood up. "Hey, wait a minute!" Bobby said.

"Yup?"

"What's your hurry? Hang out here for a while. We can play cards with Doctor J."

"I'm a busy man," I pointed out. "Besides, Doctor J always wins. See you tonight." Then I recalled the promise I'd made yesterday. "But before I go I have to relay a message from one of your many admirers." I told him what Janice Kohl had to say at the Salvage Market.

Bobby thought this was the funniest thing he'd ever heard. "Janice has some mouth on her, I'll give her that. 'Tiny little needle-nose dick.' Very impressive. I should get back together with her. She's my kind of woman."

Bobby is a strong believer in his power to charm. I shook my head and went back downstairs past an annoyed Brutus and checked again with Mickey on the van. "You and Bobby and I are going for a little trip tonight, if everything is OK."

"The van will be good to go, Walter. Don't you worry."

Outside, Doctor J was still sitting in the sunlight, reading about civilization and its discontents. "Not stayin' long, eh, Walter?" he said.

"Gotta run, Doctor J. Why don't you read some novels?"

"Novels are nothing but a way of escaping reality."

I pondered that for a moment. "Exactly," I replied. I got on my bike and pedaled away.

Where to? I'd been hoping to return to the Church, but with the van still out of commission I had no way to get there. I decided to go back downtown to one of my favorite places in the world, Art's Filthy Bookstore. My friend Art had cornered the local market on one of the most sought-after products of pre-War civilization: pornography. In a grim world filled with birth defects and bad teeth, what young man doesn't want to fantasize about a very different world filled with flawless, willing blondes eager to give him pleasure? Art himself is not a young man—he looks like a Santa Claus who doesn't get enough to eat. And he has no particular interest in pornography, except as a way of ensuring that he does have enough to eat.

What he cares about is literature—great works of art that nourish your spirit and ennoble your character. The most sublime achievements of our greatest poets and novelists. Not much of a market for them, alas. But there's always me.

As always, Art was delighted to see me. "Walter, Walter, so good of you to stop by."

His shop is small and cozy. He keeps the pornography out front. In the back, where he lives, are the stacks of books he really cares about, the ones he reads and re-reads by candlelight deep into the night. Like me, when I don't have two cases to deal with at the same time. "How's business?" I asked.

"Brisk, as ever," he replied. "I've branched out into romance novels. Just another kind of fantasy."

"Sounds like a good idea."

"But you know what I really want, Walter," he said. "Those cases of yours—you have to write them up. The world needs new books, new authors, new inspiration. We can't live in the past forever."

"I'm trying, Art. I have a typewriter Gwen gave me. It's in my office, and sometimes when I'm not too busy I put together a few pages. But, you know, writing's a lot of work. Besides, I'm a man of action, not a writer."

Art grinned. "You're a man of action who spends most of his days sitting at a desk in an empty room waiting for something to happen. Quit reading books and start writing them."

"Hmm, well, I guess that's a fair point. But I'm here because something actually did happen. I'm working on a case, and I need your literary assistance."

"Really? I'd be delighted to help. Come sit down."

Art moved some priceless *Playboys* off a couple of stools, and we sat. I told him the story of Brother Flynn's mysterious disappearance from the Church of the New Beginning, and the enigmatic words that he left on a sheet of paper in his room.

"*Down where all the ladders start*," Art repeated. "You recognize the quote, right?"

I nodded. "Sure. Yeats. 'The Circus Animals' Desertion.'"

"Indeed. Is Brother Flynn a literary sort?"

"I don't really know. I saw a quote from *Gone with the Wind* on the wall of the meditation room at his Church. Does that count?"

"Well, you don't quote Yeats without liking poetry. Stay right there." Art went into the back room of his store and returned in a minute with an ancient paperback, open to the poem. We re-

read it together. "One of his last poems," Art said.

"A friend of mine might point out that it's somewhat irrelevant to our present condition," I said.

"Great poetry is relevant to all conditions," Art responded, rather pretentiously. Not that I disagreed with him.

I recited the line that followed Dobler's quote—the final line of the poem, where all the ladders start. "*The foul rag-and-bone shop of the heart,*" I said. "What does that mean?"

"Yeats is leaving behind the airy themes that served him so well for so long," Art explained. "They no longer give him inspiration. He no longer wants to be the ring-master for those particular circus animals. And now he has to go deep inside himself in search of new inspiration."

I thought about the poem, and about Flynn Dobler. "Things have obviously been getting difficult at the Church of the New Beginning," I said. "There's dissent and intrigue and jealousy and maybe sexual tension. His ideas aren't working. People are leaving."

"Probably not what Flynn Dobler had in mind when he started the thing," Art suggested.

"Wouldn't think so."

"So he decided to leave. To search for a new inspiration."

"That makes sense," I said. "But where? What's the foul rag-and-bone shop of Flynn Dobler's heart?"

"What do you know about his background?"

Art asked.

"That's the problem," I said. "I don't know anything. He seemed to go out of his way to hide his past from Church members."

"Sounds to me like you're going to have to find this out."

It was the conclusion I had already come to myself. I just needed someone else to say it. "But how?" I wondered.

"That's why you're the private eye and I'm a lowly bookseller," Art replied. "What would Sam Spade do? What would Philip Marlowe do?"

"I sometimes wonder if my role models are appropriate for our present condition."

"Great private eyes are relevant to all conditions," Art informed me.

Again, I couldn't disagree. "I suppose they'd expend some shoe leather," I said. "Continue the investigation. Talk to their sources. But only if they got paid, of course."

"You're not getting paid?"

"I still owe my client a couple of days' work. But this isn't the answer he's looking for. So he might just tell me to knock it off and stay home."

"That would be a shame, wouldn't it? Stories should have endings."

"I'll give it my best shot. I like endings, too."

I said goodbye to Art and rode back to Louisburg Square.

A beat-up old police car was parked in front of our house. Never a good sign. Pete Callahan, whom I had last seen watching over the Food Market, was sitting on the front steps. He looked glum and worried.

I got off my bike. "Hey, Pete. What's up?"

"I'm sorry, Walter. It's not my fault."

"What isn't your fault?"

Actually, he looked close to tears. "I've gotta bring you down to headquarters."

"Huh? Why is that?"

"Well, you know, they think you murdered somebody."

CHAPTER 18

"Um, who did I murder?" I asked Pete.

"Look, Walter, could we just go there and straighten this out?" He stood up and motioned to the cruiser.

"Okay, fine. But can I leave a note for Gwen and Stretch, in case I'm not home for supper?"

"Sure, I guess so."

I went inside, hauling my bicycle up the stairs with me. Pete followed. I scrawled an uninformative note and left it on the kitchen table. "I didn't murder anybody, you know," I said to Pete.

"Of course you didn't. You just need to explain everything to Chris Mull."

I knew Detective Mull. "*He* doesn't think I murdered anybody, does he?"

"Walter, let's go clear it up."

"Fine."

We left the house, got in Pete's cruiser, and headed off. The car needed new springs or shocks or something; I'd never had such a bumpy ride. The glove compartment was taped shut; the rearview mirror on my side was tilted and cracked. The car probably needed new everything. "How's Mary Beth?" I asked.

Pete shrugged. "The same."

That didn't sound good.

We fell silent. What was going on? Why would Chris Mull think I had murdered someone? At any rate, I needed to clear this up before Mickey and Bobby showed up with the van.

Police headquarters are over at Roxbury Crossing, in a building that is way too large for its current needs. Pete parked the cruiser out front and we went inside. He waved to the cop at the front desk and led me past a deserted line of counters, where once upon a time you could obtain permits and IDs and fingerprints and other stuff no one needs anymore. We went upstairs and down a gray corridor, and we stopped outside a gray door.

Pete opened the door without knocking. I expected to see Chris Mull. Instead, I found myself staring at Cleanthony.

His eyes widened with fear. "That's the one!" he exclaimed. "That's him! Walter Sands!"

I looked past Cleanthony and spotted Detective Christopher Mull, slumped in his chair behind a desk piled high with papers. The office had one small window. On the wall was a clock and a bulletin board with more papers pinned to it. There was a telephone on the desk amid all the papers.

Mull glared back at me and then turned his gaze to Cleanthony. "You're sure this is the man who visited your boarding house yesterday, Mr. Overstreet?" he asked.

"'Course I'm sure. Looking for Scott." He shook his head. "Why would anyone want to do something like this? Scott never hurt nobody."

"Brother Scott's been murdered?" I asked.

Detective Mull ignored me. "Thank you for your time, Mr. Overstreet," he said to Cleanthony. "We'll take care of this from here. Officer Callahan will drive you home."

"It just don't make no sense," Cleanthony said. "What did Scott ever do to deserve gettin' himself killed? Why'd you do this, Wally?"

"I didn't kill him, Cleanthony. You've got to believe me."

Cleanthony just shook his head sadly, his faith in humanity shattered.

I moved out of the doorway, and Pete beckoned to Cleanthony. "Come with me, sir," Pete said.

Cleanthony obeyed. Pete gave me a nod as they left. And then I was alone with Detective Mull.

Mull is a tall man with sandy brown hair and sad eyes that always look like they are on the verge of tears. He never raises his voice. He is not unacquainted with profanity, however. "Walter," he said softly, "you fucking shit-for-brains retard moron. What have you done now?"

"Nothing. Honest, Chris. What's going on?"

"Call me Detective Mull, asshole. You admit that you visited Scott Parker yesterday?"

"Is that his last name? I just knew him as

'Brother Scott.'"

"So, are you admitting you visited him?"

"Yes, sir. I'm admitting that."

He glared at me, rightly suspecting mockery in my use of the word *sir*. I had called him "Chris" since the day I met him. "What in God's name for?"

"Did you read the *Globe* this morning?"

Mull shook his head. "Did it talk about the guy?"

"No, but it explains the case I'm on. Brother Scott belonged to the Church of the New Beginning, up in Concord. The founder, Flynn Dobler, disappeared about a week ago. I was brought in to investigate. The night after I talked to Scott—this was like three days ago—he disappeared from the Church. Yesterday afternoon I managed to track him down at Cleanthony's boarding house and we had a chat. Can I sit?"

Mull ignored my request. "You and your fucking 'cases,'" he grumbled. Like many of my acquaintances, he is not a fan of my career choice. "Mr. Overstreet says this guy was really upset after you left."

"He was upset about having to leave the Church. Plus, I took back some money he stole when he left."

"Why did he leave?"

"It was his job to hold on to the Church's money. He claimed—to me, anyway—that Flynn Dobler took it all when he disappeared. But no one else at the Church is going to believe that—

Brother Flynn's a saint to them. He thought everyone was going to blame him when they found out, and he was right about that. So when I showed up to investigate, he decided to take whatever cash had come in since Dobler left and hit the road himself. But he's really not very bright, and he returned to the rooming house he lived in before he joined the Church. That's where I found him. So what happened, Chr— Detective Mull?"

Mull grudgingly gestured to a chair, and I sat down. "Mr. Overstreet says he entered Mr. Parker's room this morning, since he hadn't come down for breakfast," he said. "He discovered the victim's body. The guy had been beaten to death. The room had been ransacked."

I considered. "Everyone in the rooming house was going out to celebrate Cleanthony's birthday last night. Did Brother Scott stay behind?"

"That's right. Apparently he was still too upset, by you or whatever. He was in the house alone from nine to midnight, approximately. So the killer had three hours to do his business. Got an alibi, by any chance?"

"I do, actually."

Did I detect a hint of relief on Mull's face? "Okay, let me have it," he said.

"I was on a case for Governor Bolton." I replied. "Give him a call. He can tell you where I was last night."

Mull glared at me again. "Don't bullshit me, Walter. Bolton thinks you're an idiot. That makes two of us. I'm sure there are a lot more."

"I never bullshit you, Detective Mull."

"I can't begin to count the number of times you—oh, never mind."

Detective Mull worked in a youth camp where Pete and I once spent a few dismal months. He was the one solid, caring person we encountered in what was otherwise a never-ending nightmare. Brother Flynn had been Marva's savior; Chris Mull had been mine. If he can't count the number of times I lied to him and let him down, I can't count the number of times he gave me good advice, most of which I didn't take. It's an odd relationship.

"Governor Bolton has great respect for my abilities," I said. "Unlike some people I could mention."

"Didn't you stake out his house and fall into his window when you thought he had kidnapped the president—and all he was up to was fucking the brains out of that pudgy secretary of his?"

"Governor Bolton has a strong belief in giving people a second chance. Unlike some people I could mention."

Mull sighed. "I have given you so many chances, Walter." And then the detective called the governor. Telephones aren't a device that mere mortals have around here, so it always comes as a bit of a shock to me when someone can just pick one up and talk to a person on the other side of the city.

Anyway, Mull got through to Governor Bolton. He briefly explained the situation, and then the conversation became one-sided, with a lot of

"Yes, sirs" and "No, sirs" on our end. And then Mull held the phone out to me. "He wants to talk to you," he said.

I leaned forward and took the receiver. "Governor Bolton, how are you, sir?"

"I told you not to let Fenwick know you were tailing him," Bolton squawked at me. "And keep the government out of it."

"Yes, sir. It was unavoidable. He was attacked, and—"

"Well, never mind. Whatever you did last night, you made Fenwick happy. He was singing your praises today."

"I'm very glad to hear that."

"You didn't have anything to do with this murder Mull is investigating, did you?"

"No, sir. Just an unfortunate misunderstanding. The murder took place when I was with Fen— with our friend."

"Don't screw this up, Sands. Nothing is more important than keeping Fenwick safe and happy. And don't go blabbing to Mull about what's going on. Understood?"

"Understood, sir."

"All right, then. Let me talk to Mull again."

I passed the phone back to Mull, who offered a couple more "Yes, sirs" and "No, sirs" and then hung up.

He gave me a puzzled look. "Bolton actually seems to think you're doing a great job on whatever this case is he's got you working on."

"I accept your apology," I replied graciously.

"I'm actually very glad to hear this, Walter. I

want to believe in you."

"You've got to follow the leads where they take you," I allowed.

"So, what happened? Did someone from the Church of the New Beginning track the guy down looking for their money? Kill him when he claimed he didn't have it?"

"That's the theory I'd start with. They have a guy—big bruiser named Brother Reggie—who seems capable of murder. He certainly talked that way about Brother Scott when he drove me home from the Church the other day."

Mull considered. "Have to go up there and have a chat with him, I guess."

"It's possible he's at the Food Market—the Church has a cart there. We might still catch him if we leave right now."

"*We?*" Mull said.

"Mind if I tag along? I can probably help—I know all the players. I want to find out who killed Brother Scott as much as you do."

Mull sighed. "All right," he said. "But you really ought to join the police instead of keeping up this private-eye nonsense."

"Would I get a pension?" I had read about pensions somewhere.

"Fuck me," he replied. "We're lucky to get a paycheck. Let's go."

I followed the detective outside, where we got into another cruiser; this one was in marginally better shape than Pete's. We jounced our way over to the Food Market, which seemed to be winding down a bit for the day. It occurred to me that I had missed lunch. "Buy me an apple?" I asked Mull.

"You're the highly sought-after private eye working two cases," he pointed out. "You buy the goddamn apples."

I bought us each an apple from a vendor by the gate. Mine was lousy.

Mull chatted briefly with the two policemen who were guarding the place today, and then we headed for the Church's cart.

It was in the same spot as it had been the day I started working on the case. But again Brother Harold was with Sister Marva. "No Brother Reggie," I said to Mull, and I explained who the two Church members were.

"Well," he said, "can't hurt to talk to them."

So we approached.

"Walter!" Sister Marva said when she spotted me. She gave me her warmest smile. Brother Harold nodded to me.

"Hi," I said. "This is Detective Christopher Mull of the Boston Police Department."

Mull flashed a badge at them. "Good afternoon," he said. "I'm sorry to have to inform you that one of your fellow Church members, Brother Scott Parker, has been murdered."

"Oh no!" Marva exclaimed, and her eyes teared up.

"God help us," Harold murmured, shaking his head.

"I understand that Brother Scott had stolen money from the Church," Mull said.

"That's true, but Brother Flynn taught us to

forgive," Harold intoned. "Even when great evil has been done to us."

Detective Mull did not look impressed by his piety. "You don't think anyone at the Church would feel different about Brother Scott?"

"There are as many personalities in the Church as there are disciples," Harold said. "But I can't imagine that anyone would murder Brother Scott—that's just not what the Church is all about. What time did the murder take place?"

"Last night, between nine and midnight," Mull responded.

"Then it certainly couldn't have been any of us, no matter how angry we may have been with him. Disciples are occasionally in the city during the day, as we are. But they're always back by nightfall."

"You're sure that was the case last night?"

"I can't be positive, of course. But if someone wasn't there, it would have been noticed."

"What about Brother Reggie? Was he there?"

"Everyone was there."

"Any other ideas about who might have murdered Brother Scott?"

"Some common thief, I imagine," Brother Harold said. "Was any of the money recovered?"

Mull shook his head. "Not a penny."

"Then I'm sure that a thug found out about the money, killed Scott, and stole it. Doesn't that sound plausible?"

Mull shrugged. "It does."

Brother Harold smiled triumphantly, as if he had solved the case. Mull took a bite out of his apple.

"We'll do whatever we can to help you," Marva said. "This is just terrible."

"I'd appreciate that," Mull replied. "Walter, got any questions?"

"That was quite an article in the *Globe* this morning," I remarked to Brother Harold.

He nodded. "Mr. Hendrikson does very good work."

"Were you the source of his information?"

"I was happy to tell him what I knew. His conclusions, of course, were his own."

"But how did he find out that Brother Flynn was missing? How did he know about Sister Lucy? Did you tell him?"

"Yes, I told him," Brother Harold said. "Was there something wrong with that, Walter?"

"Nope, not at all. Just checking."

I turned to Sister Marva. "I tracked Brother Scott down, Sister Marva," I said. "I spoke to him yesterday afternoon, before he was murdered."

"Oh. Did you find anything out, Walter?"

"He claims Brother Flynn was the one who stole the money, the night he disappeared. He said he did it so that Scott would get the blame. He said that you would know why."

Marva blushed. Her eyes widened and she brought her hands to her face. She shook her head. "No, Walter. I don't know why."

"Do you have any idea why Scott would say that?"

Marva shook her head and began to cry.

"Brother Scott has always been attracted to Sister Marva," Brother Harold explained to us rather primly. "You can ask anyone at the Church. Of course, she always rejected his advances."

"But what did he think Sister Marva knew?"

Sister Marva sank to the ground sobbing then. No more decorative tears you longed to wipe from her cheeks—this was the kind of sorrow that left her choking and gasping for breath. "He wouldn't...leave me...alone," she managed to say. She wrapped her arms tightly around herself, as if trying to protect herself—and her baby—from some unseen harm.

Brother Harold looked uncomfortable; he pushed his glasses up his nose, then reached down and patted Sister Marva ineffectually on the back.

Mull gave me a *What the fuck?* look.

Sister Marva recovered soon enough. She got to her feet, wiped her face, and apologized. "I'm so sorry," she whispered. "I didn't mean to..."

"Is there anything you want to tell us about Brother Scott?" I asked her.

She shook her head. "No, no, I—we all have our flaws, Walter. That's what Brother Flynn always said. Brother Scott was no different."

"I get the feeling there's more than a flaw involved here," Mull said.

"Please leave her alone," Brother Harold begged us. "She is with child."

"Fine," Mull said. "I'll be up at the Church tomorrow, though, if either of you have anything to add."

"Of course, of course."

And so Mull and I left the Food Market. Mull looked glum, as usual. "Tell me more about those two," he said.

I gave him a quick summary of Brother Harold, Sister Marva, and the rest of the cast of characters in my case. "They'll all have alibis," I pointed out. "The Church doesn't have any cars—no easy way of getting from Concord to Boston and back at night."

We had reached the police cruiser. Mull threw his apple away. "That apple sucked," he said.

"Sorry."

"What was all that about back there?"

"I'm not sure," I said. "It's pretty clear Brother Scott was lacking in social skills. Maybe he was obnoxious to Marva."

"Seemed like he might have been more than obnoxious."

"Could be."

We got in the car. Mull sat behind the wheel and didn't move. I noticed that his brown hair had flecks of gray in it.

"So, you're going up to the Church tomorrow?" I asked.

"I suppose."

"Can I come with you?"

"I suppose."

We sat there some more. When you're a kid, you don't think much about what's going on inside the heads of grown-ups. You just accept them as they are. That's the way I'd been with Chris Mull in that youth camp. I never questioned why he was so much wiser and more helpful than everyone else. He just was. But now, I thought: how had he pulled that off? It must have been tough. Really tough. "You OK, Chris?" I asked.

He slowly shook his head. "I'm not going to solve this murder, Walter," he responded softly. "It'll end up like all the other motherfucking cases around here. Before the War we had DNA testing, we had fingerprints, cell phone logs, surveillance cameras, national crime databases....No one could get away with anything. Now what've we got? No staff, no money, no resources, fucked-up government, fucked-up legal system. If there aren't a bunch of eyewitnesses or a confession or we catch the guy standing over the body with a bloody goddamn knife in his hand, we've got fuck-all chance of a conviction. Those loonies up in Concord will stonewall us tomorrow, and then what? Maybe one of them murdered this guy. Maybe the murderer was some other fine citizen of whatever the fuck country this is we live in nowadays. We'll never find out."

"Like whoever killed Biff Fitzgerald," I remarked.

"Yeah, like him," Mull sighed. Biff had been a murder victim in my neighborhood a few months ago. I had tried to solve the case, because I liked Biff's mother; Chris had tried to solve the case, because it was his job. But we got nowhere.

"You've got to do it for Cleanthony," I

murmured.

Mull looked over at me. "Yeah," he said. "Cleanthony. He's a good guy, and he deserves a world with some justice in it. I only wish I could give it to him."

"Gotta try."

"I suppose."

Mull started up the cruiser then, and he drove me home.

CHAPTER 19

———————◆ ◆ ◆ ◆————————

Back in Louisburg Square, I remembered that it was my turn to cook supper. I busied myself with that while pondering Brother Scott's murder. I don't like murder. Brother Scott wasn't the finest person on the planet, but he didn't deserve to be beaten to death.

And then, after a while, I started thinking about Abby Fenwick. And that made me feel a little better.

Stretch and Gwen arrived home at the usual time. I described my day while we ate.

"If someone killed this guy," Gwen said, "could you be in danger too?"

That had occurred to me. "I don't see why," I replied. "There's no reason I should have the missing money."

"You were the last person to see him," she noted. "If the murderer thought Brother Scott had the money, and it turned out he didn't, wouldn't you be the next target?"

Have I mentioned that Gwen is smarter than me?

"I'll be fine," I said, using my most reassuring voice.

"Please be careful," Gwen said.

She says that to me a lot.

"Negotiations with the Federal delegation went a lot better today," Stretch remarked, eager to change the subject. "Bolton and Fenwick issued a joint statement at the end of the meeting. It was very encouraging."

"That's great." I wondered if I had played a part in softening up Fenwick. We finished supper, and Gwen played old Beatles' songs on the piano while Stretch and I did the dishes. Finally I kissed Gwen good-bye, waved to Stretch, and went outside to wait for Bobby and Mickey.

I hadn't told either Gwen or Stretch about their participation in the night's events. Gwen's opinion of Bobby Gallagher was not much higher than that of his ex-girlfriend Janice, and of course Stretch wouldn't approve of my bringing more people into the case without Bolton's approval.

"Hey, Walter," Mickey said with a smile when the van arrived and I got in. He was always happy when the van was fixed and he was driving it.

"Hey, Mickey. Let's go to Charles River Park."

"Sure thing."

Bobby, on the other hand, wasn't happy at all. He didn't like it when he wasn't in charge. "This better be worth my time," he muttered.

"Think of it as an investment," I said.

"Then it better be a good investment."

When we got to Charles River Park, Fenwick was already waiting on the street for us. He looked nervous. I got out and made the introductions. "Roger Fenwick, this is Bobby Gallagher and Mickey McKenzie. I've known them forever and would trust them with my life."

This was probably a bit of a lie when it came to Bobby, but he certainly seemed pleased by the remark. "Fenwick," he said. "Aren't you the—"

"I'm up here from Atlanta with the Federal government's delegation," Fenwick replied. "And I'm very grateful for your assistance."

Bobby glanced at me, finally understanding the nature of his investment. It could only be good for business to have a guy like Roger Fenwick indebted to you.

"Of course," Fenwick went on, "if there are any costs associated with—"

Bobby waved off the suggestion before I had a chance to. "Not at all, not at all," he said. "Gasoline is quite expensive nowadays, naturally, but what of it? Everyone just wants to make sure you're safe."

We reconfigured ourselves so that Fenwick sat up front next to Mickey, and then I announced our first stop: "Over the river to Kendall Square, Mickey. We're headed to One-Eyed Joe's."

This got a puzzled look from Bobby, sitting next to me in the back seat. I ignored him. Mickey started the van, and off we went.

Mickey is a slow, careful driver at night, when the potholes and roadway debris are tough to spot. Even so, the route that had taken Fenwick and me an hour or so on foot took us a quarter of that in the van. When we pulled up in front of One-Eyed Joe's, Fenwick got out and went to talk to the security guys.

Bobby turned to me. "We're driving this guy to a fuckin' whorehouse? That's what this is all about? We have to wait around until he's through getting laid? What's this country comin' to?"

"Shut up," I informed him.

Fenwick got back into the van a few minutes later with the usual satchel of food. "Lamb," he said. "I got some extra in case you guys are hungry."

This certainly met with Mickey's approval. Bobby gave me yet another look.

"Keep going down Main Street," I told Mickey. "I'll tell you when to turn."

We drove in silence, except for my directions. The food smelled great, but we didn't eat it. Instead we all hunched down and kept a lookout for crazies. Driving is in some ways just as dangerous as walking in these abandoned neighborhoods, especially because nothing is more valuable than a working motor vehicle.

Anyway, we managed to arrive safely at Fenwick's street. "Right here, Mickey," I said as we pulled up in front of his house, in darkness like the rest of the street.

"Thank you," Fenwick said from the front seat. "This has been a big help. Let me give you some of the food."

"Bobby and I have this idea," I said.

Fenwick turned to look at us. "Yes?"

"See, Bobby and Mickey live and work in a warehouse over in South Boston. They deal in valuable merchandise that gets scavenged from here and there. There's plenty of room, and someone is always guarding the building. So we were thinking Abby could stay there until you figure out what to do next."

Fenwick shook his head. "That's very generous of you, but—"

I could sense Bobby getting ready to explode, but he managed to keep quiet. "Bobby and I talked it over," I lied. "The rooms aren't great, but we could fix one of them up. She'd have plenty to eat. She'd be safe. And most of all, she'd have human companionship."

"It will be difficult just getting her there," Fenwick pointed out. "She'll resist."

"Sure. But she can't stay here. You know that, right?"

Even in the darkness I could see the tears glistening in Fenwick's eyes. "Give me a moment," he said. He got out of the van and stared up at the dark second-floor windows behind which Abby lived her life.

Bobby grabbed my arm. "What the fucking fuck?" he whispered to me, not unreasonably. "Who's this Abby?"

"Fenwick's sister. She lives here. It's no place to live. You're making a friend for life."

"She's a crazy? Why didn't you tell me what you were up to this morning?"

"She's not a crazy. And if I told you, then you'd have had a chance to say no."

"Of course I would have."

"It'll be fine," I reassured him. And I got out of the van so I wouldn't have to argue with him anymore.

Fenwick was still staring up at the second floor.

"You've gotta do it," I said. "Let her eat dinner. Ease her into it."

He nodded but didn't move. "What if she doesn't survive? What if leaving here kills her?"

"She'll survive. Look at what she's survived already."

Finally Fenwick opened the van door again, took some of the food out of the satchel and left it for us, and then walked up the front steps and into the house. After a moment I saw the lamp flicker on.

I turned away. "Help yourself," I said to Mickey, who was eyeing the food.

Mickey helped himself.

"Why is this person living here if she's not a crazy?" Bobby demanded.

"This is the house where she grew up. Apparently she made her way back here after the War, and she's been living in the house ever since."

"Jesus H. Christ Electrical. And you want me to let her live in my warehouse?"

"She's not a crazy. It's just that her social skills are somewhat...atrophied."

"Does she talk?"

"Well, that's one of the skills that's atrophied."

"Does she, like, respond when you talk to her?"

"A little bit. Maybe."

Bobby shook his head. "Why are you doing this to me, Walter? I'm a businessman, not a nursemaid. I can't have a crazy livin' with me."

"It won't be for long. Fenwick will probably take her back to Atlanta when he leaves, and that may be pretty soon, from what Stretch tells me about the negotiations. I'd take her myself, except there's no one around my place during the day, and you've always got someone at the warehouse. Doctor J will be great with her. Anyway, have some lamb. I hear One-Eyed Joe has a good chef."

"One-Eyed Joe can fuck himself sideways," Bobby observed. He and Detective Mull don't get along, but both of them sure enjoy profanity.

Anyway, it was clear I had won when Bobby quit complaining and ordered Mickey to pass him a plate of food. I hadn't really expected him to put up much of a fight. He is reasonably soft-hearted under his gruff exterior, and he wasn't going to abandon someone's sister in the abandoned ruins of Somerville if he could help it.

So now it was up to Fenwick to convince Abby. The three of us finished the food and waited, watching the lamp glow in the second-floor window. "Is this gonna take all night?" Bobby muttered after a while. "I got stuff to do."

"You've got nothing whatsoever to do."

"How do you know?" he demanded.

I ignored him.

And then the screaming began.

"Jesus fuck!" Bobby exclaimed. "What's going

on in there?"

I thought for a second. I got out of the van and shot my gun into the air twice. Then I raced inside the house. At the bottom of the stairs I looked up and saw Fenwick struggling with Abby, who was howling in uncontrollable agony. Finally he gave up, and Abby retreated towards the living room. Fenwick sat down at the top of the stairs and put his head in his hands. "It's no use," he sobbed. "It's no use."

I went up the stairs to him.

"She won't come," he went on. "I tried to explain. I put my arm around her. I held her hand. But she wouldn't go down the stairs. I tried to—to force her, but—if she doesn't want to go…"

I put a hand on his shoulder and then walked past him, down the hallway into the living room. Abby was crouched in the far corner of the room, staring at me, quivering with fear.

She was clutching her Maid of the Mist poncho.

"Abby, you can bring the poncho," I told her. "Actually, you can bring anything you want. It's up to you. But you've got to hurry. You heard the gunfire. The crazies are coming, and if we don't get you out of here real soon, we're all going to die. Or worse."

She seemed to quiver faster.

"We're here to save you, Abby. But we don't have much time. We saw them heading this way—a lot of them. I think I shot one of them, but I'm not sure. Abby, I know you're scared. I'm scared too."

She stayed in her crouch in the corner of the

room. Now what?

"Abby, please—they're going to burn the place down." It was Fenwick speaking, behind me in the living room, suddenly playing along.

Abby looked from me to her brother, and then back to me. And then she bolted past us, down the hall into her bedroom. Fenwick and I exchanged a despairing glance.

"It's not going to work," he whispered.

"Give her a minute," I said.

We waited, and in a few seconds she was back out of the room, holding a teddy bear and a framed photograph along with the poncho.

"Oh Abby," Fenwick said. "Oh my darling Abby."

He held out her hand, but she wouldn't take it. Instead she raced down the front stairs and out to the street. We raced after her.

On the street she stopped and stared at the van. Fenwick came up behind her and opened the rear door. "Get in, Abby," he said to her. "You'll be safe. We'll protect you."

I could see Bobby sitting on the other side of the back seat. He didn't look happy. Abby stared at him like he was an alien. Then she turned and looked at the house where she had lived for so long. "Quick, Abby," I whispered. "The crazies."

She turned back and got into the van, staying as far away from Bobby as she could.

Now Fenwick looked at me. "The lamp," he said softly.

I nodded. The lamp was still glowing in the second-floor window. "What do you want me to do?"

He moved a couple of steps away from the van, to make sure Abby couldn't hear. "Burn the place," he commanded. "Make sure there's nothing to come back to."

I hurried back inside. Upstairs, the lamp sat on the coffee table next to the remains of Abby's supper. I picked it up, carefully removed the glass chimney, and brought the flame over to the living room curtains. I set one ablaze, then another. Then I ripped pages out of some books and set them on fire on the floor. Finally, I went into one of the bedrooms and set fire to the pile of old papers lying in the corner. I watched as the top sheet burned: "*Great Expectations* as a Coming of Age Novel." *A-,* the teacher had written at the top. *Good job, Abby!*

I thought of Miss Havisham, and the fire that almost consumed her.

OK, then.

Smoke was starting to billow out of the living room when I walked back down the hall. I smashed the lamp on the floor, spreading the oil towards the fire, and then went back downstairs and outside.

Fenwick was in the back seat of the van, holding on to Abby, who was staring up at the house, clutching her treasures. He nodded to me. I got into the front seat, moving the food out of the way.

I turned to the back seat. "Abby, they came," I said. "I couldn't stop them. I'm sorry. The house is on fire."

She looked out the van's window. You could see the flames consuming the living room. I wondered if the entire neighborhood would burn down. Was Abby its only resident? I sure hoped so.

"Time to get out of here," Fenwick said.

"Where to?" Mickey asked.

"Home," I said. "Let's go home."

CHAPTER 20

"You took her to Bobby Gallagher's warehouse?" Gwen demanded later that night. "What gave you that moronic fucking idea?"

Unlike Bobby Gallagher and Chris Mull, Gwen rarely swears. And she rarely gets angry. If she ever gets angry at me (and she's had plenty of reason to over the years), she gives me only the subtlest of hints, which maybe I don't always pick up on. So this was something of a first. I guess I'd had a vague sense that my idea was something less than perfect, but I'd been pretty sure that Gwen would at least approve of my good intentions. It wasn't as if I had a wide range of options to choose from.

We had driven to Bobby's warehouse in South Boston and brought Abby inside. Doctor J had been surprised by the new arrival, of course, but he quickly got into the spirit of things, helping us haul some furniture into a spare room on the second floor. Even Brutus didn't seem to mind the excitement, although he growled at me with his usual distrust. Abby was shaking the whole time, although oddly, the sight of Brutus seemed to calm her down—oddly, because feral packs of dogs are not uncommon in neighborhoods like hers, and she couldn't have avoided a run-in with one of them over the years.

Anyway, before long she had a room, and she was sitting quietly in it clutching her teddy bear, and she had even let her brother take the photo away from her and set it up on a nightstand next to her bed. It was their family, Fenwick explained, standing in front of Niagara Falls.

There wasn't much for me to do at that point. I left Fenwick sitting with his sister, and I went downstairs to let Bobby yell at me for a while. Finally he got tired of that, and Mickey drove me back to Louisburg Square.

Gwen was still up, so I sat next to her on the sofa in the parlor and told her what was going on. I thought she'd approve of my solicitude, my cleverness, my all-around good-guy charm. I was wrong. "We couldn't leave her in that house over in Somerville," I explained. "You said so yourself."

"Of course not. But why Bobby Gallagher's place?" Gwen demanded. "Why not bring her to a real home? Why not bring her here?"

"Because she's going to need people to help her, to stay with her, and there's no one around here during the day. Someone's always at the warehouse. I can tell that she and Doctor J are going to get along great."

"I could stay home sometimes," Gwen pointed out. "And you could certainly stay home, instead of going off to that stupid office of yours every day."

Her characterization of my office seemed a bit harsh, but I let it pass. "Look," I said, "it's only going to be for a few days. At the warehouse Fenwick told us he's going to bring Abby back to Atlanta with him as soon as they've finished work on the treaty. So that'll be the best outcome for everyone."

And then Gwen started to cry. Gwen never gets angry, and she never cries. This was a night of firsts. "That poor woman," she said. "That poor, poor woman."

Abby didn't seem terribly different to me from a million other lost souls in this godforsaken world, but I let that insight pass as well. Gwen continued to sob for a bit, and then I said, "Would it help if you punched me?"

Gwen looked up. "Huh?"

"In the stomach. Or somewhere. Take out your frustrations."

Gwen considered. "Yes," she said finally. "Yes, that would help." And then she considered some more. "How's your head?"

I had forgotten about my head. It still hurt a bit, I decided. "Fine," I replied. "But don't punch me there. Just to be safe."

We stood up, and she punched me in the stomach. It really wasn't a very good punch. I was pretty sure she hadn't given it her all. "Feel better?" I asked.

In reply she put her arms around me and laid her head against my chest. "Life sucks, you know?" she murmured.

"I can't disagree. But Abby Fenwick's life is going to get better. I'm sure of that."

"If you say so. Let's go to bed."

So we went upstairs and lay in each other's arms through the long night.

The next morning I hung around after Gwen and Stretch left for work. I cleaned up the kitchen, got the milk from the milkman and put it in the icebox, washed some clothes and hung them out to dry, and generally made myself useful until Chris Mull showed up in his police cruiser.

"Ready?" he asked.

"Ready."

And so we made our way up to Concord. It was a relief to be in a car instead of the Church's cart, even if Mull's police cruiser was only marginally better than Pete Callahan's. Mull seemed to be in a slightly better mood than yesterday, although I doubted I was going to get a smile out of him. He was just doing this because it was his duty. But doing your duty is OK; it's better than the opposite.

When we reached the Church, there were a couple of cars parked outside the gate. We parked behind them and approached Brother Willis and Brother Duane. They seemed nonplussed at the sight of a police car. "Hi guys," I said. "We're here to talk to people about Brother Scott."

Brother Willis nodded. "I heard about what

happened to him," he said. "That was just terrible."

"Got what he deserved," Brother Duane responded.

"No one deserves to die like that."

"Can you let us in?" Mull asked, not eager to hear the rest of the debate.

"Sure thing." They opened the gate.

"Who do those other cars belong to?" I asked them.

"Folks who want to see the spot," Brother Willis explained.

"What spot?"

"You know—where Brother Flynn ascended into heaven," Brother Duane said.

"Where he got *assumed*," Brother Willis corrected him. "People read about it in the paper, I guess."

"You mean it's, like, a *shrine*?" I asked.

"Well, I don't know what a shrine is, exactly," Brother Willis said, "but folks want to see where it happened."

Mull and I walked along the path that led to the Church's main building. Sure enough, just past the building, on the way to the barn, a few people, mostly older women, were listening raptly to Sister Lucy, who was gesturing to the sky, her eyes shining.

"Fucking morons," Mull muttered.

Sister Lucy spotted me and smiled. "The wonder!" she called out.

Mull and I went into the main building and

upstairs to talk to Brother Joseph, who was sitting behind his crowded desk studying papers. As usual, he looked tired, and his hands were shaking. "I should have expected the police," he said when Mull introduced himself. "But somehow I didn't."

"I assume Sister Marva and Brother Harold told you about what happened," Mull replied.

"Yes, they did."

"So you know he was murdered the night before last. Walter here visited Brother Scott that afternoon."

Joseph looked at me, surprised. "You found him?"

"I did. Marva and Harold didn't mention that?"

"No. Did he have the money?"

"He didn't. At least, only the past few days' worth of money." I placed it on the desk. "He said that he saw Brother Flynn steal the rest before he disappeared."

Joseph stared at the money. "That's absurd," he said. "Brother Scott must have spent it or—or something."

"Was anyone from the Church in Boston the night Brother Scott was murdered?" Mull asked.

"Of course not," Joseph replied.

"Could anyone get to Boston and back during the night without being noticed?"

"Impossible. As you may know, we don't believe in cars, and it's too far to walk. I suppose someone might be able to sneak off on one of our horses, but it would be tough going in the dark, and we'd surely notice the effects on the horse the next day."

"Mind if I ask around, see what people have to say?"

"Be my guest. You'll find a lot of confused, unhappy disciples, but you won't find any murderers."

"One more thing: Brother Scott told Walter that he thought Brother Flynn took the Church's money to frame him. He said that Sister Marva would understand why. Does that make any sense to you?"

"What? No, of course not. Brother Flynn wouldn't do that. And he wouldn't leave us."

"Sister Marva seemed pretty upset by the idea," I pointed out.

"Well, I wouldn't know anything about that."

"Brother Harold said that everyone knew Scott was attracted to Marva," I persisted. "Is it possible that he raped her? Is it possible that she's carrying Scott's baby—and that's why she doesn't want to talk about who the father is?"

Brother Joseph covered his face with his hands. "No, no," he said. "That's absurd. That's impossible."

It didn't seem impossible to me, but I didn't push the idea.

Brother Joseph took his hands down finally. "Is there anything else?" he asked wearily.

"I still owe you some time on this case," I said. "I'd like to pursue my theory about Dobler—see if I can track him down, wherever he is. Is that OK?"

"Do what you like," Joseph said with a sigh.

"You won't have any more success finding Brother Flynn than you'll have finding Brother Scott's murderer. It's all beyond me."

"I have to keep asking: do you know anything at all about his background? Where he grew up? Was he originally from Boston?"

"No, he never talked about things like that. Leave the past behind, he'd say. You're wasting your time."

"OK, but I'm going to give it a try."

Brother Joseph sighed again. "Did you see those people out there listening to Sister Lucy?"

"Hard to miss them."

"They're not interested in Brother Flynn's past. They just want to believe in a miracle."

"Can't blame them, I guess."

Brother Joseph put the money in a drawer. "Sister Lucy has never been happier," he replied. And then he went back to work.

"Not much help," Mull observed when we left Joseph's room.

"I feel sorry for the guy. His life is kind of falling apart."

"You don't think it's possible he could have orchestrated something—you know, order someone to ride into Boston and kill Scott and have everyone else keep quiet about it?"

I shook my head. "He doesn't have that kind of authority. And I doubt he knew where Scott was—I was only able to find him because when I interviewed him he mentioned that he used to live on Clarendon Street. And then I had to knock on just about every door on the street before I reached Cleanthony's place."

"But it's possible that someone here could have known the address," Mull said.

"Sure. He wasn't hiding his past like Brother Flynn was. Anyway, I wonder if Brother Reggie is here, or if he's in town at the Food Market with Sister Marva."

We found him in the barn, rubbing down one of the horses and looking unhappy. He glowered at us as we approached. "Brother Reggie, hi," I said cheerfully. "This is Detective Mull of the Boston Police Department."

Mull showed his badge. "You've heard about Brother Scott's murder?" he began.

Reggie didn't respond.

"I wonder if you can tell us anything about it."

He gave an almost imperceptible shake of his head.

"Can you tell us where you were the night before last?"

"Here," Reggie muttered. "Where else would I be?"

"Do you have any witnesses who can verify that you were here?"

He gave an almost imperceptible shrug.

"What's your last name?" Mull asked.

"What?"

"You heard me. I want to know what your last name is. Let's hear it."

Brother Reggie looked like he wanted to rip Mull's head off. "I don't have to tell you that," he said.

"Nothing would give me more pleasure than to arrest you," Mull said. "It's your choice."

Brother Reggie glared at Mull. "Hurlburt," he said finally.

"What was that?"

"Hurlburt," Reggie replied, a bit more loudly. "Reggie Hurlburt."

"That's better," Mull said. "Thank you, Mr. Hurlburt. That will be all." He turned and walked away. I followed. "Sometimes you just gotta show them you're the boss," he murmured to me.

I doubted whether Brother Reggie had learned his lesson.

Then we started wandering around, talking to the same disconsolate folks I had interviewed a few days before. Plenty of them could verify that Reggie had been at the Church the night of Brother Scott's murder. None of them had any idea who might have killed Scott. And, of course, all of them had alibis themselves. They had been here together at the Church. They couldn't possibly have made the trip from Concord to Boston and back in the dead of night. They had all forgiven Brother Scott, even if they found it hard to do so. Anyway, wasn't it exciting about the pilgrims coming up from Boston to see the spot where Brother Flynn left this world?

I asked them about Brother Flynn's background, but got nothing. Many of them had never given a moment's thought to where Dobler had come from. Some even seemed uncomfortable with the idea that he had lived a life before starting the Church of the New

Beginning. A couple offered a few hints—he didn't have a Boston accent; he knew little about pre-War Boston sports teams. But beyond that, his past was a blank.

Finally we gave up. "Fuck-all," Mull said as we headed back to the cruiser. "Just what I expected."

I couldn't disagree. "What happens next?"

"Pete Callahan is interviewing the neighbors on Clarendon Street," Mull replied as we got in the car and headed back to Boston. "Maybe we'll get lucky and someone saw the murderer. More likely, nobody noticed anything, and at that point we're pretty much done. We add the murder of Brother Scott Parker to our growing list of unsolved crimes and hope we do better on the next one. What about you? How do you find Dobler?"

"Well, I can think of one person who might know something about Dobler's past."

"Who's that?"

"The Angriest Man in America."

"Ha! Henry Fisher—shouldn't he be the Angriest Man in New England, now that we're no longer exactly part of America?"

"Doesn't seem to do justice to his anger, exactly."

"True. Want me to drop you there?"

"I'm not sure how welcome Boston police cruisers are in Charlestown," I said. "Just bring me home. I'll ride my bike over."

"Suit yourself. And Walter?"

"Yeah?"

"There's a murderer on the loose. I have no idea if he's got anything to do with Flynn Dobler and the Church and that missing money. But I wouldn't be surprised. And that means you could be a target."

"Yeah, Gwen made the same point. Thanks, Chris."

Mull glanced at me, trying to decide if it was OK for me to call him Chris again. Apparently he decided it was, because he didn't swear at me, and we parted friends in Louisburg Square.

CHAPTER 21

At home I grabbed a sandwich and then biked over to Henry Fisher's tailor shop in the shadow of the Bunker Hill Monument.

Henry's goal in life is not to mend old clothes (which is a worthy and lucrative goal, by the way) but to write the definitive work on the War and how we managed to blunder our way into it. If he ever manages to finish his book, he is convinced it will change the world forever. In this conviction I'm pretty sure he is completely mistaken.

As usual, his daughter Ann was busy actually running the shop while her father was upstairs working on his magnum opus. Ann is a beautiful dark-eyed girl who has never forgiven her father for naming her "Anarchy." I wouldn't be inclined to forgive him, either. Still, like Cleanthony, she has better things to do than to brood too much on the injustice of having been given a weird first name. "Walter!" she exclaimed when I walked into the shop. "How's the private-eye business?"

"Not as good as the tailoring business," I said, gesturing at the women behind the counter working away on valuable old manual sewing machines.

"We fill a need," Ann said modestly. "Do you want something mended, or are you here to consult the AMA?"

If Ann hates the name Anarchy, she loves the name "Angriest Man in America."

"I need to talk to your father, although I'd much rather spend the time with you."

"You're sweet. Go on upstairs and surprise him. He loves being surprised."

We exchanged a smile. We both knew that was a lie. She opened a section of counter for me, and I made my way upstairs to the office where Henry was hard at work explaining everything that had gone wrong with civilization.

The AMA is a little bald man with glasses perched on the end of his nose. He was sitting at his desk examining some document, too engrossed to notice me standing in the doorway.

"I've heard that romance novels are big sellers nowadays," I said. "Why don't you try writing one of those instead of this thing you've been working on? I'm sure my friend Art will pay you handsomely."

He looked up and glared at me. "This isn't about money and you know it, Walter. It's about our future."

I came in and sat down on an uncomfortable wooden chair opposite him. The room was piled high with books and papers. I like this sort of room, even though the books here are the sort I'd never dream of reading. Doctor J might like some of them, though. "How's it going?" I asked.

"You don't care how it's going."

"Yes I do. It's vital we learn from the mistakes of the past so that we never repeat them."

Henry eyed me suspiciously. "You're just parroting back something I said to you once."

"Of course I am. Doesn't mean I don't believe it, though. Your words made a deep impression on me."

"What do you want, Walter? As you can see, I'm a very busy man."

"You owe me a favor," I pointed out. "Because of my brilliant private-eye work New England rejected that referendum and didn't formally join the United States. Score one for the anarchists."

"That's a stretch," Henry replied. "I doubt the referendum would have passed even if the president hadn't been such an idiot. And before you know it there'll be another referendum, or an invasion, or a coup, and we'll be back where we started. In the meantime, Bolton is probably negotiating away our pitiful sovereignty as we speak."

"Henry, just do me the favor, OK?"

He shrugged an if-I-have-to shrug. "What do you want, then?"

"Remember last time I was here, you thought Flynn Dobler might be plotting against the government? Well, turns out that wasn't true, but now I want you to tell me everything you know about him."

"Why in the world do you want to know about Flynn Dobler?"

"Don't you read the *Globe*? Because he's gone missing, and my job is to find him."

"Missing? From that Church of his up in Concord?"

"That's right. Some people at the Church believe he ascended into heaven. I'm thinking that's unlikely. My theory is that he stole the Church's money and took off."

"Took off? Took off where?"

"That's what I'm trying to figure out. I have an idea that he might have gone home, or to some place like home that's deeply meaningful to him."

"Why would he do that? He had a good thing going up there."

"Actually, the Church hasn't been doing all that well," I said. "Internal tensions, practical people versus idealists, everyday administrative issues. Seems like he didn't enjoy dealing with that sort of thing."

"Yes, I suppose that makes sense. Dobler is a visionary, not a bureaucrat." Henry put down the document he'd been examining and got that far-away thinking-of-the-old-days look in his eyes. "I first ran into him sometime after the Federal troops arrived and things were starting to quiet down around here."

Two armies graced our presence after the War. The Brits were here for a while to restore order, but they had their own problems back home, and eventually they pulled out—too soon, as luck would have it. Things promptly fell apart, and we endured (or participated in) what came to be called the Frenzy. Eventually the Federal government, reconstituted in Atlanta, got its act together and sent up enough troops to return us to something like normal life.

This of course presented a dilemma for an anarchist like Henry. How do you reconcile your hatred of the government with the way it rescued us from chaos? Well, that was for him to figure out.

"You were a soldier not so long ago, weren't you, Walter?" he asked me.

"Sure. They sent me down to Washington to help in the cleanup."

"And you were a terrible soldier, I assume?"

I considered. "I think that's your idea of a compliment, right, Henry? Can we get back to Dobler, please?"

"He had recently arrived in Boston, and of course he heard about me."

"Of course."

"He wanted to know if Boston would be receptive to an anti-technology, anti-government message. I said that *I* certainly was, although it was unclear how the general populace felt about such things. I also said that technology, while part of the problem, was obviously an incomplete explanation of—"

"Yes, I'm sure it is," I agreed, eager to head off a lecture. "Did Dobler talk about starting a religion?"

"He alluded to it, although he spoke of it more as a kind of commune—people living together in peace and harmony and simplicity. Which sounds attractive, but it's an absurd idea, Walter, and I told him so. You can't just live on a farm someplace and assume the government won't bother you—won't force you to pay taxes and send your children to school and put sprinkler systems in your buildings. Even if you call yourself a religion. And what's a religion but another kind of government, with rules and regulations and punishments if you disobey?"

I had no idea what a sprinkler system was, but I let it pass. "You said he'd just arrived in Boston, Henry. Did he say where he came from? What he did before the War? What happened to him after the War? He was pretty guarded about all that once he started his Church."

Henry pondered my questions. "New York City," he said finally. "He came here from New York City. He said they wouldn't listen to his message, and that's why he came to Boston. That doesn't surprise me—New York is filled with plutocrats and people who want to become plutocrats."

"Was New York his home? Or was it just another place where he'd been preaching?"

Henry pondered some more. "I believe it was his home. I got the impression that he himself was a plutocrat, or perhaps the offspring of plutocrats. And he wanted to turn his back on them. Which is, of course, admirable."

Henry enjoyed saying the word *plutocrat*, I

think. "Do you think Dobler might have given up on his Church and returned to New York?" I asked.

"How would I know?" Henry responded. "New York is better off than Boston, but it has its own problems. For all I know he could be anywhere else on the planet. Maybe he's gone to Florida for the winter. That's what I'd do."

"But *home*, Henry. Home matters, at least to some people."

"I suppose." He didn't look convinced, although he himself had never lived more than five miles from where he was born. "You need to get a real job, Walter," he said. "Change the world."

"Changing the world is your job, isn't it?"

"Yes, and I need to get back to it. Is there anything else?"

"No, that oughta do it. Good luck with the book. Let me know when it's done, so I can be the first to read it."

"You're never going to read it," he growled.

I thought of replying: *That's because you're never going to finish it.* But I didn't want to be cruel. Henry resumed examining his document, and I left him to his life's work.

Ann greeted me when I arrived back downstairs. "The AMA give you what you needed?" she asked.

"As always, he was an enormous help," I replied. "And needless to say, he was a pleasure to talk to."

She smiled. "Don't be a stranger, Walter."

I smiled back at Ann and left the tailor shop.

As I unlocked my bike I pondered my next move. Now, at last, I had a scrap of a clue. What should I do with it? *Since I'm in the neighborhood*...I had survived the Angriest Man in America, so I figured I was ready to have a chat with my worst enemy.

What could go wrong with that?

CHAPTER 22

Jim O'Malley is what you end up with if Henry Fisher's dream and Francis Bolton's nightmare come true and you don't have a strong central government. If he doesn't exactly run Charlestown, he makes sure that no one else has more influence there than he does—not rival entrepreneurs, and certainly not the government. He's just smarter and tougher than everyone else in the neighborhood, and that means nothing happens there if he doesn't want it to happen.

The last time O'Malley and I spoke, I turned down an offer to join his enterprise, which was more or less along the lines of Bobby Gallagher's operation, except on a much larger scale, and with many fewer scruples. He had not taken kindly to my refusal. Shortly thereafter I took the liberty of killing two of his henchmen—well, actually, Gwen had killed one of them. Anyway, it's something I don't remember at all fondly, but it had been necessary at the time. It wasn't clear to me how he would react to those deaths. Some explanation might be in order. Would he give me the chance to offer one? If not, this might turn out to be one of the stupider decisions of my career.

I biked over to his beautiful Victorian mansion a few blocks away from Henry's shop. As usual, a couple of thugs sat on the porch guarding the front door. I didn't know these particular thugs. They stood up when I approached. "Hiya!" I called out. "I'm here to see the boss. Is he here?"

"You got an appointment?" the smaller thug demanded. He had a thick black beard and no visible neck.

"No, but he'll want to see me. Just tell him it's Walter Sands."

"I know who you are," he said, as if this knowledge was a burden he was forced to carry throughout life. "Stay here," he ordered. "Gary, keep your eye on this guy."

The taller thug nodded vigorously, obviously thrilled to be given such a responsibility. "Sure thing, Matt."

"And search him."

"Sure thing, Matt."

Matt disappeared inside the house. Before Gary could search me I handed him my gun. "Take good care of this," I instructed him. "And keep an eye on my bike while I'm inside. If anything happens to it, I'm holding you personally responsible."

Gary nodded uncertainly. "OK."

I was not impressed with Gary.

Matt returned to the porch before long. "Inside,

asshole," he said.

He went back inside, and I followed. He ushered me into O'Malley's first-floor office. It was beautiful, with a polished parquet floor covered by thick Oriental rugs, a large mahogany desk, and tall windows through which the late fall sunlight streamed. O'Malley himself was elegantly dressed, as always, in a three-piece suit and starched white shirt. All his tailoring was done at Henry's shop, I knew. There was something a bit odd about that relationship, but business is business, I suppose.

"If it isn't the Sandman," O'Malley said by way of greeting. "Nice of you to stop by, after you murdered two of my best guys."

"Hi, Jim," I replied, sitting down opposite him without being invited. I decided to set things straight without any preliminaries. "Anyway, you and I both know that Eddie and Pete were two of your worst guys. And they were two-timing you with the Feds so they could get visas and go as far away from here as possible. And the reason I killed them is because they were trying to kill me. And the result of all my efforts is that you're freer than ever to be a law unto yourself and oppress the good people of Charlestown. So how are you, anyway?"

O'Malley nodded slowly in response. "Life is good. Did you practice that speech?"

"No need. It's all self-evident. You owe me a favor. And I'm here to collect it."

"I owe you a favor? That's a stretch. What is it?"

"I just need some information. Know a guy named Flynn Dobler?"

"The one they wrote about in the *Globe*?"

"Uh-huh."

"That reporter is an idiot, by the way."

"I don't disagree. But Dobler."

O'Malley considered. "Never had anything to do with him that I can recall. He must have been honest. So, you're still looking for him? You don't believe God called him to be by His side in heaven or whatever the fuck?"

"Yeah. I'm proceeding under that assumption, and I'm assuming he may have gone home. I could be wrong, of course. Henry Fisher thinks Dobler told him once he grew up in New York City."

"I'd trust Henry about something like that. He doesn't forget anything."

"So if Dobler wanted to go back there, how would he do it?"

"Does he have money?" O'Malley asked.

"My theory is he has lots of it. He stole it from the Church."

O'Malley nodded. "I'm impressed. If he has money, then he has options. He could just apply for a visa from the Feds, of course. It's expensive, but not too bad if you're rich. Problem is, he'd have to wait around while it makes its way through the system. They're slow-walking everything lately to show how upset they are with New England."

That's how I had gotten my visa when I went to England on my first case, traveling with a rich client who didn't care about money. But I didn't think Flynn Dobler was sitting around somewhere in Boston waiting for his visa application to be approved. "What are his other options?" I asked.

"Well, if he paid me enough I could get him to New York City. Your annoying friend Bobby Gallagher could get him there too, I suppose. Anyone with a working vehicle and enough gasoline could probably do the job. There's a border between us and the rest of America, but it's easy enough to sneak across. You'd need protection against the bandits and the crazies, though. There's a lot of risk, so the trip wouldn't be cheap."

"But what if he wants to stay in New York? Wouldn't he need the visa?"

O'Malley leaned back in his chair. "Yeah, that's the problem. If he wants to live in the city, or anywhere the Federal government has any authority, he needs that visa, or he risks being deported or thrown in prison. It's not a huge risk if you lie low and stay out of trouble, but it is a risk. So if he needs to get a visa and leave town fast, his best bet would be to just go bribe someone in Immigration to move him up to the top of the list. They're very bribable nowadays, I'm told—they barely know which government they work for. Once he has the visa, he can just buy himself a ticket—there's a plane that flies down to New York City every day. And once he's in America proper, he can go wherever he likes."

O'Malley's analysis sounded about right. So now I knew what to do next. "Okay thanks," I said. "You've returned the favor." I stood up.

O'Malley held up a hand. "Not so fast," he said.

I sighed and sat back down.

"That offer I made last time you were here—it still stands."

Well, at least he wasn't going to have Matt and Gary beat me up. "You still want me to become one of your henchmen? Sorry, Jim. I really don't feel like sitting on your front porch and looking mean, or going around town hassling people for protection money."

O'Malley waved away my objection. "No, no. You're too smart for that. I get it. Look, I've got opportunities here. The government is weak, the negotiations with the Feds aren't going well, people are nervous. There's talk about coups, revolutions, what have you. Bolton can't hold things together. That's clear. But I can."

"You're going to take over New England?" I said. "That seems like a stretch, Jim, even for you."

"Fuck New England," he replied. "Who cares about friggin' Vermont and Maine? I'm just talking about *here*." He stabbed a forefinger at his desk. "Boston. Massachusetts. Maybe the metropolitan area—east of, I dunno, Worcester. The modern world isn't built for big governments. Everything is local nowadays. People want police departments, not armies. They want to be protected from the lunatics next door, not the lunatics in China or wherever."

"So you're going to, um, take over eastern Massachusetts?"

"Why not?"

"And my role would be what? Vice president? Lieutenant governor?"

Again O'Malley dismissed my words with a wave of his hand. "Let's not put you in a box, Walter. You're smart. You know the city. People like you. After that case of yours with the president, even people who don't know you personally think you're terrific. Together we can accomplish great things. All you need to do is get past this stupid private eye obsession of yours and start taking advantage of your talent."

"I've been doing pretty well as a private eye, thank you very much."

"You're just piddling around. You need to think big. Like me."

"No offense, Jim, but you're kind of a creep. You, like, beat people up and stuff."

O'Malley stood up. I thought he was going to throw me out, but instead he walked over and stared out the tall windows behind his desk. "You could think of me like that, Walter," he said after a minute. "Or you could take the position that I'm exactly the kind of person this world needs. Look at Charlestown. You feel pretty safe riding your bike around here?"

"Moderately safe."

"That's no thanks to the governor or the mayor or anyone like that. It's because, if someone gets out of line in my neighborhood, they know they'll have to answer to me. I don't need my business screwed up by chaos in the streets. What if everyplace else around here was as safe as Charlestown? Wouldn't that be worth a few cracked skulls?"

I thought of the burnt-out, abandoned wasteland that was Somerville, right next door to Charlestown. Maybe, if Somerville had found itself a Jim O'Malley, it wouldn't be a wasteland. "You'd have to do a lot more than crack some skulls to take over the government," I pointed out.

O'Malley turned back to me and shrugged. "Depends on how much support I've got. Have the right friends in the right places, maybe you don't have to crack any skulls at all. You just show up one day and the job is yours."

"Um, you do know that my friend Stretch is one of Governor Bolton's advisers, right?"

"Sure. I like Stretch—I could use him on my side too. But look, you think Bolton isn't already worried about me? He knows that I'm the guy he needs to watch out for, not the crackpot leader of some ragtag army invading from New Hampshire or someplace."

I hadn't really thought about that. Politics and revolutions were not my strong suit. Which was precisely why I had no intention of taking O'Malley up on his offer. "Well, this sounds like an exciting career opportunity," I replied, "and I'll certainly give it serious consideration. Once I've tracked down Flynn Dobler."

O'Malley sighed. He knew I wasn't going to give the opportunity any consideration whatsoever. "Run along then," he said. "Solve your little case. It won't make a bit of difference to anyone, and you'll spend the rest of your life wondering why you pissed off the most important guy you ever met."

I stood up. "Jim, I think you may be overestimating my talents. But anyway, thanks for the offer."

He waved a hand in dismissal and turned his back.

Outside, the goons on the porch stared warily at me. "Gun, please?" I asked Gary. He looked at Matt, who nodded with a sneer. I took the gun. "Thanks for watching my bike for me," I said to Gary. "You did a good job."

I gave them a wave and pedaled off towards Government Center.

I was still making progress, I thought. And I had time to stop in at the Federal immigration office before supper.

That, I figured, should do it.

I should not have been so optimistic.

CHAPTER 23

The immigration office is located in the Saltonstall Building, a dreary old high-rise in Government Center. The building was heavily guarded by troops who, like O'Malley's thugs, confiscated my gun before letting me inside. The elevator wasn't working, so I had to walk up to the fourth floor, then down a corridor that had the usual old-building smell of piss and mold. The door to the office was guarded by a bored-looking soldier who searched me to make sure the guards outside hadn't screwed up and let me through with a weapon. Visas are valuable.

The office was dim and musty and filled with file cabinets. By the door were a bunch of uncomfortable-looking plastic chairs, all empty. Behind the counter sat a little man with thin black hair and a thin black mustache. He wore a suit jacket, a bow tie, and a crisp white shirt, and he paid no attention to me. When I approached, I noticed that he was reading the yellowed pages of a paperback. The mere sight of the book made me reverse my original impression and start to like the guy.

He put the book down when he noticed me looming over him and gave me an annoyed look. "We're about to close," he said, pointing at the clock on the wall to the left of the counter. "Come back tomorrow."

"*Taken by a Rake*," I replied, reading the cover upside down. "Sounds like a romance novel. Did you get it at Art's Filthy Bookstore, by any chance?"

He reddened and glared at me. "Come back tomorrow," he repeated.

A name plate on the counter said *N. Morgenstern*. "Mr. Morgenstern, my name is Walter Sands, and I'm just looking for some information. It won't take a minute."

"What information? We don't give out information."

"I just need to know if a guy named Flynn Dobler was issued a visa in the past couple of weeks. He was probably going to New York City."

"Flynn Dobler? Never heard of him. A lot of people get visas nowadays."

"Could you just check your records?"

Mr. Morgenstern looked outraged at the idea; his mustache bristled with indignation. "Of course I can't do that! Visas are highly sensitive, private information! You can't just walk in here and expect to see them. Now leave this instant, or else I'll call the guard!"

I considered trying to bribe the guy, but bribes weren't in my budget. So I decided I would have to try a different approach. "What time do you open up in the morning, Mr. Morgenstern?" I asked him.

His gaze turned suspicious. "The information isn't going to become public overnight," he pointed out.

"Understood. But your hours of operation are public information, right?"

"We open promptly at nine o'clock," he said. "Now please leave. I need to close the office."

"See you tomorrow, Mr. Morgenstern."

The prospect didn't appear to fill him with pleasure.

I walked back downstairs, collected my gun from the guards, and rode my bike home. There was a note from Gwen on the kitchen table:

Won't be home for supper. XOXO Gwen

Missing supper was a bit unusual for Gwen, but not unprecedented. Gwen on a story was like me on a case, except that she was talented in addition to being relentless. So I made supper just for Stretch and me. When he arrived, an hour or so later, he was in a jubilant mood.

"We did it, Walter!" he exclaimed. "We reached an agreement!" He was practically dancing.

"Congratulations," I said. "Did Bolton get what he wanted?"

"Close enough. Food shipments, medical aid, diplomatic recognition—this is a great day for

New England—and America!"

"What about Fenwick—is he happy with the agreement?"

"I think so. He said he might have a hard job selling it back in Atlanta, but he thinks he can convince enough people to get it approved. No one wants another Frenzy, and that's what people on both sides are starting to worry about. Stability matters. Law and order matters. We compromised on some sovereignty issues— nothing the Executive Council won't accept."

I thought about Jim O'Malley. He probably wouldn't take the news well.

We washed up and sat down to eat. Stretch didn't know where Gwen was—he figured she was off writing up something about the treaty. This was big news, of course, and the *Globe* was going to be all over it. "Do you know when Fenwick is returning to Atlanta?" I asked him.

"As soon as possible, I guess—no reason to stick around here. He really has great things to say about you, Walter. I don't know what you did for him, but he sure does appreciate it."

"It was nothing. But could you remind Bolton to pay me, Stretch? I don't do this stuff for free."

"Sure thing, Walter."

I was on Fenwick's case again tonight. But tonight, I figured, the case would be easy. After supper I read a book while I waited for Mickey to arrive with the van.

Hadn't had much chance to read lately, what with my busy work schedule, and the sight of Mr. Morgenstern alone in his office with an ancient paperback had reminded me of what I'd been missing. I was sort of sorry when Mickey pulled up at eight o'clock—Harry Bosch had just come up with a break in the cold case he was investigating—but duty called.

Mickey was alone in the van, which was what I expected—Bobby would be back at the warehouse with his guest. "How's Abby doing?" I asked him.

"Seems okay, Walter," he replied.

Something in his tone was a little off. "You sure?"

"Yeah, she's settling in nicely."

Still a little off. I didn't press him; I'd find out for myself soon enough.

Fenwick was waiting for us on the street outside Charles River Park. He was dressed up in a suit and tie and looked almost as excited as Stretch. "I can't stay long," he said. "We're having a formal dinner tonight to celebrate the agreement. Did you hear about it?"

"I did. Does this mean—"

"We're flying back to Atlanta tomorrow afternoon. And I'm going to take Abby with me."

"That's great. I hope she'll be happy there."

"She'll be fine—I hope," Fenwick said. "I know the transition will be hard. But I'll find good people to look after her during the day. And I'm sure there are specialists in Atlanta who can treat the—the kind of trauma she's suffered. I'll do whatever it takes to heal her."

"She's very lucky to have a brother like you."

"I wouldn't call her lucky. But yes, I suppose it

could have been worse for her. It's been worse for a lot of people."

We arrived at Bobby's warehouse in no time. Mickey parked the van inside. We got out, and it wasn't hard to tell what was different.

Music wafted through the gritty warehouse. Piano music. The Beatles. "Yesterday."

...all my troubles seemed so far away...

"Um, Gwen stopped by," Mickey said.

It's never been clear to me how Gwen managed to learn to play the piano. She says she just picked it up at some house where she was hiding out during the Frenzy, drawn irresistibly to the instrument despite the danger of making noise that would attract the crazies. How do you just "pick up" a skill like that? But she had. She had even managed to figure out how to tune pianos, which seems to me to be unimaginably complicated, but pretty much a necessity if they're going to sound good after sitting around for a couple of decades.

I had never noticed that Bobby possessed a piano, but he did, along with all the other useless stuff on the first floor of his warehouse. How had he managed to move it from wherever he'd found it? Another mystery. But it was sitting there, in a far corner, amid all the junk. And Gwen was playing it by lamp light.

And Abby was sitting next to her, her eyes moist and riveted on Gwen, her hands pressed together prayer-like in front of her lips. She was wearing a blue dress that wasn't quite the right size. Her gray hair looked freshly washed.

Fenwick and I stood silently to one side. We watched and listened. When Gwen finished the song she looked up. "Hello," she said to Fenwick. "I'm a friend of Walter's. It's been a long time since your sister has heard any music, I think."

"I'm sure you're right," he said softly. "Thank you. She always liked the Beatles."

Fenwick pulled up a chair and sat next to Abby. I stood behind Gwen at the piano and kissed the top of her head. She leaned back against me. "I can't stay long, Abby," Fenwick said to his sister, "but tomorrow I'm going to come back and get you, and I'm going to take you home with me to Atlanta. I know it may not be where you want to live, but we'll be together, and I'll take care of you, and you'll never have to be scared or lonely or hungry again. Will that be all right, my darling?"

Abby looked at her brother but didn't say anything. I could feel Gwen stiffen when Fenwick mentioned that he was taking his sister home.

Fenwick grasped Abby's hands. "Have you eaten?" he asked her.

"Doctor J and I cooked supper for her," Gwen responded when Abby didn't. "I think she liked it."

"How long have you been here?" I asked Gwen.

"A while. I gave her a bath, cut her nails—stuff you guys wouldn't think of doing. I also brought a doctor over to check her out. It was a bit difficult getting Abby to cooperate with that, but we got through it. Physically, she seems OK."

"Huh." After her tirade this morning, Gwen had apparently decided to take over. I wonder if Mickey thought I'd be mad at her—or at him.

"That's wonderful of you," Fenwick said.

"It was my pleasure," Gwen said.

Fenwick sat with Abby a while longer, and then he got up to go. "Tomorrow," he repeated to his sister. "I'm coming back for you tomorrow. You'll be safe here."

Abby glanced at him, and then back at the piano.

"Gwen, are you coming?" I asked her. "I'm going to hitch a ride with Mickey and Mr. Fenwick."

She shook her head. "I'm staying here with Abby tonight," she replied. "I can sleep on the floor next to her, in case she needs anything. Bobby has plenty of blankets and pillows."

Gwen, it occurred to me, was in love. "Well OK, then," I said. I kissed her again.

Bobby was standing by the van with Mickey. "Your sister's been great," he said to Fenwick. "She was a little shaky after you left, but she got to sleep okay. Then she was kinda scared in the morning when she woke up, but Doctor J stayed with her and calmed her down. Later on Gwen came over, and the two of them really seemed to click."

"Gwen seems like an angel."

"Yeah, Gwen's the best. It was my idea to ask her to help out."

This was, of course, a blatant lie, but I let it pass.

"I appreciate everything that all of you have done," Fenwick replied. "You've been unbelievable."

Bobby beamed. In the far corner of the warehouse, Gwen started playing "Fool on the Hill."

Mickey and I got in the van with Fenwick, and we headed back to Charles River Park. That was when I asked Fenwick for my favor. "I know you're a busy guy," I said, "and you're getting ready to go back to Atlanta, but I could use some help on a case."

"Of course," Fenwick replied. "I'll do whatever I can."

"I'm trying to track down this guy, and I think he may have gone to New York City. But the person in charge at the Federal immigration office—his name is Morgenstern—won't give me any information. I suppose that's the policy, but a call from you—"

"Certainly. I'll phone him first thing in the morning. I can't see the harm."

"Thanks," I said. "There's one other thing."

"Yes?"

"Well, I might need a visa to go after the guy. Apparently it, uh, costs quite a bit to get a visa nowadays, if you don't want to wait forever."

Fenwick nodded his understanding. "I'll make sure Mr. Morgenstern takes care of you. Some of these Federal employees haven't been paid regularly since the referendum. I'm not surprised that they've gotten, er, resourceful. That's something the new agreement should help remedy. Anyway, don't worry. You'll be treated well. But—will you be able to take Abby to the airport tomorrow? She'll need all the friends there that she can get."

"Sure, we can do that. Right, Mickey?"

"Not a problem. What time?"

"Two o'clock," Fenwick said. "I can't wait."

"It's great about the agreement," I said.

"Yes, I think we accomplished a lot. Everyone is going to have something to complain about, which is a sign that we did our job."

We left Fenwick at Charles River Park, and then Mickey drove me back to Louisburg Square. When I went inside, the downstairs was empty; Stretch had already gone up to bed. I gazed at the piano in the parlor, and I started to miss Gwen. She sometimes doesn't come home for supper, but she almost never spends the night away from home. Unlike me.

I put out the lights and went upstairs, but I knew there was no chance of getting to sleep without Gwen lying next to me in our bed. So I headed directly to the third floor, where I had my version of Henry Fisher's book-lined office.

So many books. This was how I had survived through the bad years, losing myself in worlds impossibly different from my own, fantasizing that I was part of those worlds, solving cases for mysterious blondes….

I finished the Harry Bosch novel, and then decided I needed a change of pace. So I re-read *Great Expectations* and thought of Abby's term paper, which I had set on fire the night before.

Poor Pip. Poor Miss Havisham. Poor Abby.

It was near dawn when I when back downstairs and collapsed on my bed, fully clothed, to get a little sleep before morning finally came.

And it couldn't have been long after that when I felt myself being shaken. I opened my eyes to look up at Stretch, dressed for work and very upset.

"Walter, come on, get up," he said.

"What's going on?" I mumbled.

"Downstairs. The front door. Come on."

"All right, all right." I rolled out of bed and followed him downstairs.

He led me outside. "Look," he said, pointing to the front door. "It was here when I was leaving for work just now. I came back to show it to you."

I looked. A piece of paper was tacked to the door. A message had been scrawled on it in red ink. I studied it for a good long while. Here is what the message said:

> *Sandman Stop! If you know whats good for you!*

"Missing an apostrophe there, huh, Stretch?" I asked him.

Stretch just shook his head.

CHAPTER 24

Finally I took the paper down from the door and walked back inside.

Stretch followed me. "What's it about, Walter?" he asked.

"I expect it's a warning from the Church of the New Beginning," I said. "To quit looking for Flynn Dobler. Or maybe to quit looking for Brother Scott's murderer. Chris Mull and I went back up there yesterday."

"Are you in danger? Should I stick around?"

"No, there's no reason to. I'm sure you're busy at work."

"Where's Gwen, by the way?" Stretch asked. "Did she leave early?"

"She didn't come home last night, actually. She was helping Bobby Gallagher over at the warehouse. It's a long story—she'll tell you when she's around."

Stretch finally left, worried about me but unable to figure out a way to help. I sat at the kitchen table, ate breakfast, and stared at the warning, trying to make sense of it. It wasn't easy: my mind was fuzzy from waking up too early. Finally I was interrupted by someone banging on the front door.

It was Detective Mull, and he was mighty pissed. He showed me a piece of paper. "Tacked to my door this morning," he said.

I showed him my piece of paper.

The message on each was much the same.

"Want some breakfast?" I asked.

"I want to nail the bastard who did this," he replied. "Coming to my house and putting this thing on my door—that is really not a good idea. I have a wife. I have kids."

"Whoever did it is an idiot," I pointed out. "You were about to shove the case into a file cabinet and move on. Now it's clear this isn't some random crime."

"Exactly. What do those religious freaks up in Concord know about police work?"

"Maybe they panicked when we visited them yesterday."

"I suppose. How do you think they managed to put these up?"

I considered. "Same way they murdered Brother Scott, I guess. I was thinking: it's not like we have a membership list for the Church, Chris. Maybe they have a follower who lives in Boston. Somebody who supports them, without exactly being a member. It doesn't have to be anyone in Concord."

"Well, I'm going back up there and ream their

asses. Want to come?"

"Sorry, I wish I could. I've got stuff to do in Boston today. But good luck."

"Suit yourself. Bastards."

Mull stomped off.

I considered my situation a while longer. Then I did the breakfast dishes, grabbed the newspaper with Dobler's photo in it, and bicycled off to the bookstore to see Art.

The day was overcast and had started to drip cold rain. But as usual the bookstore was warm and inviting, and Art was delighted to see me. "How's the case?" he asked.

"Could be better," I said. "But you may be able to help. Do you happen to know a guy named Morgenstern? N. Morgenstern—don't know what the *N* stands for. Works for the Feds in the immigration office."

"Natty Morgenstern? Of course I know Natty. He's one of my best customers."

Natty? "He seems to be a reader of romances."

"Indeed he is. Regencies and Georgians, mainly."

"Um, what are they?"

"Just subgenres, Walter. Like those mysteries you read—you've got police procedurals, hardboiled private eye novels, and so on. Regencies are romances set in Britain during, I don't know, the early 1800s sometime, and Georgians are set in the late 1700s. You should try them—they're pretty good."

"No, thanks. But I'd like to buy one for, uh, Natty."

"Sure thing. It might be tough finding one he hasn't read, though. He seems to have a lot of free time on his hands. Like you. Let me take a look." He studied his New Arrivals shelf for a minute, and then grabbed a tattered paperback. "*Seduction in Silk*—just in. Georgian, I guess. Nice cover. I think he'll like this one. Although, if you ask me, they're all pretty similar. But I suppose you could say that all private eye novels are pretty similar."

No, you couldn't. Anyway, a beautiful auburn-tressed woman in a long blue off-the-shoulder gown gazed longingly from the cover. Clearly she needed a strong man like me to give her the love she deserved. "Well, OK," I said dubiously. "How much do I owe you?"

Art waved away the question. "For you, no charge, of course. Is this a gift for Natty?"

"Sort of. More of a bribe, actually."

Art nodded. "It's a good one."

I took the book, returned to the Saltonstall Building, and went through the same routine with the guards as the day before. This time Morgenstern was busy with a couple of customers, so I had to wait around for a while until it was my turn at the counter. He was wearing a bow tie and a crisp white shirt, the same as yesterday. Did he spend his evenings doing laundry?

He eyed me coldly. "I've been informed I have to cooperate with you," he said without enthusiasm.

"Sorry to go over your head. But anyway, I

brought you a present." I handed him *Seduction in Silk.* He tried, but failed, to hide his delight. "It's a Georgian," I pointed out. "Just in. Art said you liked Georgians. And Regencies."

Morgenstern took the book and fondled it. "You know Art?" he asked.

"Art and I go way back. I'm more of a mystery guy myself. But mainly I just like books."

"Yes. Books are…wonderful. Especially nowadays."

"Especially now," I agreed. "Sometimes I think I wouldn't have survived without books."

"I wasn't born to live in a world like this," he said. "Books let mc lcavc it. At least for a while." He managed to put the book down and look up at me. "So, what was it you needed again, Mr.—"

"Sands. But call me Walter."

"Yes. Walter. I'm Nathaniel. But people call me Natty."

That name was going to take some getting used to. "Natty, like I said yesterday, I want to check the visas you've issued for the past couple of weeks to see if a guy named Flynn Dobler left New England to go to the United States— possibly to New York City."

"Yes, yes. I can do that for you, Walter." Natty got up and went over to a file cabinet, which he pawed through for a few minutes. Then he returned, looking disappointed. "I'm very sorry, but no one by that name has been issued a visa recently."

I took out the copy of the *Globe* and showed Natty Dobler's photograph. "This is what he looks like," I said. "He might have used a phony name on the visa application."

Natty took a look. "Oh, yes, of course," he said without hesitation. "He was in quite a hurry. Um, he may have offered me a small gratuity to expedite the process. Books aren't cheap, as you well know. And our paychecks have been somewhat irregular in arriving lately."

"Perfectly understandable. We all have to make a living."

"Let me just verify his destination."

He went back to the file cabinet. A couple of people were in line behind me now, and they were getting restless. "Yes, here it is," he called out to me. "Francis Donovan. Visa issued on the thirteenth. As you say, his destination was New York City."

"Perfect. You've been a big help."

Natty was smiling as he returned to the counter. "Any time, Walter. We book-lovers have to stick together. Mr. Fenwick suggested that you might need your own visa."

"I'm not sure yet. I'll be back if I do. With another book."

Natty beamed. "I like paranormals, too."

"Um—?"

"You know—romances about ghosts? Vampires? Witches? Shapeshifters?"

"Everyone needs to be loved, I guess. Thanks again, Natty."

"Come back soon, Walter."

So, progress. I had made a new friend and confirmed yesterday's theory about Dobler. He had gone to New York City. He had returned home.

From the Saltonstall Building I biked over to Bobby's warehouse. The rain was coming down a little harder now. Doctor J had migrated inside from his usual seat by the entrance. "Gonna miss Abby," he said when I arrived.

"Me too," I agreed. "But this isn't much of a place for her."

"It is with Gwen around. She'd've gotten us all into shape before long."

"You guys are hopeless. Besides, Gwen has better things to do."

"Maybe Bobby and Mickey and me are hopeless. Not so sure about Abby. They're upstairs, gettin' ready."

"Thanks, Doctor J." I went upstairs, dodging Brutus when he lunged at me.

Gwen was with Abby in her room, helping her try on shoes. Abby was wearing a white blouse and a gray skirt. Her hair had been arranged in a bun. "You look great, Abby," I said.

She didn't respond.

"Doctor J picked up some clothes for her at the Salvage Market," Gwen said. "He does good work."

"So do you."

She didn't look happy at the compliment, and I knew why—her beloved was going away. "Abby is such a pretty lady," she said. "We just want to do right by her. This is a big day for her, after all."

Abby's eyes flicked toward Gwen, and then

flicked away. Did she understand what was happening?

"Is Stan OK with your taking the day off, Gwen?"

Stan Wolsey is Gwen's editor at the *Globe*. Gwen didn't seem interested in what Stan thought. "Doesn't matter" was all she had to say about that. Her attention was focused on Abby. "Abby darling, the gray shoes are prettier, but these black ones look like they fit you better. What do you think?"

Abby didn't respond.

Bobby popped his head into the room. "Hey, Walter, glad you're here. You coming with us to the airport?"

"Sure."

"Leaving in about fifteen minutes. Gwen, is Abby ready?"

"All dressed. I want to pack some of the clothes Doctor J bought her. Just in case she needs them in Atlanta."

"Okay. Come downstairs when you're done."

"He's certainly in a take-charge mood," I said to Gwen when Bobby had left.

"He's a happy man," Gwen replied. "Huge new vistas are opening for him, what with Fenwick being his new best friend."

"Well, Bobby does good work, too."

I went back downstairs while Gwen set about packing clothes for Abby, using an old suitcase she had probably found among Bobby's many random possessions. I ate some bread and cheese with Doctor J and Mickey, then hung around until everyone made their way downstairs a few minutes later. Brutus wagged his tail with delight as Gwen and Abby passed by.

"I'll stay in the back seat with Abby," Gwen said. "In case the ride is difficult for her."

"She'll do just fine," Bobby replied, calling upon his nonexistent experience with people who had spent twenty years hiding from civilization.

Abby was clutching her Maid of the Mist poncho and teddy bear. She looked nervous. Gwen helped her into the back seat of the van. Bobby got in the other side. I rode up front with Mickey. Doctor J stayed behind to hold the fort.

The airport is in East Boston, across the harbor from Bobby's warehouse in South Boston. There used to be tunnels under the harbor you could use to get there, I'm told, but a couple of maintenance-free decades have done their damage, and now you have to take a longish route through Charlestown and Chelsea to get there. The airport itself, like everything else in the city, is nothing like it used to be, with a couple of runways handling a small number of flights each day. Not that long ago we had driven in this van to the airport so I could fly to England on my first case, and we were all convinced I would never come back. Gwen, I knew, would also be recalling that drive.

The rain slowed us down, but still we were a bit early; Fenwick and the rest of the Federal delegation hadn't arrived at the terminal yet. I wandered off after a few minutes, telling Gwen I had to find a bathroom.

I don't like lying to Gwen.

Instead I went to find the person selling tickets for the daily flight to New York City. I had vaguely thought it would be the same one who sold tickets to England, but this woman was tall and thin and looked terrified of me.

"Hi," I said.

"Yes?" she quavered.

I'm not going to kill you, I wanted to reassure her. But that would have probably terrified her even more. "I just wanted to find out how much the flight to New York costs."

"Oh. Oh, yes. Twenty dollars." She looked relieved, as if now I would leave her alone.

But the interrogation had to continue. "And do you have to book in advance?"

"What?" she asked, her eyes widening with panic.

"You know: do the flights fill up? Do I have to buy a ticket ahead of time?"

She shook her head vigorously. "No, no, of course not. No, not at all. Never. But today's flight just left. You can't go there today."

Well, that all seemed reasonably clear. "OK, then," I responded with a smile. "Have a nice day."

She just kept shaking her head, as if such an idea was inconceivable.

When I got back, the waiting area was jammed. Fenwick and the Feds were there, and so were Bolton and a bunch of New England officials, including Stretch. A few reporters had also shown up; one of them was Ken Hendrikson from the *Globe*. Fenwick was sitting with his sister. He looked nervous, and she looked decidedly unhappy amid the crowd. Bobby had put himself in charge of keeping everyone away from them.

Hendrikson came over to me. "What are you doing here, Walter?"

"Nothing," I said.

"Well, what's Gwen doing here? She's not covering the story."

"Dunno."

"She didn't show up for work yesterday. Know anything about that?"

"Nope."

"Who's that woman sitting with Fenwick?"

"No idea."

Hendrikson shook his head. "Thanks, Walter. You've been a big help."

"Anytime, Ken. By the way, I enjoyed your story about the Church. Very even-handed."

Hendrikson eyed me suspiciously, correctly sensing sarcasm. "That story got a terrific response," he pointed out.

"I'm sure it did. But how come you didn't cover the murder of Brother Scott? Didn't your sources tell you about that?"

He shrugged. "I looked into it. The police have nothing. Sounds like a run-of-the-mill robbery—happens all the time, sad to say. Not worth more than a paragraph. Have you found Flynn Dobler yet?"

No way I was going to give Hendrikson a scoop about Dobler being in New York City. "Nope," I said. "Not a clue. But I'll find him. Don't worry."

Hendrikson simply smiled and wandered off to interview someone else. Next in line for enlightenment was Stretch. "What's going on, Walter? Why are you and Gwen here?"

"Tell you later, Stretch. By the way, have you talked to Bolton about getting my pay?"

"Sure. I have it in my pocket, actually. Want me to give it to you?"

"No, hold onto it. It's safer with you than with me."

Then I found a spot with Mickey in a corner of the waiting area and…waited. I could hear the rain drumming on the roof. Outside the window I could see the plane that would take Abby to Atlanta. Crew members came and went via the walkway that connected the plane and the waiting area. I looked at Abby clutching her teddy bear and poncho. She was starting to quiver. What would Hendrikson and the other reporters make of that? Gwen sat on the other side of Abby from Fenwick. She was leaning close to Abby, and I could tell she was whispering soothing words into her ear. *It's all right, Abby. These people will be gone soon, and you'll be fine.*

I looked out at the rain. And then I remembered something, and I started to get as nervous as Abby.

Fenwick got up and joined Bolton near the walkway, and they each made a statement to the press and the delegations and whoever else had shown up. I don't remember exactly what they said—something about close bonds and bright futures. A few questions were asked and answered. There was applause; there were smiles and waves and handshakes. Fenwick returned to Abby and helped her to her feet. I moved towards them.

"Let's go, my darling," he said to his sister.

Gwen hugged Abby. Bobby hugged her. I hugged her. Abby didn't hug back; she clutched her poncho and her teddy bear and her suitcase, and her eyes were frightened. After the hugs she headed off into the walkway with her brother. Gwen stood beside me, holding onto my arm so hard I thought she'd break it.

We watched them disappear from view. People started to leave. Bobby said something; I didn't listen. I waited. Maybe I said a prayer to a God I didn't believe in.

He wasn't listening.

I heard a low rumble in the distance.

I saw a flash of lightning.

And then I heard the scream.

CHAPTER 25

———— • ♦ • ————

I had heard that scream before. Gwen and I rushed down the walkway. Fenwick and Abby were just emerging from the plane. He had his arm around his sister, propping her up. Abby could barely walk. When she saw Gwen, she collapsed sobbing into her arms. Fenwick stood beside her, looking helpless and scared.

"Lightning," I murmured to him.

He nodded. "It was such a long time ago. I hoped…"

His voice trailed off. The trip back from Orlando that he had recalled in his long monologue the other night—lightning hitting the plane, and Abby hiding her head in her mother's lap. The childhood memories that apparently never go away. *You were always scared to fly after that.*

"I have to get back to Atlanta," Fenwick said. "I don't know what to do."

I looked at Gwen. She was stroking Abby's

hair. "It's OK, it's OK," she murmured. "We'll keep you safe." She looked up at us finally. "Abby will stay here," she announced. "We'll take care of her."

"Are you sure?" Fenwick asked.

"This is her home," Gwen said. "This is where she belongs."

"Maybe if we delayed the flight until after the storm…" But again he didn't finish the thought. He could see what we saw: Abby had been through enough—today, and in her life. Flying wasn't an option.

He tried again. "I can't ask you to do this," he said.

Gwen shook her head. "We're doing this," she replied, in that way of hers that brooked no argument.

Fenwick looked like he wanted to object some more, but finally he capitulated. "You are the best people in the world," he said.

This applied only to Gwen, but I didn't argue the point.

"I'll come back," he went on. "As soon as I can. The Federal government is going to need a permanent presence in Boston—an ambassador, if that's what they want to call it. Someone who knows New England. It might as well be me, if I haven't made too many enemies in Atlanta with this agreement."

Gwen nodded. "We'll keep her safe till then," she said.

And then Fenwick hugged Abby in turn, told her he loved her, told her he would be back before long....Did she understand? Did this make her feel better? I couldn't tell. She wasn't as upset as she had been. But maybe that was just because she wasn't on the plane anymore, facing a flight into a thunderstorm.

Finally Fenwick headed back down the walkway and disappeared. A few moments later the plane taxied away from the gate, and we watched it until we couldn't see it anymore. There was no more lightning. By the time the plane took off, the sun was starting to break through the clouds.

"Um, back to the warehouse, I guess?" Bobby asked. He was standing next to us, looking unusually subdued.

Gwen shook her head. "Louisburg Square. Abby is coming home with us."

It occurred to me to object. But it also occurred to me that my objection would be instantly overruled.

Bobby looked relieved. "Sure. Sure thing. Mickey, let's go."

When we turned around I noticed that Ken Hendrikson was still in the waiting area, looking like he really wanted to ask some questions. What's going on here? Who is this woman? But he, too, knew better than to mess with Gwen.

Stretch had already left, along with Governor Bolton and the rest of the New England government leaders. So the explanation we would have to give him could wait.

We all went outside, piled into Bobby's van, and headed out of the airport. Nobody said anything. Abby sat quietly in Gwen's arms, quivering just a bit. Back in Louisburg Square, Gwen brought Abby upstairs and installed her in the bedroom that used to belong to Linc, another member of our little family who had suffered for years until finally he decided not to suffer anymore. His death had left a hole in our lives, I knew, and perhaps Gwen saw Abby as a way of filling that hole. Or, looking at the situation from a different angle, perhaps Abby was the baby that Gwen couldn't have—a person on whom she could shower all the maternal care and devotion she had bottled up inside her. An odd sort of baby, but this is an odd sort of world. Not that I was going to ask Gwen about my theories; she would just dismiss them as absurd. Because it was also true that Abby was simply a person who needed help, and Gwen was able to give it to her. And so she did.

Gwen stayed for a long time with Abby in the darkened bedroom. I busied myself around the house. Everything felt odd, out of whack, as if the structure of the cosmos had changed with Abby's arrival. But it was more than Abby. I studied the warning that had been pinned to our door in the middle of the night. *Sandman Stop!* That hadn't helped. I thought about Flynn Dobler down in New York City, and the flights there. Every day. Twenty dollars. That wasn't helping either.

Eventually I settled down and made supper. Stretch arrived home, and it was time to fill him in.

Gwen brought Abby down to eat, and Stretch

started in with his questions. Unlike Ken Hendrikson (or, for that matter, me), Stretch had no compunctions about grilling Gwen. After we had established who Abby was and why she was staying with us, Stretch asked, "But how are we going to take care of her, Gwen? We all work."

"I'll take a vacation."

"Does the *Globe* even give you vacation time?" Stretch persisted.

Gwen glared at him, but Stretch was oblivious. "Of course they do," she said. Then: "I don't know. I'll find out. It doesn't matter."

"But what happens when your vacation is used up?"

"Then you can use your vacation. And Walter can help too. He doesn't need to go to his office every day. He can stay here. People know where to find him."

Stretch didn't bother disputing that assertion. Instead he veered off in another, equally unhelpful direction. "Did Walter tell you about the paper someone stuck on our front door last night? Probably from that Church, warning him to quit investigating."

Gwen looked at me. I shrugged. "That's a pretty complicated situation up there in Concord," I said. "I wouldn't worry about it."

"Are you still on the case?"

"I guess so," I replied. "I actually made some progress this morning." I told them about the discovery I had made when I visited Natty.

"So what are you going to do?" she asked. "Follow Dobler to New York?"

Her tone of voice suggested that this idea was misguided, if not completely insane.

"I need to ask Brother Joseph up at the Church what he wants to do. It's his case."

"You can always resign," she said. "In fact, you should resign. That case has been nothing but trouble. And then you can help out with Abby."

"Happy to do what I can," I replied. "But I really do have to tell him what I found out."

Gwen seemed unconvinced, but she didn't argue the point. I looked at Abby. Her attention had been focused on eating the meal I had prepared, so she probably hadn't even heard Stretch's interrogation. Scrambled eggs probably weren't the best choice for someone who had forgotten how to use a knife and fork, but she did OK, and Gwen was quick to wipe her face when she left food on her cheeks or lips. She was much calmer than she had been at the airport. Would we ever be able to leave her by herself? Maybe. But it also seemed possible that she would always need someone with her, to keep her safe from the terrors in the world and in her mind.

Unlike a baby, maybe this was as far as she was going to come.

Gwen slept on the floor in Abby's room that night. "It's only temporary," she explained. "Just till Abby settles in."

What if she never settles in? I wanted to ask. But I didn't. "Of course," I said.

Gwen gave me one of her looks. "Walter, are you sure you're OK with all this?"

"I don't see that we have any other options," I

replied. "I never meant for her to stay at Bobby's warehouse for more than a few days."

She gave me a hug then, leaning her head against my chest. I kissed her fragrant hair. And we left it there. Gwen went off to care for Abby. I was unable to sleep, of course, so I went up to my chilly third-floor library and dipped into my vast collection for another book to read. I read till near dawn, and then slept in my chair. What was the point of going downstairs to an empty bed? When I awoke, Stretch had already left for work, and Gwen was with Abby in the kitchen. Gwen greeted me cheerily. Abby had slept well, had eaten well. And didn't she look great?

"She looks fabulous," I said, equally cheerily. "What have we got to eat?"

Gwen served me breakfast. Abby sat silently at the table. She seemed a bit on edge, constantly clasping and unclasping her hands, but I wasn't going to mention it. She kept looking at Gwen, as if to make sure her protector was still there. *Gwen isn't going to let you down*, I wanted to tell her. But I didn't.

After breakfast Gwen and I discussed the day. I agreed not to go to the Church, and in return she gave me my assignments. Go to Bobby's warehouse to pick up the clothes and toiletries they had left there. Go to the *Globe* office downtown and explain her absence. Go to the Food Market and buy supper.

Yes, ma'am.

First I went to my office, which I hadn't visited for days. There was no sign anyone had been there while I'd been gone. I hadn't really expected any. I thought about leaving a note giving people my home address and telling them to look for me there. But I didn't bother. Gwen was right; people knew where to find me.

So I began my chores. I went to Bobby's warehouse to get the stuff Gwen wanted. Everyone seemed sad that Abby wasn't staying there—even Bobby. I managed to change his mood by asking for a favor. "I need Mickey to drive me up to the Church of the New Beginning tomorrow."

"Oh, come on, Walter," he said. "Times are tough. I can't afford to be your taxi service."

"Fine. I'll pay for the gasoline. It's not like I've ever done anything for you."

"Just shut the fuck up, would you? Can you do it in the morning? Mickey's got a pickup scheduled for the afternoon."

"That would be perfect. Thank you so much. I don't deserve your generosity."

"*Please* shut the fuck up."

I returned home with the stuff for Abby, and then I went to the *Globe*'s downtown office near South Station with the news about Gwen's whereabouts And what were they going to say? Everyone loved Gwen; they would relay the information to Stan at *Globe* headquarters in Dorchester, but they were sure there wouldn't be a problem.

And then I went to the Food Market.

It was still outdoors, although that wouldn't last much longer. Thanksgiving was coming soon, and the market would move indoors by then. There were fewer vendors in attendance, and everyone looked cold and cranky. Pete Callahan was standing guard at the entrance. "What's up, Walter?" he asked.

"Nothing much. How's Mary Beth?"

He shook his head. "I don't know. OK. Hanging in there."

He sounded scared.

"You hang in there too."

"Tryin'."

"I don't see the Church's cart here today," I said. "Did they leave already?"

He shrugged. "Never showed up. Maybe they ran out of food. Maybe it's too cold for them."

Didn't matter. I was here to shop. It didn't take me long to buy the bread and potatoes and onions and carrots that Gwen had ordered me to obtain. It was odd buying for four again, especially when the fourth had as big an appetite as Abby did. I had to haggle a bit to get the prices down to what I thought supper was worth. Federal food aid couldn't come soon enough for me.

I brought the food home. With my chores done, I headed out yet again. To Police Headquarters. I found Chris Mull sitting in his office, contemplating the pile of papers on his desk. "Hey, Chris."

He nodded to me. "Hey."

"I was wondering if you made any progress on those warnings we got."

"I asked around my neighborhood," Mull said. "Nobody saw anything. I went up to the Church.

Nobody claimed to know anything. Nobody had been in Boston. Everyone was home in bed. Just what I expected."

"Well, I have this theory."

"Yeah?"

"Remember what I said yesterday—about the Church having supporters in Boston? It occurred to me that we know one—Ken Hendrikson of the *Globe*. He wrote that story the other day about the supposed miracle. And that's not the first favorable article he's written about the Church."

"Hendrikson? Isn't he a shrimpy guy who wears tweed jackets? You think he's a murderer?"

"OK, yeah, he doesn't look the part. But I was thinking—nobody from the Church knows where I live. They came to my office when they hired me. But Hendrikson has been to my house. He probably knows where you live, too. And if he didn't know already, he probably could have found out. It'd be easy for him to put up those signs."

Mull thought about it. "I can imagine the guy sneaking around in the middle of the night to do something like that," he said. "I can't imagine him beating someone to death, though. But sure, I'll look into it. It's more than I've got."

"Thanks. Also, for what it's worth, I've got proof that Flynn Dobler flew down to New York City after he disappeared."

"Why New York?"

"He apparently comes from there. Going back home."

"You going after him?"

"I don't know. It's up to my client. You ever been to New York?"

"Oh, in the old days, sure. It was a fucking sewer."

"Nice to know."

We fell silent, contemplating our cases. "I'm going back up to Concord tomorrow," I said finally. "Have to find out what they want me to do."

"Give them a kick in the balls from me," Mull replied. "Bastards."

"Will do."

I didn't really want to go back there. But it was my case, and I had to see it through.

CHAPTER 26

The next day didn't begin well. I made the mistake of buying a *Globe* on my way to Bobby's place. The news out of Atlanta was actually pretty encouraging—Fenwick's proposed treaty had received a generally favorable response from Congress and the new president. But it was Ken Hendrikson's latest article about the Church of the New Beginning that got my blood boiling. The substance was straightforward—it was about the crowds now flocking to the Church to visit the spot where Brother Flynn had been assumed into heaven. He included quotes from a couple of the pilgrims and the usual Church disciples. And me.

> *Private Investigator Walter Sands continues to be baffled by Flynn Dobler's disappearance. When asked if he had any idea where Dobler was, Sands responded that he hadn't a clue. Brother Harold Utley noted that the detective's inability to*

find the Church's beloved leader was telling. "We have gone out of our way to determine if there could be a natural explanation for Brother Flynn's disappearance," he pointed out. "If you can rule out the natural, only the supernatural remains."

That was the last time I was going to talk to a reporter, I vowed, although I decided I would make an exception for Gwen.

At the warehouse, Mickey had the van ready to go. Doctor J was reading *On the Genealogy of Morals* by Friedrich Nietzsche. Bobby did his usual grumbling about the price of gasoline, but it was clear his heart wasn't in it. I parked my bicycle near the door, and in a few minutes Mickey and I were off.

The day was cold but sunny. Mickey was happy; he loved daytime trips, since obstacles were easier to spot in daylight and there was less risk of being ambushed. He also didn't mind getting away from Bobby for a bit. But he didn't like going to the Church of the New Beginning. "Those people creep me out, Walter," he said.

"Why is that?"

"It's their uniforms, mainly. I don't like uniforms."

I hadn't considered that angle. I wasn't fond of uniforms myself. "You can stay in the van, Mickey. No need to see any of them. I just need to talk to a guy."

"Appreciate it."

We made good time up to Concord. There were even more cars parked on the road leading up to the Church than had been there the other day, along with a few carts and buggies. All the vehicles were ancient, but that's where the similarities ended. There was a dented monstrosity painted in rainbow colors, a long convertible with a ripped top, a tractor, a golf cart—basically, anything that moved. "Popular place," Mickey noted.

"I guess some people are OK with uniforms. I won't be long."

"Good luck, Walter."

I got out and was greeted by Brother Willis at the gate. "Unbelievable, isn't it?" he said, gesturing at the menagerie of cars.

"Is it like this all the time now?"

"Bigger crowd today. There was an another article in the paper."

"Yeah, I saw it. Is Brother Joseph around?"

"Sure. Where else would he be?"

I walked through the gate. As I had the other day with Detective Mull, I first walked over to the people surrounding Dobler's shrine. Some folks were on their knees; others stood with clasped hands and glistening eyes. I made my way through the crowd. Sister Lucy wasn't there recounting the story this time. The area had been roped off, and in the center stood the Church's symbol–that cross with the horizontal arms tilted down, so it looked sort of like an arrow pointing to the sky. Before, I'd assumed this was supposed to symbolize the future, or progress, or something like that. But now it seemed to mean something different; now it seemed to say: *Look up! That's where Flynn Dobler went! Ponder the mystery of his assumption, or ascension, or whatever.*

"They say his son will be born any day now," I heard a woman murmur.

"Another miracle!" her companion responded.

"Amen!" said someone else.

Since when was it a miracle for a baby to be born?

"Isn't it exciting, Walter?" a voice behind me said.

I turned. It was Brother Harold, looking very devout. "You must be very happy," I said.

"I'm happy that we will have a chance to spread our message to these wonderful people."

"Good luck getting them to give up their tractors and golf carts."

He smiled. "It will be a long process. But we'll be here."

I excused myself and went to find Brother Joseph. This time he wasn't in his room. I asked a couple of people, and finally I found him sitting by himself in the refectory, staring into the fire. "Has that shrine out there been good for recruiting?" I asked.

He looked up, and then he motioned to me to sit down across from him. "Recruiting? No. Most of those people don't want to devote their lives to building a new world. They want magic. They want to say a prayer to Brother Flynn and have him cure their disease, or put food on their table, or just make life the way it used to be. But

Brother Harold put a collection box out there, and it's overflowing with cash."

"That'll help, I suppose."

Brother Joseph didn't respond. Instead, he said: "Before the war, Sister Lucy was an advertising executive—did anyone tell you that? Do you even know what an advertising executive is?"

"Vaguely."

"She had a husband, two kids, a house, a swimming pool. They went to Disney World during school vacation. Do you know what Disney World was? Doesn't matter. On winter weekends they drove up to their condo in Vermont and skied. Condos, skiing. She was an accomplished modern woman. She had it all. And now it's all gone, every bit of it, and she's reduced to memories and dreams and fantasies."

"If it makes her happy…" I murmured. *The heart of a heartless world.* I recalled someone saying that about religion. Had it been Henry Fisher?

"Yes, of course. It's all that can make her happy. Why are you here, Walter?"

"I've found Flynn Dobler," I replied.

That got his attention. "Where? Where is he? Is he alive?"

"As far as I know. He boarded a plane for New York City a couple of days after he disappeared. He used a fake name, but I talked to the immigration guy that he bribed to get a visa, and he ID'd Dobler from a photo."

"Why New York City?"

"That's where he grew up. That's where he was

before he came to Boston. Maybe he just decided to go home."

"But you haven't seen him, you haven't talked to him."

"No. That's why I'm here. I can try to track him down in New York, but it would be a bit expensive—airfare, meals, a place to stay. I'd need, say, eighty dollars up front. In addition to my usual per diem rate."

"How would you find him?"

"I'd start by tracking his past residences—they should have directories, tax records, stuff like that from the old days. New York is doing a lot better than Boston. We still have some of that information, so they should too. Obviously I can't guarantee I'll find him. But I have pretty solid evidence that he's there. I know you don't like the idea that he deserted you, but these are the facts."

Brother Joseph stared into the fire. "Eighty dollars is a lot of money," he said.

"Plus my per diem," I reminded him. "But it sounds like you have some money now."

"You don't understand," Joseph replied, not looking at me.

"What don't I understand?"

He shook his head. "You must have made a mistake," he said. "Brother Flynn is not in New York City. He can't be."

"But I told you, I—"

"He's not there!" Joseph insisted.

And then I understood. "He's beaten you, hasn't he?"

"I have no idea what—"

"Brother Harold. He's won. Brother Flynn is worth more to you in heaven than he is alive. Well, it's your choice, I suppose."

Brother Joseph didn't respond. I waited for a moment to see if he had something more to say, but he didn't. And I found that I didn't have anything more to say either, so I got up and walked out of the refectory.

I stood in the entrance hall. Disciples passed by, busy with their daily tasks. Occasionally they greeted me. Occasionally they gave me a puzzled look: *why are you still coming here, bothering us?* I decided to go upstairs in search of Sister Marva.

I found her in her room, sitting on her bed, knitting. Her belly seemed to be a lot larger than when I had last seen her.

She gave me a serene smile and put down her knitting. "Walter, how nice to see you!" she said.

"Hello, Sister Marva. How are you feeling?"

"I feel blessed. As always."

"You're due soon, looks like."

"I believe so." She patted her belly. "They won't let me go to the Food Market anymore. I suppose that's wise."

"I just wanted to tell you something. About Brother Flynn. I know everyone wants to believe that Sister Lucy's vision is true. But it isn't. I've tracked him down. Brother Flynn is alive. He went to New York City. I'm not exactly sure why, but I have proof."

Marva looked at me. Her jaw trembled; her

eyes watered. "He's alive?" she whispered in disbelief.

"He is. I'd go there and find him, if Brother Joseph would pay for it. You need to convince him it's worth while. He seems pretty depressed about the situation. But maybe you can talk some sense into him."

She reached out and grabbed my hands. "I'll try, Walter. I'll try." And then she kissed my hands, the way she had kissed Sister Lucy's that night when I had begun my work on the case. "God bless you," she said. "I knew you could help us. You're a good man, Walter."

"Good luck with the birth, Sister Marva," I replied. "Take care of yourself."

She let go of me and placed her hands back on her belly. "I will, Walter. It won't be long now. And Walter? I'm sorry about the other day, the way I reacted when you asked me about Brother Scott. That wasn't like me."

"Did he do anything to you, Sister Marva?"

"No, he didn't. Just…sometimes…he looked at me. I didn't like the way he looked at me."

"I understand."

I left her and went back downstairs. Outside, the crowd around the shrine seemed to have grown. And on its outskirts, I saw Brother Joseph and Brother Harold deep in conversation.

I watched them for a few minutes, and then I walked back to Mickey and the van.

"How did it go?" he asked when I got inside.

"I have no idea," I admitted. "Let's go home, Mickey. I'm sick of this place."

CHAPTER 27

———◆◆◆◀———

What I needed was another case to take my mind off the Church. But no clients showed up in Louisburg Square. Governor Bolton was delighted with my work protecting Fenwick, but he had nothing to offer me. Bobby asked me to come along on a couple of his forays out into some desolate area in search of salvage, but that didn't count as private eye work; I might just as well have been a security guy at One-Eyed Joe's.

So mostly I did the errands and the cooking and the laundry and made myself useful.

And I helped take care of Abby.

This was mainly Gwen's job, but even Gwen couldn't do it full-time. And eventually she had to go back to work, because the *Globe* needed her and we all needed the money.

The first day Gwen was gone, Abby was her usual scared self. She had nothing to say; it was beginning to look like she was never going to have anything to say. So I had to do the talking.

For a while I just said the usual reassuring stuff: *Don't worry, Abby. Gwen will be home in a few hours. Nothing bad is going to happen.* But eventually I found myself talking about other things. Like, well, me.

"Everyone wants me to be something different, Abby. Everyone wants to mold me into their own image. Chris Mull wants me to be a policeman. Jim O'Malley wants me to help him take over eastern Massachusetts. Henry Fisher wants me to be an intellectual revolutionary or something. Even Gwen—who I'm sure you'll agree is the greatest human being who ever lived—even Gwen doesn't want me to be a private eye. Not really. She'd prefer that I had a nice boring job that got me home at night so we could all wash the dishes together and listen to music and read books and keep each other safe against the dark. Okay, there's nothing wrong with that. There's nothing wrong with a thousand lives you can imagine. It's just that this is the life that I want to lead. It may be stupid and pointless and dangerous, but it's mine—not Henry's or Chris's or Jim's. Or Gwen's. Can you understand that?"

Abby just stared at me with wide eyes, and before long she looked away, ultimately uninterested in my boring career problems. And then she wrapped her arms around herself and closed her eyes and started to quiver, trapped in some horrible memory from which she couldn't escape.

What, really, did I have to complain about?

"You're right," I said. "I should be grateful for

Gwen, for Stretch, for a lot of things. Never let me forget that. Still…"

I kept quiet about all this with Gwen. For once she wasn't especially interested in my problems. Her life had become fuller, richer, more satisfying. Her job remained interesting—there were lots of stories to be written about the new political order: Fenwick had gotten Atlanta to ratify the treaty, which meant that Bolton's position was secure, the threat of chaos and revolution had been averted, and food and medical aid would start to arrive before the onset of winter. And after work, there was the satisfaction of caring for the new member of our family—there was Abby to be groomed and dressed and fed. Abby to play the piano for. Abby to be comforted in the middle of the night when she began screaming in Linc's old bedroom.

Fenwick wrote us frequently from Atlanta—the only mail we ever got, actually. He was trying to get back up to Boston, but so far had been unable to do so. Now that Atlanta had agreed to the treaty, there was jockeying over who would be appointed ambassador to New England. He had his enemies, apparently—people who thought the treaty was too favorable to New England; people who questioned his loyalty to the United States. So the decision was taking some time. He wanted to know: could we please care for Abby just a while longer?

Yes, we could. Gwen didn't say anything much about Fenwick's letters. She dutifully read them to Abby and made the right comments to her afterwards. "Your brother is coming back as soon as he can, Abby, and you'll be together again. He loves you very much...." But it wasn't hard to sense her fear—fear that Fenwick would return and take Abby away from us, casually reclaiming his sister like a weapon he'd checked in at a government building.

"He's a good guy," I told Gwen. "Things will work out."

"This is Abby's home," was all she would say. "We're her family, too."

I wasn't going to disagree.

I waited for someone from the Church to get in touch with me, to tell me that Sister Marva had convinced Brother Joseph to let me go to New York City and track Brother Flynn down. But no one came. And I couldn't help remembering the way Brother Joseph and Brother Harold had stood together, talking, while they watched the crowds worshipping at Brother Flynn's shrine.

And so it went as Thanksgiving approached.

Gwen and I like the holiday well enough, but to Stretch celebrating Thanksgiving is a sacred duty. This is something we haven't lost, he liked to point out, a connection to the very beginnings of our land. Despite everything that had happened, we should show some gratitude for what America did for us, and what the Earth has given us.

Stretch always wanted us to invite someone less fortunate to join us for the meal. This year's winner was clearly Abby, but he also wanted to invite the runner-up, and that choice was obvious, too: Mrs. Fitz.

I found out once that her full name was Samantha Lally Fitzgerald, but people scarcely knew or cared that she had a first name, or a maiden name, or that her married name had a couple of additional syllables that no one used. She was born to be called Mrs. Fitz, and that's all there was to it. She was about sixty, with white hair and ruddy cheeks and a perpetual smile. She had suffered as much as any of us since the War, but that didn't mean that today wasn't a great day, or that tomorrow wouldn't be even better. God would provide. Things would work out.

She and Stretch were kindred spirits.

Mrs. Fitz had nothing in the way of survival skills to go along with her optimism, but her son Biff certainly possessed them, and that may have contributed to her sunny disposition. It wasn't actually God who was doing the providing; it was Biff. If something went wrong in her life, Biff was sure to fix it. It was Biff who early on had commandeered for her one of the empty houses in Louisburg Square, a tony location where the Fitzgeralds never would have set foot before the War. It was Biff who made sure she had food and firewood and clothing, who found her new glasses when she broke a pair and a Christmas tree for the front parlor because wouldn't that be nice.

Biff was a great son, but otherwise a complete jerk. Not that anyone would mention this to Mrs. Fitz, who wouldn't have been able to comprehend a universe in which her offspring could do any wrong. It's one thing to take stuff from long-abandoned houses; we've all done that. It's another thing altogether to steal stuff from your neighbors. Biff presumably hadn't taken part in the Frenzy. He wasn't crazy; he wasn't an anarchist. But surviving those years had apparently led him to the conclusion that rules were for sissies. What he (or his mother) needed, he would take. Didn't matter if it was food to keep his mother alive or firewood to keep her warm or a Christmas tree to brighten up her holidays. If you had a problem with that, try and stop him.

Eventually someone did. His body was found stuffed into a rubbish barrel in a Beacon Hill alley a few blocks away from us. The left side of his face was caved in; most of his ribs had been broken. Whoever had murdered him had been really unhappy with the guy. This turned into yet another one of Detective Mull's unsolved cases— no witnesses, no clues, and pretty much everyone had a motive. It was one of my unsolved cases, too—I had done a *pro bono* investigation for Mrs. Fitz that led nowhere.

The neighborhood certainly didn't mind that the murderer hadn't been found. Maybe Biff Fitzgerald didn't deserved to be murdered, but no one was sorry to see him go.

Except, of course, Mrs. Fitz. Beyond her grief over the loss of her only son, she now faced a difficult future. She didn't have a job; she didn't have any possessions to sell. In the old days there had apparently been something called Social Security, but there was no security of any sort nowadays. So she had to rely on the kindness of her neighbors.

The neighbors were happy to help. After all, Biff hadn't been her fault, exactly. So we gave her what previously Biff had simply taken, and everyone felt better about the situation. And now Mrs. Fitz was delighted to come to our place for Thanksgiving.

She arrived early, along with an apple pie and her perpetually upbeat if somewhat vague disposition. Although we tried to explain to her who Abby was and where she'd been living and why she didn't speak, it wasn't clear to me that Mrs. Fitz quite got it. Didn't matter. She was happy to prattle on, safe from interruption. Mostly she prattled on about how much she missed her son. "You didn't know my son Biff, did you?" she asked Abby. "No, I don't suppose you did. He was such a good boy. He'd do anything for me. He would say to me, 'Ma, just tell me what you need, and it's yours. You want the moon? I'll go get it for you.' Imagine that— the moon! I believed him, too. Such a good boy. He's gone now. Taken from us too young. But he's with God now. And, Lord knows, I'll be joining him soon enough."

She'd been told her son had been brutally murdered, of course, but that memory had fogged over until it was just a blur, lost amid all the platitudes stuffed into her brain.

So, not the most stimulating dinner companion. But neither was Abby. And Thanksgiving isn't about stimulation; it's about family. And, well, here we were, eating our turkey and potatoes and beans and drinking our cider, and it was hard for me not to have some platitudes buzzing around my own brain. So what if my private eye career wasn't exactly taking off? Would I trade that career for Gwen or Stretch? Would I trade this world for any other?

We ate our apple pie in the front parlor while Gwen softly played the piano. Abby closed her eyes, delighted as ever by the music. Mrs. Fitz started talking about the old days—there had been a Mr. Fitz, and a daughter, and a house in Weymouth with a lovely backyard, you should have seen her garden, and a Toyota that got good gas mileage, and everything went in and out of focus, and then she was remembering Biff as a baby. "Oh, he was the cutest thing. There was nobody like my little Biff. You could just tell he was going to grow up to be someone special. Like that other baby."

"What other baby is that, Mrs. Fitz?" Stretch asked. He really enjoyed her stories.

"You know, the one at the Church. The one everyone is talking about."

"The Church of the New Beginning?" he asked.

Mrs. Fitz beamed. "Yes, that's the one. I think. A beautiful baby boy. I read about it in the *Globe* this morning. They say his father has gone up to heaven. Like my Biff. But they say the baby is going to grow up to be a great leader. He's going to make all these problems go away. We need someone like that, don't you think? So many problems nowadays, with the disease and the crime and all the bad people. We need—we need someone. Don't you think?"

"Um, I guess so," Stretch replied.

Mrs. Fitz smiled and nodded to herself, having summed things up to her satisfaction.

And that's how I found out that Sister Marva had given birth to a son.

Later Stretch and I walked Mrs. Fitz home. She was in a wonderful mood, still yakking about her Biff and the new baby. "Does the baby have a name, Mrs. Fitz?" Stretch asked.

"I don't think so. But I'm sure it'll be a fine name."

We made sure Mrs. Fitz was safe and then walked back to our own home.

"That's pretty interesting about the baby, huh, Walter?" Stretch said.

"Sure is."

"What do you think is going to happen?"

"No idea, Stretch."

That didn't mean I wasn't going to think about it, though. At home, Gwen had something else on her mind. She greeted us as soon as we opened the door. "Guess what Abby just did!" she said in a low, excited voice.

"What?"

"I was cleaning up—you know, just bringing the dishes over to the sink, wrapping up the leftovers to put in the icebox—and I turned around, and there was Abby, holding out a plate to me. She was helping! She cleared the table for me!"

"That's great!" Stretch said. "She's really

making progress, isn't she?"

"Yes, yes she is."

There had been flashes of this before from Abby, but nothing sustained—she would pick her clothes up off the floor one day, and leave them there the next. One moment she would look like she understood exactly what you said; the next she seemed lost in her own inner world, filled with darkness and confusion. Gwen was convinced that she would come all the way back, with enough time and love, but I had my doubts. Maybe this was a turning point; maybe it wasn't. How could we know?

Anyway, Stretch and I did the rest of the cleanup while Gwen put Abby to bed. When I went upstairs to our bedroom, Gwen was still excited. "Oh, Walter, isn't it wonderful?" she asked me.

"It certainly is."

That night she had as much trouble getting to sleep as I did. But the next day life was back to normal, and I was caring for Abby once more, cooking supper, washing the clothes....What else was I good for?

And then, a few days later, I noticed a police cruiser pull up in front of my house. "I wonder who I murdered now," I said to Abby, who presumably had no idea what I was talking about.

Chris Mull got out and strode up our front steps. I let him in. He nodded to me and gave Abby a puzzled look. "This is our friend Abby," I said. "She doesn't say much."

"Pleased to meet you," Mull said. "Walter, can

we talk?"

"Sure."

"Here's the thing. Remember our friend Brother Reggie from the Church? Reggie Hurlburt?"

"Of course."

"Well, he's gone to fucking New York City."

CHAPTER 28

Mull and I went into the parlor. Abby trailed along behind.

"How do you know?" I asked him.

"I put him on a watch list with Immigration in case he decided to leave the country. You know, because of Brother Scott. Him and Hendrikson were my only two suspects—not that I had anything on either of them. And sure enough, yesterday he got on a plane to New York."

"How did he get the visa?"

"Visas are still expensive, but they're easier to obtain now that the treaty's been signed."

"New York City is where Flynn Dobler went," I pointed out.

"I remember. That's why I'm here. I don't have any evidence linking this guy to Brother Scott's murder—it just seemed like, if someone from the Church did kill him, it would be Brother Reggie. Now that he's skipped town, I'm even more suspicious of him, but I still don't have grounds to go down to New York and find him, or ask the New York police to help. I thought maybe you'd want to know, though. I figure he went down there to join his boss or guru or whatever the fuck Dobler was."

"I *do* want to know," I replied. Then I paused as I thought things through. "The thing is," I said finally, "I don't think he went down there to join Dobler. I think he went there to murder him."

"Huh?"

"Brother Harold has this plan to save the Church or take it over or something," I said. "Brother Joseph thought he murdered Dobler as part of the plan, but obviously that wasn't right. Instead, it looks like Dobler just got fed up with everything that was going on and went back home. So Brother Harold got poor Sister Lucy to think she actually witnessed Brother Flynn being assumed into heaven, and he got Sister Marva to believe Sister Lucy. And you saw the result— people are flocking to the site of the miracle, Marva's baby is born and that's big news. It's all worked out great, except for one thing."

"Dobler is still alive," Mull said.

"That's right. If people find that out, Harold's whole premise is wrecked."

"But I thought nobody at the Church knew where Dobler was."

"Yeah, except I told Brother Joseph after I found out from the guy in the immigration office. I asked him if he wanted me to go to New York and track Dobler down, and he told me not to. Seems like Joseph realizes he's been beaten. The only way the Church survives is if Brother Flynn stays out of the picture, so they can hold onto their miracle. The only way they can guarantee that he stays out of the picture is if he's dead." I thought some more and realized there was another angle. "And then there's Sister Marva."

"Good Lord," Mull muttered. "What about Sister Marva?"

"I told her about Brother Flynn too. I thought she could convince Joseph to send me down to New York and find him. But maybe he and Harold convinced her it would be a better idea to send Reggie instead."

"But she wants Brother Flynn back—right? You told me she adored him."

"Sure. But Brother Harold knows what he's doing. I bet he could convince Brother Reggie that what he really needed to do was kill Brother Flynn—he's the one who abandoned Marva, after all. And without Brother Flynn, Sister Marva and her baby become the most important people in the Church."

"Jesus Christ," Mull said. "What a mess."

"Can you ask the New York police to help?"

Mull thought about that for a few seconds, and then shook his head. "I have a contact down there, but this is just too thin, too theoretical. If I had an arrest warrant for Brother Reggie, they might try to track him and Dobler down. But not for something like this. We're on our own on this one."

"Dobler could already be dead," I pointed out.

"Yep. Or Brother Reggie could still be looking

for him. Or you could be totally mistaken about the whole thing. Frankly, Walter, that's not inconceivable."

We were both silent for a minute. "You think I should go," I said finally.

Mull shrugged. "I can't go, Walter. I've got a job to do here in Boston. But if you think your theory is right—well, who else is going to save Dobler's life?"

"No one's going to pay me to do it. And it won't be cheap."

"Up to you. But you know who you are, what you are. You know what matters. Also, I'll lend you some money."

I sighed. "Thanks, Chris. Let me think about it."

"Sure. But think fast, Walter. If you're right…"

"Yeah. I know."

I walked him to the door, and then I went back and sat down in the parlor with Abby.

"I don't know, Abby," I said. "What should I do? Private eyes don't spend their own money on cases. I'm not supposed to risk my life and inconvenience my family trying to prevent every crime that anyone's likely to commit. Flynn Dobler is not my problem anymore. Brother Joseph fired me, so all my obligations with respect to the case have ceased. Right?"

Abby didn't say anything.

"Okay, fine, I get it. It's about more than just the case. Imagine if I followed Governor Bolton's orders and didn't get involved with your brother and you. That would have been awful for everyone. But what am I going to tell Gwen? She needs me here. *You* need me here. It's one thing if I have a job to do. But this isn't a job. It's a...a quest. And probably a futile one. Gwen'll understand that right away. So how do I convince her this is a good idea?"

Abby didn't offer any suggestions. After a while I went into the kitchen to make dinner. At some point I turned from the counter to set the kitchen table, and I saw a piece of paper. On the paper was printed a single word:

GO

And next to the word was a picture of a ladder.

I took the paper and tracked down Abby, who was still sitting in the parlor, next to the Christmas tree I had put up the day before. "Did you write this?" I asked her.

Of course she had written it. But she didn't admit it. She didn't say anything.

"Did I ever talk to you about that poem? I guess I must have. This is *my* ladder, right? Like Chris said—who I am, what I am. You're a wise woman, Abby. Will you let me kiss you?"

She didn't object. So I went over and kissed the top of her head. I held her by the shoulders, and at first she was stiff, resistant. But then she let go, just a little.

And that night I had to talk to Stretch and, especially, Gwen. She didn't argue about it— what could she say, really? She knew better than anyone who I was and what I was. "When?" she asked.

"Tomorrow, if I can. I may already be too late."

She simply nodded her agreement.

That's when I showed her Abby's piece of paper. And that's when the tears came. Tears of joy. "Oh, my darling, you're here, you're with us," she said to Abby. "It's wonderful."

Abby gazed at her, and for a moment I thought that, at long last, she would speak, or at least give a smile of recognition. But instead she just looked away.

Gwen didn't seem to mind.

In bed that night, Gwen and I made love. Afterwards we held onto each other in the dark. "I'll be back," I said. "As soon as I can."

"I know," she murmured. "I know."

Eventually Gwen fell asleep, but I didn't leave her to read a book as I usually did. Instead I held her through the night, and in the morning I prepared to leave for New York.

First I went to the immigration office and picked up a visa from Natty Morgenstern.

"I'm in a hurry, Natty," I explained to him, "or else I'd have gotten something for you from Art's."

"That's OK, Walter. Happy to oblige. Be careful in New York."

"Thanks, Natty. I'm always careful."

Then I biked over to police headquarters and told Chris Mull about my decision. "You're a good man, Walter," he told me.

"I do my best."

He gave me ten dollars, plus the name and address of his contact in the New York Police

Department, a guy named Dominic Rodriguez. "Rodriguez will help with Dobler's addresses and any other records they have for him," he said, "but like I said, otherwise you're going to be on your own."

"That's the way private eyes like it."

Mull rolled his eyes. "Please don't tell Rodriquez you're a private eye, Walter. He'll think you're an idiot. I don't mind that, but then he'll probably think I'm an idiot, too."

"Got it."

"And be careful."

"I'm always careful."

Mull just shook his head.

From police headquarters I went to Bobby Gallagher's warehouse and requested a ride to the airport so I could maybe prevent an innocent man from being murdered. Bobby was not as sympathetic as Chris Mull.

"Let me get this straight: no one is paying you to go after this guy?"

"That's right. And that reminds me: can I borrow some money, too? The airfare isn't cheap."

"Holy fuck almighty, you really have a nerve. You have no idea where Dobler is?"

"Well, maybe I can get an address where he used to live."

"And you don't know anyone else in the city?"

"Well, Chris Mull gave me the name of a cop."

"And you don't know anything about the city?"

"Well, not really. I've read books…."

"Jesus, Walter. This is fucking nuts. You know that, don't you?"

"Sure. I guess."

"But you're still going?"

"Yep. If I can get a ride to the airport."

Bobby shook his head in despair. But he let Mickey take me, and he slipped me a ten-dollar bill before we left.

Mickey stopped first at Louisburg Square. Gwen was staying home with Abby, and she wasn't going to accompany me to the airport—she couldn't bring Abby back there, after all. I dropped off my bike, picked up the bag I'd packed, and got some money out of the canister in the kitchen where we keep our funds. And then it was time to go. "Please don't tell me to be careful," I said to Gwen, "and please don't tell me I'm an idiot."

Gwen smiled. "You'll be fine. And you're not an idiot. You're…eccentric."

"That's more like it."

We hugged, and then I hugged Abby, who didn't resist much. And then I got back in the van, and Mickey and I left for the airport.

Mickey let me off at the terminal, but he couldn't let me go without warning me to be careful down there in New York. The idea of being somewhere other than Boston filled him with dread. Inside the terminal, I found the ticket agent I had terrified by asking about flights to New York City. Today for some reason she was delighted to see me and overjoyed to take my money. "Have a *wonderful* flight," she chirped.

I promised that I would.

But it was a lousy flight, cold and bumpy. There were a half-dozen other passengers, and they all looked as scared as I was. Was this how it was all supposed to end, crashing in an ancient, under-maintained plane somewhere in the wilderness of Connecticut?

No, not this time. We landed at the New York airport without a problem. I half-expected the passengers to break into applause, the way they did on Abby's lightning-struck flight so long ago. But we were all too grumpy to clap. Instead, we grabbed our bags and exited the plane as quickly as we could, climbing down onto the tarmac far from the terminal.

The sky was overcast. A cold wind blew snowflakes into my eyes. I was in an unfamiliar city, with no friends to greet me, nowhere to spend the night, and little idea of how I could accomplish what I was there to do. I started walking toward the terminal. *Welcome back*, I thought, *to the United States of America*.

CHAPTER 29

Once I got through immigration, I found my way to an ancient bus that would take me to downtown Manhattan, and I got on it along with everyone else who had been on the flight from Boston. The landscape on the way was depressingly alien—the apartment buildings were too big, the traffic was too heavy, the shops in the strip-malls by the side of the road were too busy...I saw some familiar burnt-out blocks, but fewer than in Boston. Why should I have been depressed by signs of civilization?

Not for the first time, I wondered why Boston had ended up so badly. New York was still functioning reasonably well, although it had suffered actual devastation in the War—lower Manhattan was supposed to be more of a mess than Washington, D.C., which I had spent my year in the army helping to clean up. Henry Fisher had a theory about this—he had a theory about everything. In his view, it was because

Boston had been so anti-War. So when the War finally came and went, and it was time to move on, Boston was unable to do so. Boston lost its will to live, and therefore lost its ability to fight back against the crazies.

I had no idea if Henry was right. But just looking out the window of the bus, I began to feel intimidated by New York. The bus crossed the river and entered Manhattan and the traffic increased, the cars got newer, the buildings got even larger, and the late-afternoon lights even brighter. The bus let us off at a place called Grand Central Station, which only intimidated me more, as I compared its throbbing vitality to Park Street Station in Boston and the pitiful single train that plies its lonely little route under our city. We don't even have buses—who would use them? We just walk places, or ride our bikes.

The other passengers, busier and more important than I was, quickly dispersed to their destinations. I needed to figure out how to get to police headquarters and Dominic Rodriguez. I asked a couple of people and got a couple of surly shrugs. Finally a policeman pointed me in the right direction. I walked out of the station and into the city.

And this was when my attitude started to change.

The first thing I noticed was the beggars—on every street corner, in every abandoned storefront, sitting cross-legged and dull-eyed, mumbling pleas for coins, holding out their trembling hands to passersby who resolutely

ignored them. They were old and young; they
were blind and crippled and microcephalic and,
often, without any physical problem I could see;
they were cold and weary and desperate. We have
beggars in Boston, but nowhere near as many.
We know them all by name; we help them when
we can. We're all in this together.

The second thing I noticed were the guards.
Everything was guarded—the shops and the
theaters, the hotels and the restaurants. The
guards were usually uniformed but always armed.
They stood by the entrances and judged if you
were worthy to go inside.

What was going on? Who were they afraid of?

New York City was obviously busier and more
prosperous than Boston, but it was still a far cry
from a fully functioning city like London, which
I'd visited for my first case. There was a lot of
traffic, but no traffic jams. The streets were in
rough shape, and many of the stop lights weren't
working. The buildings were brightly lit—except
for the ones that were completely dark, with
windows broken and exteriors crumbling. The
city was working, but just barely. And anything
that worked had a guard.

Police headquarters, it turned out, wasn't far
from Grand Central Station, and Manhattan
streets were laid out so sensibly that I didn't have
any difficulty finding it. Here was another
difference from Boston: this was clearly a new
building, built since the War. Boston never built
anything new. The previous headquarters had
presumably been further downtown and didn't

survive the blast. This one was cold and gray and fortress-like, surrounded by a high fence. It too was guarded, which was more understandable. The burly cop inside the booth glared at me from behind the glass.

"Hi," I said. "I'm here to see Detective Dominic Rodriguez."

"Appointment?" he squawked over his microphone.

"Um, no, not an appointment, exactly, but I believe he's expecting me. My name is Walter Sands."

The cop picked up a phone. After a few seconds he put the phone down. "Ain't here," he said to me.

"Do you know when he'll be back?"

"Waddaya mean?"

"I mean, has he left for the day, or should I come back later?"

The cop seemed to find that question deeply offensive. "How should I know? He ain't here, that's all."

I got the impression that any further questions might get me arrested for excessive inquisitiveness or something. So I sighed and turned away.

Now what? It was dark; it was cold. I needed to find a place to stay for the night and start again tomorrow.

Could I even get into a hotel? I spotted a dingy hotel across from police headquarters. Its guard gave me a suspicious look but let me enter, and I quickly confirmed that Manhattan hotels were beyond my meager budget. So I wandered the streets looking for something cheaper. Eventually I found a boarding house, but the landlord wanted a week's rent in advance, at a price that would have left me no money for food—or a return flight to Boston. So I searched for a place that was more run-down than the first one. I found a likely candidate eventually—a wreck with boarded-up windows and crumbling front steps— but its rooms weren't much cheaper.

I decided that I was desperate. I asked the landlord if there was anywhere you could go in the city if you were homeless and couldn't afford a room.

The landlord was an old guy without much hair or sympathy. "Dunno," he said.

"No ideas? I'm new here—just flew in from Boston."

"Shouldna come if you don't have any money," he pointed out. He was no Cleanthony.

"I get that now. No ideas at all?"

He shrugged. "The cathedral takes people in, I've heard."

"What cathedral?"

He looked at me like I was a moron. "Saint Patrick's, of course."

"Where is it?"

He shook his head at my stupidity and grudgingly gave me directions.

I walked for half an hour past the skyscrapers until I found myself standing in front of the cathedral, a massive gray neo-Gothic building that still managed to look puny next to its towering neighbors. Across the street from it was a statue of Atlas holding up the world; good luck with that, I thought. I also saw the largest Christmas tree I could conceive of; Biff Fitzgerald wouldn't have had any luck trying to steal that one.

I turned back to the cathedral and stared at its large bronze doors, decorated with bas-reliefs of saints. Could I even open those doors to get inside? At least they weren't guarded.

Then my eye was caught by a manger scene set up next to the doors. I recognized the players: the shepherds, the wise men, the sheep, the oxen. The baby Jesus, the Virgin Mary, Saint Joseph.

The Holy Family.

Oh, I thought, as something finally clicked into place. I wondered if the Church of the New Beginning was going to have its own version of the Holy Family. Sister Marva and her unnamed baby—and Brother Joseph, finally pulled into Brother Harold's vision of a new religion for a new world.

I stood there staring at the crèche until finally the cold forced me to go up and try one of the doors. It swung open easily, and I felt the warmth rush up to greet me.

I shut the door and walked through an entranceway and another set of doors, and then stared down the long aisle to the altar, lit by dim interior light. I looked up at the stained-glass windows; a couple of them were boarded up— that felt familiar to me. I heard voices murmuring. I smelled the faint odor of furniture polish.

It was a soothing, welcoming, if somewhat overwhelming place. Like the rest of New York, I felt a bit lost in it.

I walked along the marble center aisle towards the altar. A few old women knelt in the pews, praying. Near the altar a bearded man wearing a priest's collar was giving instructions to a shriveled-up old janitor carrying a mop. I waited. Vertical rows of Christmas wreaths decorated the massive columns on both sides of the altar. Poinsettias were lined up in front of it; ornate carved wooden chairs were lined up next to it. Somewhere behind me, I figured, was an enormous organ ready to boom out a hymn. I thought of the simplicity of the architecture at the Church of the New Beginning. Was this the past, and Concord the future? Or did Brother Harold's plans include a cathedral dedicated to Saint Flynn?

The guy with the mop wandered away. The bearded priest turned his attention to me. He was thin and wore rimless glasses; his black beard was peppered with gray. He seemed intense, efficient, suspicious. He looked me up and down, and presumably wasn't impressed by what he saw. "Help you?" he asked.

"I was looking for a place to spend the night. Someone said—"

"We open at nine for overnight guests," he interrupted. "Doors locked at ten. No entrance or exit after that. No weapons, no drugs, no alcohol, no fighting. First infraction, you're banned for sixty days. Second infraction, banned for life. Clear?"

"Um, yes. Thank you, Father."

He nodded and turned away.

Well, *he* wasn't exactly soothing and welcoming. On the other hand, he had given me what I needed. I trudged back down the aisle and sat in a pew near the doors. Was that an infraction? I supposed I'd find out.

I thought about praying: *Oh Lord, help me out on this case*. But I was pretty sure God wasn't interested in my case.

Instead I found myself struggling to stay awake. Surely falling asleep in a pew was an infraction. Would New York cure me of my chronic insomnia? And then my stomach started growling. I had forgotten to eat lunch, and now it was suppertime. Finally hunger won out over sleepiness, and I left the church in search of a cheap restaurant that would let me inside.

That turned out to be easy; the area was filled with pizza places and delicatessens and diners that catered to people like me. And prices were lower than in Boston, perhaps because New York had less difficulty importing its food. So I could fill up on slices of pizza, and even splurge on a cup of coffee, without worrying that I would ruin my delicate finances.

I returned to the cathedral with time to spare, but my heart sank as I saw a line already stretching half a block back from its bronze doors. I made my way to the end of the line, taking my place behind a white-haired guy with rheumy eyes and trembling hands. "Are we guaranteed a bed if we're in line?" I asked him.

"No beds, just cots," he replied. "And nobody guarantees nothin'." And then he turned away.

I folded my arms and tried to think warm thoughts. Wasn't easy. Had I met anyone pleasant since my arrival in New York? Not that I could recall. Had coming here been a good idea? Not so far. I thought about what was happening in Louisburg Square right now: Dishes done, Abby and Stretch were probably sitting in the parlor listening to Gwen play the piano. That's where I should have been.

Eventually the line began stuttering forward, and twenty minutes or so after that I was back in the warm entranceway, where three dour men were checking us in. The dour man who processed me was short, red-faced, and bald. He glanced up at me. "New here?" he asked without interest.

"Yes, sir."

He pointed behind him at the house rules, taped haphazardly to the wall. "Can you read?"

"Yes, sir."

"Read the rules. Follow 'em." He explained again about infractions. Then: "Name?"

"Walter Sands."

He wrote it down on a list.

"Need medical attention?"

"No, sir."

"What's in the bag?"

"Clothes. Books. But also, see, I have a gun."

He rolled his eyes. "I thought you said you

could read. See what it says up there? 'No guns.'"

"I understand. I didn't know about that when I came here. I was hoping there was some way I could, you know, leave it someplace safe, and pick it up in the morning."

The man shook his head. "We don't provide weapon storage services," he said sarcastically. "You want a cot for the night, hand over the gun. Maybe it's here in the morning, maybe it isn't. No guarantees."

I took out the gun and handed it to him. Didn't see that I had much choice. He glanced at it, put it under his desk, and waved me to an inner door, where another dour man checked my bag and grudgingly let me pass.

The left-and-right-hand sides of the vast floor area were now filled with cots. Men were filling up the left side, women the right. I made my way down to the first empty cot on the left, next to the white-haired guy with trembling hands. He ignored me. The cot had a thin pillow and blanket on it. I took out the book I had brought, lay back on the cot, and tried to read.

This was going to be difficult, I realized. The way I get through the long nights—especially without Gwen lying next to me—is by reading. Would I be able to read here? At least there wasn't a rule against it. At least they hadn't confiscated my copy of *A Tale of Two Cities*. Not having a gun made me feel vulnerable, powerless. That was OK. But not having a book…

I read while I could.

…it was the epoch of belief, it was the epoch of

incredulity....

The crowd of homeless people milled and thrashed and settled themselves. There were bathrooms we could use to relieve ourselves and brush our teeth. There were a couple of nurses to check out anyone with a medical problem. Dour men patrolled the aisles, checking for infractions.

...it was the season of Light, it was the season of Darkness...

And finally a bell rang, and the lights went down, and it was time to sleep. Before long the murmur of conversation died, and I began to hear snores and snorts and coughs. It was too dark to read, so I reluctantly set Dickens down onto the marble floor next to my cot. Then I stared up at the ceiling and thought about what the new day would bring.

...it was the spring of hope, it was the winter of despair...

The night was endless, filled with memories and regrets. As usual, I drifted off to sleep for a while near dawn, but I awoke when it was finally light enough to read. I got through a couple more chapters of my book before the place started stirring. We all had to be gone by seven, the rules on the wall had said. Time for morning Mass. Time for the day to begin in this cold, unfriendly city.

Time to find Flynn Dobler.

CHAPTER 30

I changed my shirt. I stood in line for the bathroom. I wondered if my gun had been stolen. I wondered what time Dominic Rodriguez showed up for work. I thought about *A Tale of Two Cities* and pondered the similarities between Dr. Manette and Abby, between Lucie Manette and Gwen. Apparently being locked up in the Bastille for eighteen years had much the same effect on a person as hiding from the crazies in Somerville.

I went into the entrance area to reclaim my gun from a dour man who was different from last night's dour man. He produced it without a fuss. So something good had finally happened. I decided to press my luck. "Is there somewhere I could stow this bag for the day?" I asked him. "I don't want to carry it around with me."

"Well you can't store it here," he replied, sounding shocked that I could even suggest such a thing.

"OK, somewhere else, then. I'm new around here."

"I suppose you could try Grand Central. They have storage lockers there."

"Ah, thanks. I appreciate it."

The man didn't bother to respond.

The day was clear and cold. I made my way back to Grand Central Station, which was filled with morning commuters. I found the lockers, put coins into a slot to rent one, and stashed my bag and gun. What an amazing invention! Then I treated myself to a large breakfast of eggs, toast, and bacon before trekking down to police headquarters once again.

This time there was a friendly woman with dyed red hair and several earrings in the guard booth, and my day brightened. "Who you lookin' for, honey?" she asked.

"Dominic Rodriguez. I don't have an appointment, but he knows I'm coming to see him."

"Let me just give him a call, hon." She gave him a call and then flashed an encouraging smile. "He says to come right up. Third floor. External Liaison office. Can't miss it."

"Thank you so much."

"You take care now."

Maybe New York wasn't so bad after all.

Despite what the guard said, it took me a while to find the External Liaison office. There were lots of offices, lots of people, lots of activity. They probably solved lots of crimes here; Chris Mull would be jealous.

I finally tracked down Rodriguez. He was a small, compact man with a crew cut, a small gray mustache, and a no-nonsense bone-crushing handshake. His office was small and neat. His desk had a computer monitor on it and a phone with lots of buttons. "Mr. Sands," he said. "Welcome to New York. Detective Mull has good things to say about you."

"Thanks. He's a good guy."

Rodriguez nodded. "Never met him in person, but he sounds very capable. You're looking for a man named Flynn Dobler."

"Yes, sir. We think he might be in danger. I can give you the details, if you like."

"Not interested. Well, that's not exactly true. I'm interested, but it doesn't matter. I'm afraid I can't be much help." He pushed an index card across the desk to me. "That's the most recent address we have for a Flynn Dobler. But he hasn't lived there for a long time."

I looked at the address. "We had the idea that maybe he went back there after he left Boston."

"Doubt it," Rodriguez said. "Someone else lives there now—name of Benjamin Osborne. Here's the thing. This address is on the Upper West Side—very nice neighborhood. *Very* nice. The city doesn't like having abandoned residences up there. Breeds crime. Besides, we need the tax revenue. So we encourage people to buy them up from the city. Of course, it helps if you know someone at City Hall."

"Dobler abandoned the place?"

"That's what the records say. The guy who

bought it was a banker. Probably pretty well connected. Just between you and me, that's the way it usually works."

"So he wouldn't have any connection to Dobler?"

Rodriguez shook his head. "And if Dobler tried to go back there, he wouldn't have any rights to the place. Osborne owns it now."

"Any other information about Dobler?"

"Got arrested once for disturbing the peace in Central Park. Charges were dropped. Otherwise, his record is clean. And that's it from my end. If he's in the city, he could be anywhere, using any name. But look on the bright side—if someone else is trying to track him down, he's not going to have any more luck than you."

"Yeah. That is a bright side."

"So, what are you going to do?"

"Well, I suppose I'll just go up there and talk to Osborne. Maybe Dobler left something behind when he left—some clue about where he might be now."

Rodriguez shook his head. "Afraid you can't do that," he replied.

"Why not?"

"You're not familiar with New York City, right, Mr. Sands?"

"Not really. Just got here last night. You can call me Walter, by the way."

"Notice anything about the city, Walter? Anything different from Boston?"

"Lot of security—guards everywhere. Also, way too many folks begging on the streets."

Rodriguez nodded. "Yeah. Some people have become really successful here since the War— people who work for the banks, the big construction companies, people with connections to Atlanta, foreign governments, people who can import the cars and the oil and the computers, everything we can't make here....There's a lot of money to be made. For most of us working schlubs, or people who aren't able to work...not so much. We just scrape by. And when we can't scrape by, we beg. Anyway, these super-rich folks want nothing to do with us. They're afraid we'll kidnap them or rape their daughters or break into their houses and steal their vintage wines. So they make sure we never get close to them."

"So Osborne's house will be guarded?"

"Not just the house—the entire neighborhood. He lives in what we call a high-security zone. Not even the police can get in without permission. That's undoubtedly why Osborne wanted to move there when Dobler abandoned his house."

"That sounds...depressing."

The detective shrugged. "Yeah, I suppose it is. Nothing much we can do about it, though, except try to become rich ourselves."

"Wrong line of work for that," I said.

"Wrong line of work," Rodriguez agreed.

"Could I maybe give Osborne a call?" I suggested.

"Sure, if you knew his phone number. Which you don't. And I don't. He doesn't want to talk to someone like you, Walter. There's just no point in trying."

I thought for a moment, and then sighed and stood up. "Well, thank you for your time, Detective."

I reached out my hand and let Rodriguez crush it once again. "You're welcome," he said. "Sorry I couldn't be more help."

I left his office and pondered what to do next. Was I finished in New York? Could I return home with a clean conscience? If I couldn't find Dobler, Brother Reggie couldn't find him either. So he was safe. And that was all that mattered, right?

I looked at the index card once again. I decided that I needed to at least make an effort.

I took the subway. I had to stand up—something that never happened in Boston. But standing up was OK—at least I was staying out of the cold.

It was easy enough to find the security area surrounding Osborne's house. The streets were blocked off, and armed, stony-eyed guards wearing green uniforms and sunglasses stood in front of an electric gate. An occasional car or truck would approach the gate; one of the guards would make a call or examine a clipboard, and then open the gate for it. I wandered around for a bit seeing if there was an obvious way to sneak in. I couldn't find any.

So I tried a different approach. I walked up to the guards at the gate and gave them a smile. "Hi," I said. "Could you call Mrs. Osborne for me? Mrs. Benjamin Osborne?"

"Is she expecting the call?" one of them asked, politely but suspiciously.

"Just tell her I want to talk to her about Flynn Dobler."

He hesitated, taking in my ragged jacket and pants, and then he shrugged and did as I asked.

Here was my thinking: It was the middle of the day; Osborne would probably be at work. If he was married, his wife might be at home. If she knew anything about Dobler—from cleaning out old papers when they moved in, or whatever— why wouldn't she talk to me?

And, surprisingly, I was right. The guard handed the phone over to me.

"Mrs. Osborne?" I said.

"Who is this?"

"My name is Walter Sands, Mrs. Osborne. I'm trying to track down a person named Flynn Dobler, and all I have is this address. My information is that he used to live here before you moved in. I wonder if I could ask you a few questions. It won't take long."

"Why are you tracking down Flynn Dobler?"

"It's a long story, but I think he might be in danger."

"Why?"

"It's a bit hard to explain over the phone. Can I talk to you in person?" There was no response. "Mrs. Osborne?"

"Let me talk to Mangini," she said finally.

I read the small nametag on the security guard's jacket, then handed the phone back to him. He listened for a moment, said "Yes, ma'am," and hung up. He motioned to another guard. "Escort this gentleman to 57," he instructed.

"Can I leave my gun with you?" I asked. "Don't want to cause any problems."

Mangini took my gun and opened the gate. The other security guard, whose nametag identified him as Richardson, led me through.

The neighborhood was filled with well-maintained brownstones but didn't seem all that special to me—not as nice as Louisburg Square, at any rate. One thing was different, though: the spectacularly shiny, undented cars that lined the streets.

Richardson and I walked up the front steps of Osborne's brownstone, and he pressed the buzzer. The intercom above the buzzer immediately squawked to life. "Yes?"

In Boston, these intercoms never worked. "Richardson, ma'am," the guard said. "With your guest?"

The door buzzed open.

I stepped inside and found myself in a large, ornate entranceway: marble floor, a chandelier, flocked green wallpaper, several poinsettias. I waited, and a moment later the inner door opened, and I found myself facing the woman I'd been speaking with.

I mentioned at the beginning of this account that Sister Marva was the most beautiful woman in the world. I stand by that statement, but the woman I was now looking at was a close second. Marva was maybe ten years younger, but this woman was more elegant and better dressed. She reeked of wealth and power. Her hair was black; her cheekbones were high; she looked as if she could have been Hispanic or native American. She was wearing a powder-blue silk blouse and black pants. Her jewelry was all gold—necklace, several bracelets, a slim wedding ring. Her nails were painted red; nobody in Boston wore nail polish. I was sure when I got close enough to her I would smell a subtle but alluring perfume.

"Thank you, Richardson," she said to the guard, who came close to bowing before he left.

"Come in," she ordered me. She turned and walked away, leaving the door open behind her. I followed. Through another entrance area, with a stairway curving upstairs. This room, too, was beautiful: Persian rugs on the polished hardwood floor, another poinsettia on a mahogany table beneath a gilt-framed mirror. We walked on, into a huge living room. A Christmas tree with tasteful white lights nestled in its branches. Modern paintings on the walls. Leather furniture. The whole place looked like it had been *designed,* not thrown together. I had never seen anything like it. She motioned to a long couch. I took off my jacket and sat. She sat opposite me, and that's when her perfume wafted its way over to me. Oh, my.

"I'm Angelique Osborne," she said.

"Walter Sands, as I said on the phone," I replied. "You can call me Walter."

"About Flynn Dobler," she said. "You said he was in danger."

"Yes, ma'am. Again, my information is that he

used to live here."

"I'm aware of that. What kind of danger?"

And that's when I heard footsteps in the next room. We both looked toward the door, and in strode a man wearing a dark suit, white shirt, and silk tie. He was tall, and his black hair was streaked with silver. If he wasn't the most distinguished man in the world, he was in the top three. I didn't see people like him—or his wife—in Boston.

I stood up. He stared at me, and I'm pretty sure he didn't like what he saw. "Walter Sands," I said, extending my hand.

He shook my hand—a bit reluctantly, I think. He was wearing cufflinks. That was another new experience for me. He didn't bother identifying himself. "What's this all about?"

"Mr. Sands is looking for Flynn Dobler," Angelique said softly.

Osborne looked at her and then back at me. "Sorry, can't help you," he said to me.

I sat back down. Osborne stayed standing, letting me know that he didn't have time for this nonsense in his important life. "He hasn't come here in the past few weeks?" I asked.

"No, of course not. I know he used to live here, but he abandoned the place years ago."

"No one else has come here looking for him—a big guy? Maybe not very bright? His name is Brother Reggie."

"*Brother Reggie?* This is absurd. No, no one has come here looking for him, especially not someone with the ridiculous name of 'Brother

Reggie.' Now—"

"What's going on?" Angelique interrupted. "Why do you think Flynn Dobler is in danger? And why do you think he's here?"

Osborne glared at her. I don't think he was used to being interrupted.

"After he left New York," I explained, "Dobler went to Boston and started a Church there—kind of a cult, I suppose. Recently he disappeared from the Church. We have reason to believe he came back to New York. And we think someone from the Church is tracking him down. Possibly to murder him."

Everyone was quiet for a moment. Angelique looked up at her husband. He looked down at her, and then folded his arms and turned back to me. "And what's your role in this, Mr. Sands?" he asked.

"I'm from Boston. I'm investigating Dobler's disappearance on behalf of the Church." That was a bit of a lie at this point, but they weren't going to know.

"Well, we can assure you that neither Dobler nor anyone looking for him has come here. We have nothing to do with the man, or his so-called 'Church.'"

"I understand that. But I was wondering if Dobler left behind some papers when he abandoned this place. If so, could I take a look at them? I might find some information I could use."

"There aren't any papers," Osborne said. "They're long gone by now. He left here years ago. This isn't a museum. This is our home. I'm sorry, but we can't help you. Now if there's nothing more…?"

I could take a hint; I stood up. "Thank you both for your time. If you happen to think of something, I'm staying at Saint Patrick's Cathedral. Sorry I don't have a better address, but I'm doing this on the cheap."

"With the homeless people? That must be very distressing for you," Osborne said, clearly uninterested in my distress.

I shrugged. "I've stayed in worse places."

"May I ask you a question?"

"Of course."

"You're the one, aren't you?" he said. "The one who brought down President Kramer in Boston."

This frankly shocked me. Fenwick knew about my role in the case, but he was part of the government. Osborne, as far as I could tell, was just some rich guy. Was I famous?

"Yes," I replied. "That was me."

Osborne gave me an appraising gaze, and then appeared to dismiss me as unimportant. "Too bad," he said. "New England would have been far better off as part of America."

"I'm sure some people have had some second thoughts about that. Anyway, I'm sorry to have bothered you."

"Not at all. Let me see you to the door."

I looked over at Angelique. She made no move to rise from her chair. She barely even glanced at me. More New York rudeness?

I couldn't tell. But there had been a moment

when she and her husband had exchanged glances…or maybe it had been nothing. What did I know about how people like them thought and lived?

There was a small suitcase on the floor in the entrance hall. "Just on my way to the airport when you arrived," Osborne explained. "Business in Atlanta."

"With the government?"

"A bit, yes."

"Say hello to Roger Fenwick if you run into him. He's a friend of mine."

Osborne raised an eyebrow. "Really? You get around, don't you, Mr. Sands."

"It's a small world. Merry Christmas, Mr. Osborne."

Osborne nodded and ushered me out the door.

Richardson was waiting at the bottom of the steps to escort me back to the gate. It crossed my mind to ask him if we could visit some more houses in the high-security zone. Maybe there were neighbors who remembered Dobler, who could give me clues to his whereabouts. But Richardson already looked cold and bored and annoyed that he'd had to deal with the likes of me. I couldn't imagine that he'd allow me to ring random doorbells and bother more people who looked and acted like the Osbornes.

I followed him back to the gate. I had done my best, but I had run into a blank wall.

It was time to admit defeat and go home.

CHAPTER 31

I got my gun back from Mangini and took the subway to Grand Central. I went to my storage locker, stashed the gun there, and got *A Tale of Two Cities* out of my bag. Then I had lunch in the best restaurant that would allow me inside. I ordered a pastrami sandwich and a Coke. I had never had those items before, and after I tasted them I decided that I never want to have either of them again.

The flight back to Boston left at ten in the morning. If I caught that flight tomorrow, I could be home in time to make supper for my family.

No one would say a word of criticism. No one would complain about the wasted money. I had done what I needed to do—I had gone to New York and found Dobler's childhood home, but he wasn't there. That wasn't where his ladders started. Maybe those ladders didn't have anything to do with his disappearance. Maybe there were no ladders. Maybe poetry and private investigation don't mix.

So, that was that. I had failed. Back to everyday life.

I read my book until they threw me out of the restaurant, and then I returned to Grand Central, found an empty bench, and kept on reading. I decided that the Frenzy had nothing on the French Revolution.

I should have been sightseeing, I supposed— when would I get to New York City again? But it was cold out, and I didn't like New York City. I was lonely and depressed, and reading was my solace.

I finished the book at around rush hour. I ate again, and then made my way back to the cathedral—past the beggars and cripples, past the skyscrapers with their windows boarded up, past the shop windows displaying fancy clothes I would never own, past the sparkling Christmas decorations.

I joined the line of tired, shivering, shuffling homeless people outside the cathedral. At nine o'clock the doors opened and before long I was back in the warmth again. Yet another dour man processed me—yes, I knew the rules; no, I had no medical problems—and I found my way to an open cot.

After lights-out, amid the coughing and creaking and snoring, I tried to think about the case. But what was there to think about? Dobler had disappeared. Brother Reggie had either found him or he hadn't. Maybe Brother Harold had information about Dobler's whereabouts that I

didn't have—Harold was the guy writing
Dobler's biography, after all. Maybe Reggie had
already done his job. Or maybe Reggie had run
into the same brick wall I had encountered and
returned to the Church.

Or maybe my theory had been all wrong.

When I finally fell asleep, I dreamed of Brother
Reggie stalking *me* through the streets of New
York. I spotted a high-security zone where I'd be
safe, but when I reached it the gate was locked,
no one would let me in, and he grinned
demonically at me as he approached, gun in hand,
ready to kill....

Great. In the morning I got up, groggily stood
in line for the toilets, splashed some water on my
face, and then made my way down the center
aisle towards the exit. Time to pick up my bag at
Grand Central Station and go home.

And that's when someone whispered my name.
"Mr. Sands."

The voice came from my right. I looked. And
there was Angelique Osborne sitting in a pew.
She was wearing a long black coat and a woolen
hat. She looked gorgeous. She motioned to me to
sit next to her. I obeyed.

"Can we talk?" she asked.

"Of course. Here?"

"Have you eaten breakfast?"

"No. We're just being kicked out."

"Let's go, then."

We exited the pew. Angelique genuflected
towards the altar before turning to leave. The
scruffy derelicts I had spent the night with stared

at us as we strode out of the cathedral. Was I a French nobleman just pretending to be homeless?

We found a fancy restaurant across the street. The security guard looked at me dubiously, but Angelique said, "He's my guest," and brushed past the guy without slowing down. We were seated immediately. She took off her hat and coat; she was wearing a white turtleneck sweater and yesterday's gold necklace and bracelets—or maybe they were more of the same. Her hair was tied up into a bun. I could smell the same expensive perfume she had worn in her home. There was something about the turtleneck....

"What's it like sleeping in the cathedral?" she asked me as she glanced at the menu.

"It's OK. Lot of coughing. I don't think they have a very healthy clientele."

That seemed to exhaust her small talk. I ordered bacon and eggs. Angelique just had coffee. She said nothing. When the coffee came, she just stared at it. Still she said nothing.

"Your husband did most of the talking yesterday," I noted.

"That's generally the case," she replied.

"So maybe there's something you didn't have a chance to bring up?" I suggested. "Something you'd like to talk about now? You're obviously not here to enjoy my company."

"I think I may know where Flynn Dobler is," she said to her coffee.

"Where?"

She looked up at me finally. "His family had a summer house in the Hamptons—out on Long

Island. If he came back to New York—if he thought someone was hunting him down—he might have gone there. Of course, I have no way of knowing that for sure. I just thought I'd pass it along."

"How do you know about this summer house?" I asked.

"What you said yesterday—he left papers behind when he abandoned the house. Documents, bills…"

"Your husband said there weren't any," I pointed out.

"Benjamin didn't clean up the place when we moved in. I did. Or, at least, I supervised the people doing the cleanup. I read some of the papers. It felt wrong—it felt like I was spying on someone else's life. But I did it. It's not like I ever expected Flynn Dobler to return."

"Why didn't you tell me about this yesterday?"

"Because I knew Benjamin wouldn't want me to."

"Why not?"

"Well, the fact is that we didn't entirely follow the law when we bought the house. There's a waiting period to ensure that a residence is truly abandoned, that the owner or his heirs aren't going to show up someday. A lot of people were displaced by the War, obviously; there was a lot of chaos. So people return home unexpectedly sometimes."

I thought about Abby. Not quite the same situation. "My understanding is that Dobler didn't leave New York till some time after the War," I said.

"That's right. So when Benjamin decided he wanted the house, the waiting period hadn't expired. But Benjamin is powerful enough that he could, well, bend the law a bit in this case."

"So yesterday he was hiding his shady business transaction," I summed up. "And you felt bad because that might be putting Dobler's life in danger."

Angelique nodded. "Yes, I suppose. Something like that."

My food came. I took a few bites. It was delicious. "Is that why he choked you afterwards," I asked, "—to warn you to keep your mouth shut about his shady business transaction?"

Angelique flushed, and her hand moved involuntarily to her neck.

"Your turtleneck doesn't quite hide all the bruising," I pointed out. "It's a very lovely turtleneck, though. Is that what they call cashmere? I don't see much cashmere up in Boston."

Her eyes teared up, but she didn't cry. "My relationship with my husband is none of your business, Mr. Sands," she said after a moment.

"Of course it isn't. I really don't want to cause you any trouble, Angelique—may I call you Angelique?"

She inclined her head slightly.

"And you can call me Walter. Do you by any chance remember where Dobler's summer house was, Angelique? Just the name of the town would be helpful."

"I remember the address, actually. At least, I think I do. For some reason it's stayed with me."

"Fabulous. Just give me that, and I'll take it from there. Your husband won't ever have to know we ate breakfast together."

"I can drive you, if you like."

She said this to her coffee, flushing once again.

"Really, that's not necessary," I replied, even though I had no idea how I would get to the Hamptons. Did the subway go there? Could I take a cab? How much would that cost?

Angelique shrugged. "It's no trouble," she said, looking up at me. "I don't have much chance to do good deeds—at least, good deeds that involve something more than hosting fund-raisers and giving money to the occasional beggar. If Flynn Dobler is in danger, I'd like to help warn him."

"It could be dangerous," I pointed out.

"Why? This other fellow who's looking for him—Brother Reggie? Was that his name? He couldn't possibly know about the place in the Hamptons, could he?"

"I have no idea. It seems unlikely, but I have no idea what people in the Church know about Dobler's past. They claim to know nothing, but they could be lying. I can't say there's no risk."

"This Church—it sounds…strange."

"There's plenty of strangeness to go around nowadays, I guess." I gave her a quick summary of the Church of the New Beginning's beliefs.

Angelique was less scornful of them than I had expected. "I suppose starting over is not unreasonable, given all that's happened," she remarked when I'd finished. "And Dobler got a lot of people to follow him?"

"He's a very charismatic guy. The trouble is, the whole project hasn't turned out to be terribly practical."

"You've met Dobler?"

"I met him last summer. He makes quite an impression."

"But he left the Church, you said. He came back here."

"I think he got tired of the problems, the people, the politics. I think he wanted to come home. That's just a theory, of course."

"Of course. Well, I'll still drive you. If you like. I'm willing to take the risk."

"You're not worried that your husband might find out?" I asked. "Seems like that's another risk."

Angelique shook her head. "Benjamin's in Atlanta," she replied. "That won't be a problem."

She said this with a steady voice, but her hand moved to her neck once again, and I knew she was lying. Or deluding herself. Or...well, I knew that something wasn't quite right. But I couldn't think of a reason to turn down a favor like this from a gorgeous woman like her. "Then sure," I said. "That would be great."

Angelique was ready to go right then, but I wanted to finish my breakfast first. It was an excellent breakfast. Besides, the odds were still slim that I would find Dobler at his summer house, and even slimmer that Brother Reggie would be able to track him down there. So what exactly was the point of the trip? Why stay in New York another day? Just to prove something about ladders, maybe.

I finished in a couple of minutes, Angelique paid the check, and we left the restaurant. The sky was leaden and spitting snow, and the biting wind made me long for a warmer jacket as we walked to her car. It was in a nearby parking garage. Heavily guarded, of course. We have parking garages in Boston, but none of them are actually used for parking; they're not used for much of anything, in fact. Her car was white and sleek and looked like it had never been driven.

"Is this new?" I asked. "We don't have new cars where I come from."

"Fairly new," Angelique replied, obviously uninterested in the subject.

"Why don't you have a chauffeur?"

"I don't like chauffeurs."

"Do you have a bodyguard?"

"If I want one. Today I didn't want one."

We got in. The car was spotless. It smelled delightful. Angelique turned it on, and the engine emitted a low, powerful thrumming noise. It was almost enough to make me want to learn how to drive.

"Are the Hamptons far away?" I asked.

"Not far, but it depends on the road conditions, the snow, how often I get lost. I've got an old map in the glove compartment. You can take a look."

"Can we stop off at Grand Central Station first?"

"Why?"

"I left my gun in a locker there. Even if there's not much risk, you can't be too careful."

She drove over to Grand Central and waited outside while I fetched the gun. Then I got back in the car, and we were on our way.

"You're really a private eye?" she asked me. "Like in the old movies?"

"I really am."

"Benjamin thinks that's an idiotic line of work."

"He's probably right about that."

"Why do you do it, if it's idiotic?"

I shrugged. I didn't feel like getting into my life story with her. "Some people start Churches," I said. "Some people become bankers and live in high-security zones. It takes all kinds."

She flushed a bit. I wondered what her life story was. Her beauty was undoubtedly a big part of it. She had an expensive home, a new car, beautiful clothes, nice jewelry. And a husband who choked her. Not a good tradeoff, I thought. But I wasn't her.

I decided not to ask for her story. She'd tell me if she wanted to.

The snow got worse as we headed out of Manhattan. The Long Island Expressway was better than New England highways, but it had its share of potholes and downed tree limbs and other hazards. There was little traffic. Angelique drove slowly, hunching forward, her hands clenching the steering wheel as if it were a life preserver. "I'm not used to this," she muttered. "Mostly I drive in the city. They have snow plows in the city."

I was not familiar with snow plows.

The trip seemed to take forever. The snow started to accumulate. Eventually we got off the expressway and onto smaller roads that were lined with abandoned car dealerships and fast-food restaurants. Occasionally we encountered traffic lights, but none of them were working. Angelique slowed at the lights but didn't stop. The scenery became more rustic. We passed through a small town center, where the stores looked fancier. Some of them were even open, with Christmas lights twinkling in the windows. I got out the map and figured out where we were.

"Not long now," I said.

Angelique said nothing, concentrating fiercely on the road.

"I'm sorry about the snow. This probably isn't what you bargained for."

She didn't respond.

We finally reached the town Angelique remembered, but then we couldn't find the street. We drove randomly through the town looking for Dune Road. Had she gotten it wrong? I looked over at her; her eyes had teared up. "We'll find it," I assured her, although I was pretty sure we wouldn't.

But then we did. There was no sign, but a faded little address plaque on a low stone wall at the end of a long driveway, half obscured by snow, told us we had found the street we were looking for.

"Thank God," Angelique whispered.

Now we had to find out if she had remembered the house number correctly. All we could see from the road were widely spaced long driveways, apparently leading off to summer homes too important to let themselves be seen by people in automobiles passing by. Some of the driveways had a number visible on a wall or a tree; others didn't.

At last we spotted the number we'd been searching for.

"This is it?" I asked Angelique.

"I hope so," she said, and she carefully turned into the driveway. It sloped up through pines and junipers, curving around until we saw a white, modernistic house, all slabs and angles, beyond high ragged hedges in the distance.

We got stuck once as we drove up the house. "Dammit," Angelique muttered. She backed up, then gunned the accelerator and raced the car forward. The tires spun helplessly for a moment, whining over the noise of the engine, and then at last we lurched forward.

And finally we came to a stop in an elegant circular drive in front of the house. There was smoke coming out of the house's chimney. A snow-covered car was parked next to the house, just off the driveway.

Angelique turned the ignition off, closed her eyes, and took a deep breath.

"Thank you," I said.

She smiled for the first time since the journey

began.

And then we heard a gunshot, and my window exploded.

"Get down!" I shouted unnecessarily. Then: "You OK?"

"Yes, I think so," Angelique replied, hunching down behind the steering wheel.

"Get out of the car," I said. "I'll follow. Stay down."

"Right." She opened her door and slid out. I crawled across the center console to the driver's side, expecting another bullet to come my way at any second. But I made it out. Still crouching down, I shut the door behind me and took stock. The car was between us and the house. Good. But whoever had shot at us would still have a clear shot from the second floor. Bad.

"You're bleeding," Angelique said. She reached over and picked a tiny piece of glass from my cheek.

"Don't worry about it."

I tried to think. It was snowing hard. Maybe we could make a run for it. Or maybe…

Angelique peeked out above the car's hood.

"Stay down!" I repeated urgently.

But she ignored me. She took her hat off and dropped it on the driveway. She shook out her long black hair. She stood up.

I grabbed at her. "Please, Angelique."

She broke away from me and walked out from behind the car, towards the house.

I got my gun out and crawled around to see what was happening.

Flynn Dobler was standing in the doorway, gun in hand. And then he was running forward across the snow towards Angelique.

And then they were in each other's arms, kissing passionately, while I sprawled on the ground, wondering what I had missed.

CHAPTER 32

I got to my feet. I was too polite to mention that I was bleeding, but after a few moments the happy couple recalled my presence and unclinched. Dobler stared at me, puzzled, with those fierce eyes of his. "Walter Sands?" he asked.

"Hiya," I replied. "Long time no see."

"What are you doing here?"

"Kind of a long story. I come in peace, though. No need to use that gun again. Listen, you wouldn't have hot water and a towel inside the house, would you? Wipe off the blood?"

"I'm sorry," he said. "Come in. This is all a bit—"

"I owe you an explanation, Walter," Angelique said, clutching Dobler's arm.

"Can't wait," I replied.

We went inside, passing through an airy hallway into a huge room with floor-to-ceiling windows offering a spectacular view of the ocean, gray and choppy in the snowstorm. All the windows were cracked, which made me feel a bit at home. A fire roared and hissed in an immense fireplace. On either side of the fireplace were bookshelves jammed with books, and they also made me feel at home. I looked for, and quickly spotted, a copy of the collected poems of William Butler Yeats.

"Making do a bit here," Dobler muttered as he ladled out some water from a pot in the fireplace.

Angelique and I took our coats off, and she cleaned the blood off my face and picked the tiny pieces of glass out of my skin. Could have been worse.

"I thought you came to kill me," Dobler explained.

"That been happening much lately?" I asked.

"Once. Once is enough."

"Brother Reggie?"

"Yes—how did you—well, obviously we all need to do some explaining."

"First tell me what happened to Brother Reggie."

Dobler considered for a moment, and then motioned to us to join him at the windows. In addition to the ocean I could now see a deck surrounding an empty swimming pool and, beyond the pool, a snow-covered yard. To the left and right were trees. "I buried him over there among the trees," Dobler said. "It wasn't easy with the ground this cold." We were silent for a moment, and then he went on. "Reggie simply wasn't smart enough to do what he was sent to do. I didn't want to kill him, but I didn't want to die, either."

"How did he know where you were?"

"I assume he found out from a man named Brother Harold. But I don't know if you—"

"I know Brother Harold. I know a lot. But I have some gaps in my knowledge."

After a moment we went back and sat by the fire. Angelique snuggled into the crook of Dobler's arm. Dobler was wearing ragged jeans and a sweatshirt; it was strange not to see him in the Church's brown robe. "It's been so long," she murmured to him.

"You two seem to know each other pretty well," I remarked astutely.

"I'm sorry, Walter," Angelique said. "This is…complicated."

So, after a moment, she began to tell the story.

Flash back a decade or so. The War was fading into the past, and New York City had divided itself into the haves and the have-nots. Angelique was a nobody, but she was young and beautiful and had her pick of rich and powerful men. She fell in love with Flynn Dobler.

He was the only child of rich parents. The blast had incinerated them, leaving him in possession of their beautiful brownstone in the city, their elegant summer home in the Hamptons. But he wasn't interested in money or power. He was determined to change the world.

He was full of idealism and full of ideas. Angelique found him irresistible. That intensity! That certainty! That air of command! She knew he was destined for greatness, but she didn't care about that; she just wanted to be with him.

She moved into the brownstone with him. She had never been happier. But...

Dobler became restless. He tried helping the multitudes of sick and abandoned children, but that was too depressing. He tried writing a book, but that was too solitary, too confining. He tried running for office, but the elites controlled politics, and they didn't like what he had to say about wealth and technology and changing the way people lived. They liked the way they were living just fine.

And that's when he started preaching in Central Park. Preaching the gospel that became the centerpiece of his new religion. Except it wasn't a religion then; it was just a message that he needed to deliver. We have to start over. Get rid of all these institutions and inventions and attitudes that have caused us so much pain.

But no one listened.

Was it New York? Or was it him?

He decided it was both.

He decided it was hypocritical of him to return every night to his beautiful home in its high-security zone, to live his comfortable life because of the riches his father had amassed running a hedge fund (whatever that was). He had to give it all up. And he had to go to someplace less obsessed with wealth and status, someplace that might respond to what he had to say.

He decided to go to Boston.

But Angelique wouldn't go with him. "I loved

my life," she said to Dobler, still sitting next to him. "I loved *you.* You didn't have to change the world. No one can change the world. We had all suffered so much already. Why did we have to suffer more?"

"I didn't want to make you suffer," he replied softly. "I wanted you to share my vision."

"I did, I did. It was just…"

She began to cry now, and Dobler stroked her hair.

"It was just too hard," she said.

Dobler looked confused, uncertain. Before today, I could not have imagined seeing that expression on his face. "I thought I could change the world," he murmured. "And in Boston I discovered how to do it. I discovered religion."

"The Church," Angelique said. "Walter told me about that."

"Religion is what you need to change the world," he said. "I understood that finally. And you don't need to win elections to start a religion; you don't need to write a book. You just need to convince people to follow you. And it turned out I was very good at that, at least in Boston. I had a message the people there wanted to hear."

"You have some very devoted followers," I said. "But you left them behind."

"Yes, I did. Starting a religion was easy in a place like Boston after the Frenzy, where people were desperate for someone to explain what had happened to them, to give them a reason to hope. Turns out that maintaining a religion is the difficult part. I hadn't thought about that. I thought—if I could gather some disciples, if we could work together, we would succeed. But I was wrong."

"What happened?" I asked. "Brother Joseph talked about the compromises the Church had to make, disciples becoming disillusioned."

"Yes, that was hard. But Brother Harold made it harder."

"Brother Joseph thought he murdered you."

Dobler shook his head. "It occurred to me that Harold might do that, but I left first. Made it easier for him, I suppose. Harold took the idea of a religion to its next step—one that never occurred to me, frankly. He is obsessed with the idea of God. He believed that my ideas, my wisdom, had come directly from God. In his mind, I was like Mohammed taking dictation for the Koran, or Saint Paul on the road to Damascus. He wanted to write my biography, you know."

"He told me."

"Well, what he really wanted to write was a gospel, filled with signs and wonders. Loaves and fishes, walking on water."

"But he doesn't really believe that stuff, right? It's just his way of getting people to join the Church."

Dobler disentangled himself from Angelique and threw a log on the fire. Then he went over to look out at the ocean. The snow was still falling. Angelique, I saw, was baffled by this conversation. "I think you don't know enough about human nature," Dobler said. "You assume people are rational, like you. They are not.

Someone like Brother Harold is perfectly capable of believing his fantasies and believing me when I tell him they're false."

"Sister Lucy is convinced that she saw you ascend into heaven the night you left, that God brought you home to Him. She's convinced most of the rest of the disciples, and a lot of other people, too. They're making pilgrimages up to Concord to see the spot where it happened."

Dobler sighed. "Sister Lucy is also convinced that I brought her back from the dead many years ago. Which I did, although not in the way she thinks. I wonder if she will tell people that story."

"Do you think Brother Harold gave her the idea of you going up to heaven?"

"Perhaps, but he didn't have to. Sister Lucy is perfectly capable of conjuring up a miracle all by herself."

"So, did you leave because of Harold?"

Dobler slowly shook his head. "No, I think I could have handled him, one way or another. Ultimately, I left because of Sister Marva."

"Who's Sister Marva?" Angelique asked.

Dobler turned away from the window and looked at Angelique. "Sister Marva," he said, "is a beautiful young woman who wanted desperately for me to love her. But I couldn't. Because I was already in love. With you."

"So why did she make you leave?" Angelique asked.

"Because someone raped her and made her pregnant, and there was nothing I could do about it."

"Brother Scott," I said.

Dobler looked at me now and nodded. "Brother Scott," he repeated. "I knew that people thought I was the father. Marva would have loved it if I were. Maybe she half-believed it, in the same way that Harold can believe and not believe at the same time. But I wasn't. When her pregnancy started to show, I saw the way Scott looked at her—that creepy, self-satisfied look of his—and I understood. He had done it. I don't know why other people didn't see what I saw—maybe they were convinced that I was the father. Anyway, she was too ashamed to say anything about it. And, I suppose, she liked it that everyone assumed that it was me. I ordered her to tell the truth. I told her I was going to throw that sniveling little bastard out of the Church. She begged me not to. She said it wasn't his fault. She said she had never told anyone I was the father, and she never would. I couldn't get her to see reason. She said she'd kill herself if I did anything to Scott."

"She just had her baby," I told him. "A boy."

"That's good," Dobler said. "I wish her no harm."

"But Scott's dead. He snuck away from the Church, like you did. Only this time someone caught up with him and beat him to death. Maybe they were looking for the money you took."

"And that's good, too. It occurred to me when I took the money that I would get him into trouble. It wasn't the reason I left, but I'm glad it happened. He should never have touched that girl."

"So you decided to give it all up and go home," I said.

He nodded.

"Down where all the ladders start," I quoted.

"Yes, exactly. Do you know Yeats?"

"Doesn't everyone?"

Angelique looked puzzled. "What does that mean?" she asked.

Dobler went back to her. "It means that I came home to find you," he said. "I realized that I never should have left you in the first place."

"You couldn't get inside the security zone, I suppose," she said.

"I'm sure I could have found a way. But I saw you leaving. In a car. With a man." He held up her left hand, the one with the slim gold wedding ring on the fourth finger. "With your husband, I assume." Angelique flushed and looked away. Dobler gently lowered her hand. "It's all right," he said. "Really it is. It's been so long. After I saw you with him, I made my way out here to ponder my future. Luckily, no one had taken over this place."

Angelique started to cry. "I made a choice," she sobbed. "You left me with some money, but not enough to pay the taxes, the guards, everything. I didn't *own* the house. I couldn't *sell* it. Benjamin offered me security. Can you understand how important security is in this world? Can you forgive me?"

"There's nothing to forgive," Dobler murmured. "Nothing to forgive."

He kissed the top of her head. He looked tired. He sounded tired.

I was feeling a bit extraneous at this point. And hungry. The snow was coming down harder now. We wouldn't be able to get back to New York City today, I realized. Did that matter? Would Osborne return from Atlanta, find Angelique missing, and track her down here?

It occurred to me that I had done my job. I had found Dobler and determined that he wasn't in any danger—no thanks to me, but so what? If I hadn't come here, I wouldn't have known he was OK, and I would have always regretted not knowing.

So why wasn't I happier?

Maybe I was just homesick. Watching Dobler and Angelique clinging to each other made me miss Gwen. I had left Gwen not so long ago to pursue a dream in England; that had turned out to be a bad idea. Dobler had found out that abandoning Angelique to save the world had also been a bad idea, except it had taken him years to come to his senses. Maybe I was just thinking about how fragile our happiness is.

I got up and threw a log onto the fire. I wondered where Dobler got the logs. Where did he buy his food? Did he have food? I studied the books on his shelves and took down a tattered paperback copy of *Middlemarch*. That would keep me out of trouble for a while.

I left Dobler and Angelique and went in search of the kitchen. I found it on the other side of the entrance hall. It was a large room with sleek appliances, lots of pots and pans hanging on the walls, and a leaky ceiling that looked like it was going to cave in on me. There was a bowl of apples on the counter. I grabbed one gratefully, took a bite, and sat down at the counter to read George Eliot.

Eventually Dobler came out to find out what I was up to. "You're hungry," he said.

"Don't know why," I replied. "Angelique bought me a big breakfast."

"Maybe getting shot at sharpens your appetite."

"You could be right."

"I have some stew here. Probably enough for the three of us."

He got a pot out of the refrigerator, and we went back go the living room, where he heated it up in the fireplace.

The stew was not as good as my breakfast, but it was good enough. I decided to get the rest of the story. "So, you've been hiding out here?" I asked Dobler.

"That's right. I can buy food and supplies in town. A couple of people even remember me from the old days. It's given me time to think, stare at the ocean, do some repairs." He gestured at the bookshelves. "I've even started reading again. It's against my principles, but perhaps my principles were too extreme."

"You think Brother Harold told Reggie where to find you ?"

"I told Brother Harold everything. Of course, he'll deny it. I didn't talk about my past with anyone else, but I was trying to make Harold see that there was nothing supernatural about my ideas. So Reggie knew where to look for me. I had a feeling Harold might come after me, so I was careful. And, as it turned out, Reggie was stupid—even stupider than I could have expected."

"What happened?"

"He just drove up and parked in front of the house—like you did. And then he came up the front door and knocked. By that time I was upstairs watching him from a second-floor window. So I went downstairs, grabbed my gun, went out the back door, and circled around to the front. As soon as he saw me he tried to shoot. But I was faster. And that was the end of Brother Reggie."

"That's awful," Angelique said.

Dobler nodded. "I loved my disciples—all of them. Reggie was not smart, but he was loyal. Or so I thought."

"Will they try again?" she asked.

"Who knows? That's certainly what I had in mind when I shot at poor Mr. Sands."

"Then you shouldn't stay here. We should leave right away."

"No one's going anywhere tonight," I said, gesturing at the snow still accumulating outside.

Dobler didn't say anything. Instead he just held Angelique closer.

I decided it was time to let the couple have some privacy. *You must have lots to catch up on. I have this book I'd really like to read.* They didn't argue. Dobler brought me to a bedroom upstairs with its own fireplace and view of the ocean. As usual, it smelled of mildew, and the walls were water-stained, and one of the windows was cracked. But otherwise it was lovely. Dobler started a fire, and soon the room was almost warm.

"I'm very grateful to you for bringing Angelique to me," Dobler said, his dark eyes blazing in the firelight. "And for trying to save me."

"You're welcome," I replied. And then I added: "You have to do something, you know. You won't be safe here. When Brother Reggie doesn't return, Brother Harold will send someone else. He can't leave you alive. And you can't keep shooting at everyone who comes up your driveway."

"Yes, I know that."

"The best way to protect yourself would be to show yourself to the world," I pointed out. "Prove that what Lucy saw was just a hallucination. I have a friend who works for the *Globe* back in Boston. If you were to just go back and give an interview to her, Harold's whole story would collapse. Once you do that, there's no point in anyone trying to kill you."

"And the Church would collapse," he pointed out in turn.

"Well, Harold's version of the Church. But not your ideas. They don't depend on miracles."

"My ideas," he said. And he sounded very tired. "I'll give it some thought."

He went downstairs and left me with my book. There are worse ways to spend the afternoon than sitting by the fire and reading *Middlemarch*. I could hear the sounds of murmured conversation from beneath me. And eventually the sounds became more, um, ardent, and I started missing Gwen again. The best way to spend the afternoon would have been reading *Middlemarch* with Gwen sitting next to me by the fire.

Later Angelique and Dobler cooked supper and fetched me back downstairs to join them. They looked flushed and satisfied, but they seemed happy to have a person to share the meal with. We talked about finding shovels. We talked about whether the roads would be plowed. We talked about the next day, but made no plans. Finally I went back to my room, put another log on the fire, listened to the ocean and the murmured conversation, and waited for morning.

CHAPTER 33

When I awoke, the sun was shining for a change. I went downstairs and found Angelique and Dobler already up and dressed. They looked subdued, like too much had happened for them to absorb. Dobler had made coffee, for which I was grateful; I wondered if coffee was easy to find out here. We had fried eggs and leftover bread for breakfast, and we talked matter-of-factly about logistics.

"I'll drive you back to New York," Angelique said. "The roads should be OK once we get to the highway."

"Are you coming with us?" I asked Dobler.

He shook his head. "I'd just as soon stay away from the city."

"The trip shouldn't take long," Angelique said, "if we don't get stuck somewhere."

After breakfast Dobler and I found a couple of snow shovels in the garage.

"I'm sorry about the broken window in the car,"

Dobler added. "It won't make the trip any more pleasant."

Didn't matter. I just wanted to get home. I wouldn't make the morning flight back to Boston, and that meant one more night in New York. I could probably stand it. "Do you mind if I hold onto your copy of *Middlemarch*?" I asked Dobler. "I haven't finished it, and it's pretty good."

"That's fine. As long as you leave me my Yeats."

"There wouldn't be any Yeats in your new world order," I pointed out. "He belongs to the old days."

"*The blood-dimmed tide is loosed*," he quoted from another Yeats poem. But that's all he said.

We set to work shoveling the driveway, clearing the snow off Angelique's car and sweeping the broken glass out of the front seats. The sun was helping to melt the snow a bit, and it certainly raised my spirits. Before long we were ready to go.

I waited by the car while Angelique and Dobler said goodbye at the front door—a long embrace, and then the briefest of kisses.

Angelique got in the car, and I went over to shake Dobler's hand. "Thank you again," he said.

"You're welcome again. Have you thought about my idea—come back to Boston and show the world you're alive?"

He shook his head. "I have my own ideas about what to do."

"I could just tell people you're living here," I

persisted. "You wouldn't even have to—"

He put a hand on my arm and gave me one of those compelling gazes of his. "It's all right, Walter. Really, it is."

"Well, good luck, then."

"And good luck to you."

I got into the soggy passenger seat next to Angelique, and we drove off with a wave. As we left Dobler extended his arms, as if offering his blessing to our journey.

The hardest part was the beginning. The road that led past Dobler's house hadn't been plowed, but fortunately a car or two had already traveled along it, leaving ruts in the snow for us to drive in. Once we reached a main road, conditions got better. A plow had made a pass, but it hadn't managed to get down to bare pavement, and Angelique had to drive slowly to avoid skidding, but we didn't get stuck. Aside from the cold wind blowing in through the hole where my window used to be, the trip was turning out to be fairly pleasant.

And then I spotted the tear on Angelique's cheek.

"Um, are you OK?" I asked.

She wiped the tear away. "It's nothing," she said.

"The roads are pretty good," I pointed out. "You could be back in the Hamptons this afternoon."

She nodded. And then, after a pause, she said, "I'm not going back, Walter." And another tear appeared. Several, in fact.

None of my business. Still…"But why?" I asked. "Dobler's the love of your life. And your husband…"

"Is an abusive prick. Yes, I know. And I know Benjamin. He'll slap me around a bit—to let me know who's boss, who's paying the bills. And then life will get back to normal. Normal isn't perfect, but it's not awful, either."

Dobler had told me I didn't know enough about human nature. I certainly felt like I was struggling a bit here. "But your husband choked you. I can still see the bruises."

Angelique wiped away the latest batch of tears. She said nothing for a while. And then she asked, "What was that thing about ladders you and Flynn were talking about yesterday?"

"*I must go down where all the ladders start,*" I quoted. "It's from a poem by Yeats. It means something like—go down to your deepest sources of inspiration. What makes you who you are."

She nodded. "You want to know where my ladders start, Walter?"

"Sure."

She paused again, and I wondered if she was changing her mind. But then she began to talk. "I was ten years old and living in New Jersey when the bomb fell on New York. My mother was in Manhattan that day and died in the blast. OK, that happened to lots of people. But other than that, we were luckier than most. My father and I were unharmed. He had a job, we had a house, we had food to eat. But then he started drinking. And he wouldn't—couldn't—stop drinking. He missed my Mom. He was depressed about the world. He had to take care of me all by himself. I get it. But I was a little girl. He had a responsibility."

"What happened?"

She shrugged. "One day he didn't come home. The next day I got scared and went to where he worked, and it turned out they had fired him weeks ago. I went to the neighbors, I went to the police. No one had seen him, no one knew where he was. No trace of him. Then, or ever. He had simply disappeared. I never saw him again. I never found out what became of him."

"So, what happened to you?"

"My aunt and uncle took me in. What else could they do? I wasn't happy about it, but it was probably all for the best. I was treated like one of the family. I got an education. I was loved. I ended up being luckier than anyone has a right to be, given all that's happened. But you know where my ladders start, Walter? Down there where my father abandoned me."

"Maybe he had an accident," I suggested. "Maybe someone murdered him."

"Sure. It's not like he left me a note. I only know what I felt—what I feel."

I thought of my own father, who would no more have abandoned me than he would have cut off a hand. "Dobler abandoned you, too," I said.

Angelique nodded. "He was such an exciting person. He still is. You listen to him, and you're convinced he's going to save the world. I was caught up in the excitement. I just wanted to be with him, to be part of his life. And then he decided that to save the world he had to go to Boston."

I recalled yesterday's conversation. "You could have gone with him," I pointed out.

"He said I could come along, but he didn't mean it. He thought I was standing in the way of his greatness—and I probably was. I didn't care about saving the world; I just wanted someone to love me. Love has always been secondary to Flynn."

"But he came back for you," I persisted. "He realized his mistake."

She shook her head. "He *thinks* he's realized his mistake, because that Church of his didn't work out. I was so desperate to see him, when you showed up and I found out he was still alive. I guess I had a dream—but after a day with him I know better. I realize that I'd make him happy for a while, and then he'd become restless, he'd start looking for something more—another challenge, another theory. And in the meantime people from the Church are trying to kill him, and he doesn't seem willing to do anything about it. One way or another, he's going to abandon me again."

"And your husband won't?" I asked. "He won't dump you when your looks start to go, or you get pregnant and put on a lot of weight? Or maybe you'll get cancer—everyone's going to get it eventually, from the fallout. What if you're desperately sick and he has to take care of you?"

"I don't know. I suppose it could all turn out awful. But you know, I think Benjamin does love me. I think I make him happy, and not just with my looks. He isn't perfect, but who is?"

Angelique left me feeling a bit baffled. I assumed she was rationalizing; I assumed she didn't want to leave her husband because she liked her gold jewelry and fine art and expensive furniture and new car. She liked being safely inside her high-security zone. I assumed she would someday regret giving up her one true love to return to all that. But what did I know? I had been orphaned and then kidnapped by crazies and mistreated at youth camps, but I had never been abandoned. "Does Dobler know?" I asked.

She nodded. "I told him this morning."

"How did he take it?"

"I think…he's confused. But he'll be all right."

We were on the expressway now, heading in to Manhattan. There was more traffic, and the plows had done a better job. I thought of the mismatched couples and unhappy marriages in *Middlemarch.* Happiness is hard, I decided. Just about as hard as saving the world.

"Do you at least want me to go back home with you?" I asked. "Maybe I can keep your husband from getting too angry. Protect you if he gets out of control."

"No, you'll have just the opposite effect. Have I mentioned that he doesn't like you?"

"Um, yeah, I think you did."

"I can handle my husband, Walter," Angelique said. "I've handled him before. It'll be all right. Now, where can I drop you off?"

"Grand Central Station, I guess. I'll have to put my gun back into my locker before they'll let me into Saint Patrick's."

"Oh God, you can't stay there another night."

"I don't really have enough—"

"I'll give you money, Walter. That's one thing I have plenty of. And I owe it to you—without you coming with me, I wouldn't have had the courage to go to the Hamptons. Please, stay in a good hotel. Take a shower—you could use one, frankly. Buy a new coat—you could use one of those, too."

"The security guards won't let me near a good hotel," I pointed out.

"I'll take care of that."

I am a weak man. The prospect of a hot shower was too much for me. "Well, thanks," I said. "I appreciate it. But speaking of coming with you— why did you lie to me yesterday at the restaurant? I guess I can understand why you'd want me to go with you to the Hamptons—Brother Reggie could have been out there, for all you knew. But why make up a story about remembering the address of the summer house from some old piece of mail? Why not just tell me you knew him?"

Angelique flushed. "If I told you the truth, and then it turned out Flynn wasn't there—if it was just the foolish hope of a foolish woman—I didn't want you feeling sorry for me. I'm not especially proud of my life, Walter. But I don't want any pity."

"Fair enough," I replied.

She drove me to a clothing store and bought me a coat, plus some new pants for good measure.

Then she took me to a hotel called The Plaza, next to Central Park. She parked at the door and escorted me past the security. The management was delighted to take good care of anyone vouched for by Mrs. Benjamin Osborne. She put the room on her charge card. Then she handed me a wad of cash and kissed me on the cheek. "Take a shower," she commanded me.

"Yes, ma'am."

"And no pity," she insisted. "I've made my choices. I know how to live with them."

"I understand."

She strode back out to her car then and drove off with a wave.

So my last day in New York turned into one of sybaritic luxury. I took the longest shower of my life. I went out for a walk, wearing the first brand new coat of my life. No more Salvage Market leftovers for Walter Sands! I recalled that Christmas was coming in a few days, and some other folks could use some new clothes. So I returned to the clothing store, where they were now happy to let me in, and bought presents for Gwen and Stretch. No leftovers for them, either!

Later I ate dinner at the fancy hotel restaurant. Then I went back up to my toasty-warm room, with its view of the park, where I read my book and counted down the hours till I could return to Boston.

CHAPTER 34

Gwen was home with Abby when I walked in. She leapt into my arms and wrapped her legs around me, hugging me so hard I could barely breathe. She felt wonderful.

"That's a new coat," she pointed out when she finally let me go.

"Yeah, well, OK, I'll tell you everything," I replied. "But first, here's a bunch of money."

I took the rest of the cash that Angelique had given me and dumped it on the kitchen table.

"This is going to be an interesting story," Gwen said.

I made myself a sandwich, and then we went into the parlor and sat down. Abby came with us, sitting silently by the fireplace. I admired the Christmas tree I had set up before I left. A real tree, decorated with homemade ornaments and strings of popcorn and cranberries. Real presents were now heaped up beneath it.

I recounted my adventure to Gwen and Abby.

Gwen was not happy to hear that I'd been shot at and got my face cut, of course, and she thought that New York City sounded like a horrible place, but she zeroed in on the one part of the story that made me feel guilty. "You left that woman Angelique to face her husband alone? Walter, he could kill her!"

"She was pretty, um, vehement about not needing any help."

"Well, you should have been vehement right back!"

As always, Gwen was right. "OK, sorry," I said. "But it's good to be back."

"It's good to have you back."

"What did I miss?"

"Nothing much. We're getting ready for Christmas Eve tomorrow. Mrs. Fitz is coming over. And Abby's brother got named ambassador—isn't that great? I assume that means he'll be returning to Boston soon."

"That is great," I said, although I wasn't sure how great Gwen really thought it was.

"Oh, and Ken Hendrikson had an article in the paper today. They're having some big public event up at the Church tomorrow night—christening that woman's baby."

"Huh. Christmas Eve. No one can say Brother Harold doesn't think big. How 'bout we go tell Ken this whole thing is based on a lie?"

Gwen shrugged. "Have you got any proof, Walter? Otherwise, you know how Ken will spin it: 'Disgruntled private eye Walter Sands now insists he has found Flynn Dobler, but when pressed for evidence was unable to provide any.' Ken is really invested in this story. He's convinced Stan Wolsey to let him bring a photographer up to Concord tomorrow."

"Why doesn't Ken just join the damn Church? He'd look good in a brown robe."

"It really doesn't matter, Walter. Let's just be grateful you're home."

Right again.

Stretch arrived home from work later, and I repeated my story to him. "Walter, you have just the most amazing life," he said.

"I'm very proud of my life," I replied.

Abby smiled but said nothing.

In bed that night, Gwen asked me, "Are you really proud of your life?"

"Well, sure. Mostly. Sort of."

"And you're glad to be back?"

That was an easier question. "I can't tell you how glad I am. I can only show you."

So I showed her. And afterward, when Gwen was asleep, I went up to our chilly attic and continued reading *Middlemarch*. And—I couldn't help it—I thought about Sister Marva's baby being christened on Christmas Eve. *The Holy Family*. Would Brother Harold stage it out in the Church's barn, amid oxen and lambs? I wouldn't put it past him.

It really didn't matter.

The next day I was back on duty taking care of Abby.

She had continued to make progress while I was gone. She still didn't talk, she still had difficulty maintaining eye contact, but she washed and dressed herself, she helped with the chores…she was part of the family.

In the middle of the day I heard a knock on the front door and went to answer it. Roger Fenwick was standing there, grinning at me.

"Mr. Ambassador," I said.

"Hello, Walter."

I stepped back and let him come in. Behind me, Abby was standing in the doorway to the parlor. He rushed over and embraced her.

She embraced him back.

After a few moments we went into the parlor and sat down.

"You heard about my appointment," Fenwick said.

"Yes. Congratulations."

"There's a lot to be worked out—where I'm going to live and so on. But it's great to be back in Boston."

"Abby's doing fine, as you can see. I've been out of town for a few days."

"So I understand. I was in a meeting with a fellow named Benjamin Osborne a couple of days ago, and he seemed interested in you for some reason. I'd have as little to do with him as possible, if I were you. He's got a lot of clout, but he's not a nice man."

"Yeah, I got that impression. My dealings with him are over."

"That's good. And it's good you could be home for Christmas."

"That means a lot to me," I said.

"And to me." He reached out and squeezed his sister's hand.

We talked for a while. I made lunch, and we ate at the kitchen table. It was clear that Fenwick wanted to stay with Abby, so eventually I took some of Angelique's money and went to finish my Christmas shopping at Art's Filthy Bookstore. Art greeted me cheerily and let me choose from his private stock of non-filthy books. "How is that case of yours coming?" he asked.

"Well, I solved it. But by the time I'd solved it my client had fired me. So, I dunno, kind of a split decision."

"You can't win 'em all. Merry Christmas, Walter."

"Merry Christmas, Art."

From Art's I bicycled over to Government Center to visit Natty Morgenstern. Natty was delighted to see me. "Walter, I'm just about to close up shop! How are you?"

"Doing fine, Natty. I brought you a little something."

I handed him one of my purchases. "*To Taste Temptation*—nice!" he exclaimed. "I haven't read this one, I think. They do run together a bit after a while."

"It's a Georgian, Art tells me."

"It is indeed. How was your trip to New York?"

"Enlightening."

"So, you convinced that guy to come back to Boston."

"Um, what?"

"I saw him on the list of re-entries from

yesterday. Francis Donovan—that was the name he used. Could be another Francis Donovan, I suppose, but the visa numbers match up. He was driving this time—he stopped at the Connecticut crossing."

"This was yesterday, you say?"

"Yeah. I just got the list this morning."

"Thanks, Natty. This is really interesting. Ambassador Fenwick is at my house right now. I'll be sure to put in a good word for you."

Natty beamed. "Thanks, Walter! And Merry Christmas!"

I wished him the same, and then I left the building and pondered this development as I stood by my bicycle in Government Center. Had Dobler changed his mind about talking to the *Globe*? If so, his timing was great. I realized I hadn't seen the *Globe* today. Maybe everyone knew about this except me. I found a news vendor and bought a copy. But there was no exclusive interview with Flynn Dobler, tracked down by the brilliant private investigator Walter Sands and convinced to reveal his continued existence to the world. No, there was just another breathless article by Ken Hendrikson about Sister Marva and her baby. What name will she give him? How large a crowd will show up for the event?

Huh.

I biked over to the *Globe*'s Boston office. It was deserted—except for Hendrikson, who greeted me cheerily. "I'm just heading up to the Church, Walter. It's going to be quite an evening."

"Yeah, um—"

"Do you have a statement? Anything I can quote you on?"

"Sorry, Ken. I've got nothing for you. Listen, just between you and me, and totally off the record, did Flynn Dobler show up today? Did he talk to anyone at the *Globe*?"

Hendrikson looked at me as if I'd started drinking early to celebrate Christmas. "You're kidding, right, Walter?"

"Well, you never know what might happen, Ken. This is an age of miracles."

Hendrikson shook his head. "The only miracles nowadays are up in Concord," he replied reverently. "See you, Walter."

"Bye."

So, if Dobler wasn't in New England to reveal himself to the *Globe*, what *was* he doing here? I had my suspicions.

I decided I was going to have to spend my Christmas Eve at the Church of the New Beginning.

I pedaled quickly over to South Boston. There was enough snow and ice on the ground to make riding a bicycle dangerous, but it was getting late in the day, and I was in a hurry. I pounded on the door of the warehouse, wishing I could remember the special knock that told them I was a friend.

Eventually a tiny slit in the door opened and Doctor J's eyes looked out at me. "Hey, Walter," he said. "Merry Christmas." He opened the door and I went inside.

"Merry Christmas, Doctor J." I handed him the book I had bought him at Art's: *The Origins of Consciousness in the Breakdown of the Bicameral Mind.* "Sorry I didn't have a chance to wrap it."

He took the book and studied it. "This is great, Walter. I'm really interested in the problem of consciousness."

"I figured you would be."

"Bobby and Mickey are upstairs. But Mickey's not too happy—the van's broken."

"Thanks." That was bad news. I went upstairs, ignoring Brutus's displeased growls. At the top of the stairs stood a giant cardboard Santa Claus enjoying a bottle of Coke. Santa and I were just going to have to agree to disagree about Coke.

I found Bobby and Mickey sitting in Bobby's office. There was a bottle of some kind of dark liquor on the desk between them. I handed them each a ten-dollar bill. "Merry Christmas, guys. I came into some money."

"Holy shit!" Bobby said. "You got a new coat, too. Who did you have to kill down in New York?"

"Thanks, Walter," Mickey said. "Merry Christmas."

"Have a drink," Bobby offered.

Bobby knew I didn't drink. "What's wrong with the van?" I asked.

"Needs a new battery," Mickey responded glumly. "I had a spare, but turns out the spare is dead too. Gonna hafta spend Christmas Day looking for one."

"I need a ride up to the Church of the New Beginning. Any ideas?"

"Tonight?" Bobby asked.

"Right now."

"That's nuts. Why do you need to go up there?"

"I think someone may be in danger."

Bobby considered. "I'm kind of stumped, Walter. No one wants to go anywhere on Christmas Eve."

"I could pay. This wouldn't have to be a favor."

"Even so."

"I'm really sorry, Walter," Mickey said. "I'd be happy to drive you, if I had a damn battery."

"That's OK, Mickey. I'll figure something out."

"Why don't you just stay here and have a drink with us?" Bobby asked. "It's Christmas, for fuck's sake."

"Some other Christmas, maybe," I said.

I went back downstairs, where Doctor J was already deeply engrossed in his book. "Walter, do you think that consciousness is merely an epiphenomenon?" he asked.

"I'm going to have to get back to you on that, Doctor J. Have a great Christmas."

"You too, Walter!"

Back outside, it was growing dark. I got on my bike and pondered some more. How was I going to get to the Church?

I decided to pay a visit to Chris Mull. That meant trekking on over to police headquarters, which looked mostly deserted when I finally got there. Mull had his coat on and was walking out the door as I approached. "Walter, you're back!" he said. "And you got a new coat! Did you find Dobler?"

"Actually, I did—not that he needed me. Turns out he'd already killed Brother Reggie by the time I tracked him down."

"Well, that's a success, I guess. Brother Reggie had it coming, if you ask me. Got to figure that he killed Brother Scott, then."

"Yeah, but here's the thing, Chris. I tried to persuade Dobler to tell the world he's still alive—give an interview to the *Globe* or something. That way, Brother Harold wouldn't have any reason to kill him, right?"

"Sure," Mull agreed. "It'd short-circuit all the lunacy with the shrine and everything."

"But he didn't want to do that, Chris. He said he could take care of himself. Now my friend in the immigration office tells me that Dobler's back in New England. But he didn't go to the *Globe*. I think he's heading up to the Church to kill Brother Harold. They're having a big event up there tonight for the christening of Sister Marva's son. Harold stole the Church from Dobler, Chris. Plain and simple. Harold's turning it into something completely different, with him running things from behind the scenes. Dobler doesn't want to just stop Harold; he wants to get his revenge."

Mull considered my theory. "Maybe he's still getting up his nerve to give an interview," he said. "Maybe he's going to crash the christening and show the world he's still alive."

"I don't think so. I—" And then I stopped. Something had occurred to me, and I didn't know what to make of it.

"What?" Mull asked.

"The garage," I said. "It was empty."

"Give me a hint, Walter. It's Christmas fucking Eve."

"Dobler told me he killed Brother Reggie at his house in the Hamptons. But there was only one car there—parked by the side of the house. I assumed that was Reggie's. But Dobler's garage was empty. There should have been two cars at the house, but there was only one. So where was the second car?"

"You think Dobler was lying? Why?"

"Well, I have no idea."

"Well, neither do I. What would you like me to do, Walter? Why are you here?"

"I just need a ride," I said. "I want to see this through to the end, Chris. And I think it's ending tonight up in Concord—one way or another."

Mull sighed. "Well, you're not getting a ride from me. Did I mention that it's Christmas Eve?"

"Sure, I understand. What about Pete? Could he drive me? I could pay him—I know he needs the money, what with Mary Beth's health problems and all. By the way, here's the ten dollars I borrowed from you."

"Keep your fucking money. That was a gift. Merry fucking Christmas."

"Merry fucking Christmas to you, too. So, what about Pete?"

Mull considered. "I think he's inside—his shift

just finished. If he's willing to go, he can tell the sergeant I said he could take one of the cruisers."

"You're the best, Chris."

"Just don't wreck the cruiser. And try not to get yourself killed."

"I'm always extremely careful. Give my best to the family."

"Sure. Tell Stretch and Gwen to keep you out of trouble."

I went inside and tracked down Pete Callahan, who was just changing out of his uniform. I quickly explained the situation to him. My explanation did not make him happy. Even the offer of sixty dollars for his services didn't improve his mood. "I don't want to do this, Walter," he said. "It's Christmas Eve. I need to spend it with Mary Beth."

"How about we bring Mary Beth over to my house?" I suggested. "Gwen and Stretch would love that. We'll go back there afterwards and join them. Also, I'm increasing my offer to seventy dollars. That's a lot of money, Pete."

"I really don't want to drive up to Concord, Walter. And I don't want anything to do with that crazy Church."

"You may help prevent a murder, Pete. Think about that."

Finally he gave in. "Fine," he muttered. "But that means we have to go argue with Sergeant Espinosa about the cruiser. This won't make him happy."

In fact, our request seemed to enrage him. Sergeant Espinosa was a burly guy with a face crisscrossed with scars. "It's starting to snow out!" he said. "You can't drive a Boston police cruiser up to Concord in this weather! Our cruisers suck!"

"Detective Mull said we could," I replied. "And Pete's a good driver."

"Callahan's a lousy driver. And Mull has his head up his ass!"

"Yeah, I know, but if someone gets murdered up there because you won't let us borrow a cruiser, you think he'll be happy?"

Espinosa turned to Pete. "Damn it, Callahan, bring the cruiser back in one piece, or you're the one who'll get murdered."

Pete nodded. "I'll be careful," he promised.

Espinosa turned away, too disgusted to say anything more.

"That wasn't bad," I said as we walked outside to where the cruiser was parked.

"Chris Mull scares him to death," Pete replied.

"Let's go pick up Mary Beth before he changes his mind."

Espinosa was right; a light snow had started to fall. "I hate driving in the snow," Pete muttered.

"It'll be OK. We'll get through it."

Pete just shook his head.

If possible, this police car was worse than the one I had ridden in with Pete when he arrested me. Whenever he stepped on the accelerator, the engine objected strenuously before agreeing to speed up. The windshield wipers randomly refused to wipe, and the heater was no damn good at all. But we made it to Pete's apartment over by Kenmore Square. He parked the car on the street. "Be right back," he said. "I hope she's OK with this."

"I'm sorry, Pete. It's important."

"Yeah, fine." He got out of the car and went into the apartment building. Ten minutes later he returned with Mary Beth. She was a small woman with curly brown hair, bright eyes, and a dimpled chin. She looked a bit like a doll. A very pale, very pregnant doll, wearing a coat that wasn't quite big enough to cover her belly.

I got out and let her sit in the front seat next to her husband. "Sorry about all this, Mary Beth," I said.

"That's all right, Walter," she said. "Pete explained. And I'm looking forward to seeing Gwen and Stretch." Mary Beth had a soft voice, and she never complained or criticized anyone.

"How are you feeling?"

"Oh, you know. Good days and bad. A bit tired right now."

I figured that meant she was feeling pretty horrible.

Pete drove us to Louisburg Square. There was a wreath on the door, and candles were burning in the windows. Pete and I both held onto Mary Beth as she walked across the snow-covered sidewalk and up the front steps.

Inside, Gwen's delight at seeing Mary Beth trumped her puzzlement at what was going on. She left Pete and me stranded in the front hall as she got Mary Beth settled in front of the fire next to Abby. "What a treat," she said when she returned. "Are you staying too, Pete?"

"Pete and I have to go up to the Church of the New Beginning," I said. "Sorry to spring this on you. Flynn Dobler's in town, and I think he may be out to kill Brother Harold. Or, you know, something."

Gwen's face fell. "Flynn Dobler? Are you sure?"

"Not really. Sure enough, I think."

"And you have to drive up to Concord? Tonight?"

"We'll be back as soon as we can. Maybe Pete will join us then."

"Please be careful, Walter."

"Of course."

She gave me a look, but then she hugged me, while Pete went into the parlor and kissed Mary Beth on the top of the head. "It's not your case anymore," Gwen whispered to me. "This is just you being you."

"I know," I replied. "I can't seem to help it."

Pete came back then, and we headed out to the cruiser.

"I'm not going into the Church," he said as we drove off. "That's not part of the deal. I just stay outside in the car."

"Transportation only," I agreed. "Besides, I'm probably wrong about everything that's going on. I often am, turns out. Or maybe we'll be too late—maybe what's going to happen has already happened."

Pete said nothing. We crossed the bridge into Cambridge. He drove much more slowly than

Mickey, who didn't drive that fast himself at night. On the other hand, Mickey's van was a much better vehicle than this stupid police cruiser. I thought about Angelique's car. You could get spoiled pretty quickly riding in a car like that.

"Remember the youth camps?" Pete asked suddenly.

"Of course I do."

"Remember the room we shared—in that apartment complex in Roslindale?"

"Yeah, sure. Wasn't the best time of my life."

"At least we got fed, most of the time," Pete said. "I remember you used to wake me up, sobbing into your pillow. I knew you were trying not to make any noise. I appreciated that."

Well, then. I had the same memory of Pete, sobbing into *his* pillow in the middle of the night. I didn't bother pointing that out. He had never comforted me, but then, I had never comforted him. We were both too tough; we didn't need comforting. We just needed to sob every once in a while.

The youth camps had not been a terrible idea. The Federal troops were coming into New England in force to try to put a stop to the Frenzy, and one problem they had to confront was what to do with all the orphaned kids running around, many of them attached to street gangs for protection, others being exploited and degraded and tortured by the crazies—and some, like me, just trying to survive on their own. So why not scoop them all up into government-run camps, feed them and educate them, and put them to work helping in the ongoing, mostly futile cleanup?

The problem was that, in most of those camps, the cure was as bad as the disease. The worst of them were run by sadistic psychopaths, the best of them by ineffectual do-gooders who were unable to control the young savages in their care. In all of them the food was pitiful, the medical care minimal, the education worthless, the work hard and unending.

But then there was the one that Christopher Mull ran—the one in Roslindale where Pete and I ended up. He actually wasn't formally in charge; he reported to some guy who hated the assignment and was happy to let Chris take on as much responsibility as he wanted. Chris was a local; he had been a Boston cop, so he knew the city. And he knew what the kids were going through. So he did his best to help. He couldn't improve the food, couldn't do much about the medical care, but he could teach us some stuff we really needed to know, like how to read and swim and ride a bike. He couldn't control the work assignments, but he could make sure that they didn't kill us. And sometimes he even let us have some fun.

"What made you think of the camps?" I asked Pete.

"I dunno. Seems like…we were so young. We thought life was so hard, and of course it was, but really, we had no idea."

"You worried about Mary Beth?"

"Every moment of every day, Walter."

"You annoyed by Sister Marva—how easy her pregnancy was?"

"No, of course not. I just wish—ah, fuck it. Everyone in that Church annoys me."

We were in Arlington now, just getting onto Route 2. Route 2 had a long uphill slope before we reached Concord. I wondered if we'd make it.

Damn Dobler. Why did he have to come back to New England? On Christmas Eve? "I'm sorry to take you away from Mary Beth," I said.

"It's OK. I'm all the time taking overtime shifts, doing whatever I can to make money. This is no diffcrent. Better, really. You're trying to do something good. I appreciate that." We skidded a bit. Pete tightened his grip on the wheel. "This is crazy, though," he said. "You know that, right?"

"Yeah, Pete," I said softly. "I know that."

We made it up the hill. There were a few other cars on the road, all heading for the same destination, I figured. How many miracle-starved people would read the *Globe* and decide to risk the snowy roads on Christmas Eve to catch a glimpse of Marva's baby and hear his name announced to the world? Were they hoping it would change their lives? Were they prepared to give up everything they still had from the old days and follow Flynn Dobler's teachings?

What did they have to lose?

Pete managed to speed up a bit once we had crested the hill. And then, finally, we reached the turn off the highway. I could see the brake lights of half a dozen cars in front of us on the road. It was like New York City! A disciple was directing traffic, and he gestured to us to park by the side of the road, well short of the Church's gate. Pete obeyed, then shut off the engine and turned to me. "Well," he said, "good luck doing whatever it is you're going to do."

"Thanks, Pete."

So I got out of the cruiser, and I went to do whatever it was I was going to do.

CHAPTER 35

I joined the people walking up to the gate. Men and women, old and young, all bundled up against the cold. I found myself next to a woman about Mrs. Fitz's age. She wore thick glasses and used a cane as she limped carefully through the snow.

"What do you think is going to happen tonight?" I asked.

"We'll get to see the baby, of course!" she replied, her voice quavering with excitement.

"But why does that matter? Why does the baby matter?"

"They say he'll save us from all this misery, all this suffering," the woman replied, gesturing with her cane, as if the misery and suffering were visible in the night sky. "Maybe he'll cure my arthritis."

"How?" I asked. "I mean, he's just a baby."

"Jesus was just a baby once."

"So, is this baby like Jesus?"

"Maybe. That's what people say, anyway."

The gate was open, and we hurried past, then along the path that led to the Church's main building. Cars were parked everywhere. Beyond the main building, I could see people kneeling in the snow around Brother Flynn's shrine.

I could hear singing from inside the main building. Did the Church have its own hymns now? I pushed my way through the crowd to the entrance, where Brother Willis and Brother Duane were standing guard. They recognized me. "Pretty exciting night, huh?" Brother Willis asked.

"I wouldn't have missed it for the world," I replied. "Any room left inside?"

"Just barely—standing room only. They're supposed to signal us when to shut the doors."

"When are things starting?"

"Pretty soon, I think."

"Thanks, guys." I went inside.

In the middle of the hall was a raised platform, decorated with evergreen boughs. On it were a couple of chairs and a holder for a torch. The chairs were for Marva and Joseph, I assumed. Around the platform were seated the brown- and blue-robed Church disciples. I spotted Sister Lucy in the front row, looking ecstatic.

Behind them stood the rest of humanity, crammed into every inch of space, buzzing with anticipation. Old people leaning on walkers, children perched on their fathers' shoulders, disfigured War victims who had somehow managed to survive all that had happened since.

For the old, life before the War was an ever-receding memory; for the young, it was nothing but a tale that approached myth. All of them were here looking for something: release from suffering, a reason to hope.

A narrow roped-off aisle led from the refectory to the platform. This was how the Holy Family would make its entrance, I supposed. I noticed Ken Hendrikson standing just inside the rope, behind the disciples, taking notes. Next to him the *Globe* photographer was snapping pictures of the scene.

The gallery above the hall was empty.

I looked around for Dobler. No sign of him. But I spotted Brother Harold standing in front of the refectory doors. I made my way through the crowd back towards him.

He smiled when he caught sight of me. "Walter Sands, what a pleasant surprise!"

"Did you know that Flynn Dobler is back in New England?"

He shook his head. "Walter, Brother Flynn is looking down from heaven and blessing us on this sacred night."

I remembered what Dobler had said about Harold: he was capable of being perfectly rational and perfectly irrational at the same time. Were there such people? Or rather: were we all such people? I stifled a desire to slug him.

"You may be in danger," I pointed out. "Dobler thinks you've stolen his Church. And really, you have, right? He could be coming here to kill you."

Brother Harold seemed unconcerned. "I'm just doing God's will. God has a plan for us all—Brother Flynn, me, Sister Marva—and you. There's no reason to resist it, because you can't."

"Well, maybe God has a plan, but that's no reason to be stupid about things," I persisted.

"All is well, Walter," he replied. "Watch and wonder, for the world is about to change forever."

He turned and gave a signal, and the oil lamps around the hall started to dim. The crowd fell silent. We waited in near darkness.

Finally he opened the refectory doors, and there was Sister Marva, backlit by the refectory lights, holding her baby in her arms, looking ethereally beautiful in her blue robe. The baby was wrapped in a blanket that covered all but his tiny, sleeping face.

The crowd gasped with excitement.

Marva saw the crowd, and her eyes widened. She took a step back. She turned. Brother Joseph was behind her, looking appropriately solemn. He leaned over and whispered to her, and then guided her forward, out of the refectory. Marva kissed the baby's forehead and nervously began walking through the crowd towards the platform. Joseph followed, a couple of paces behind.

Harold closed the doors behind them and took up the rear.

Hands reached out from the crowd to touch Marva's robe. The *Globe* photographer snapped away. Most people just looked on in awe. As Marva approached the platform she paused just once, when she bent down to kiss Sister Lucy on the top of the head. Sister Lucy clasped her hands afterwards and shook with joy. Then Brother Joseph held Marva's elbow as she proceeded up the three steps and took her seat on the platform. He sat to her left.

A disciple had lit a torch, which he passed to Brother Harold. Harold walked up the steps, put the torch in a holder, and stood in the shadows behind Joseph and Marva.

The hall was silent. Joseph and Marva sat there, and the silence seemed to grow, become intense—become holy. And then, at last, Marva looked hesitantly at Joseph, who nodded to her. She carefully took the blanket off the baby and handed it to Brother Joseph. The baby was wearing a long white garment. Marva smiled down at the baby and kissed it again. Harold took a step forward. Standing behind her, in a loud clear voice he proclaimed, "I give you Joshua— God is salvation!"

Everyone was looking at Marva and the baby. *I* was looking at Marva and the baby. But above, in the gallery, suddenly there was a light…

Sister Lucy rose to her feet and pointed up to the light. "He has returned!" she called out. "He has returned to bless his son! Oh, the wonder, the wonder!"

We all looked up, and there was Brother Flynn, standing in the light, wearing a white robe like Joshua's. His arms were outstretched as if in blessing. It was, I realized, the same pose he had struck when Angelique and I drove away from him in the Hamptons.

Abruptly the light in the gallery went out, and there was just the flickering torch on the stage. The crowd was pointing, shouting, pushing forward. Hendrickson scribbled furiously in his notebook. The photographer twirled around, trying to capture images of the chaos. And above us all Sister Marva sat motionless on the platform, serenely holding the baby Joshua in her arms.

CHAPTER 36

In that moment I felt the pull of the irrational. I knew that Dobler was alive. I knew that the woman he loved had left him, that he had lost control of the Church he had founded, that he was probably lonely and confused and angry….

And yet…

The lights came up. People had broken through the ropes protecting the aisle as they milled around, babbling excitedly. "Did you see him?" someone asked me. "He was hovering in mid-air!"

"I saw him!" someone else said. "I'm pretty sure he had a halo over his head—just like in old paintings!"

"But did you see little baby Joshua?" a third chimed in. "He was pointing up to his father—like he recognized him!"

I pushed through them and into the refectory. It was empty. Beyond it, the kitchen was empty as well. But it had a door, and the door was open.

I poked my head outside. Nobody there.

Now what?

Not my problem. The case was over. Whatever had happened, had happened. It was God's plan, after all.

But, dammit—was that really Flynn Dobler up in the gallery? Already my memories seemed to be getting cloudy, confused. Maybe I had imagined it all in the dim light and the confusion.

No, that wasn't it. I had gotten something wrong—maybe a lot of things. Suddenly I felt as if I were spotting glimmers of the truth shining through the clouds in my brain.

I made my way around the building to the rear staircase, near where Brother Scott had whacked me on the head, where Marva had gently tended my wound. The door was unguarded. I raced upstairs to the gallery overlooking the hall. I found the spot where Flynn Dobler had appeared. Behind it was a door. I opened it.

It was the usual small, plain room with a bed and a table. In it was the machinery behind the miracle. On the bed was a white robe. On the table were a couple of lamps. The window was open. Next to the window was a coil of rope, one end of it tied to a leg of the table. I looked out the window. Nothing.

Oh, the wonder, the wonder!

"The man you seek is not here," a voice behind me said, "but he is risen! Alleluia!"

I turned to face Brother Harold, standing in the doorway, his eyes shining behind his glasses.

"It's not you," I said. "It was never you."

"It has all been God's work," he replied. "Alleluia, alleluia!"

I pushed past him, back out into the gallery, and down the rear staircase. Underneath the open window I found footprints in the snow heading away from the building, and I followed them. They went behind the shrine, past the barn, and then off into the woods.

I stopped to catch my breath. I had an idea where the footprints were going. I made my way through the woods and along the barbed-wire fence till the fence stopped, then through more woods until I found the abandoned neighborhood I had explored after my talk with Sister Lucy so long ago.

It was still abandoned, except for a man in a blue parka, wiping the snow off the windshield of an ancient car. The car I thought had been Brother Reggie's.

"Why didn't I notice that there was only one car at your house when there should have been two— yours and Reggie's? Did he never even show up there? Or did he come on a different mission?"

Dobler turned. "Hello, Walter," he said. "You're very persistent, aren't you?"

"Aren't you going to stay and revel in the glory?" I asked. "After all, not many people return from the dead, or whatever it was you just did."

"The Church needs me to stay in heaven, I'm afraid. It's time for me to have a new adventure. I think there's another snow brush in the back seat. Want to clean off the other side?"

I did as I was told. "Was this the plan all along?" I asked. "If so—"

"I had no plan," he replied. "Harold had the plan. And he would claim that it was God's plan."

"I've heard that from him," I said. "So, did Reggie find you at the Hamptons?"

"He did. He came bearing a letter from Brother Harold. It explained a bit about what was going on up here. And it said: 'Come back if you want to become a god.'"

"Did you know what that meant?"

"I had an idea."

"And what did you tell Brother Reggie?"

"I told him I'd think about it. Angelique was married. I was bored; I was lonely. I was just sitting in my house, looking out at the ocean, reading poetry. The idea had its attraction. And then you showed up."

"But why did you shoot at me, if you didn't think Harold was trying to kill you?"

"Harold isn't stupid. The letter warned me that this was a limited-time offer. I figured my time to become a god had expired."

"Why didn't you tell me about all this? Why didn't you tell Angelique?"

"I needed to keep my options open. In case—"

"In case Angelique decided not to stay with you?"

Dobler paused in his brushing. "I suppose I knew that was a possibility, even the first moment when she was in my arms, after so many years. It always comes down to love, doesn't it? I still loved her, but she—well, she needed her security zone. And she knew I couldn't give it to her. Besides, Harold was right, you know? He understood where the Church had to go, even if I didn't. It was time to come back here and finish what I started."

"But I don't get it," I said. "How does anything change? I mean, I see how it changes things for the Church. Hundreds of people saw you back there. The *Globe* will devote the whole front page to it. It's another miracle, but this one has more than just Sister Lucy's word for it. So now you're completely extraneous, right?"

Dobler shrugged. "That's right. And that's why I'm leaving. Now it's time to do something else—far away, with a different name, in a different place."

"Won't you still be in danger?" I asked.

"Harold and I have an agreement. You know, before long, even if I do claim to be the real Flynn Dobler, no one will believe me. They'll believe Sister Lucy. They'll believe the story in the *Globe* tomorrow morning. They'll believe what they want to believe."

"I suppose," I said. "But I think you made your agreement with the wrong—"

I never did have a chance to explain to Dobler the nature of his mistake, because that's when I heard a shot and Dobler crumpled to the ground.

I hit the ground, too. Just in time, as another shot rang out, and a bullet once again destroyed a car window inches from my face. Good thing I was on the other side of the car from whoever was shooting. I got out my own gun and took a peek. Couldn't see anyone, just trees and houses, long-abandoned shells of cars, long-broken streetlights. That wasn't good. The shooter could already be circling his way around to get a clear shot at me. I took another peek, and spotted the gun's muzzle flash as another bullet took out the car's rear window.

I shot in the direction of the muzzle flash. Then I looked around. I was on the sidewalk. Behind me was a short driveway leading to a dilapidated garage next to a dilapidated house. Time to make a run for it.

I scrambled down the driveway. About twenty feet in, I slipped in the snow and fell to the ground. I staggered to my feet and kept running, expecting the next shot to put me on the ground again. I made it around to the back of the garage. I crouched down panting next to a rusted wheelbarrow. Now what? Behind me was a sagging wooden fence. Knock some of the slats out and find out what was on the other side? Keep running through this wasteland of a neighborhood? Or wait here and hope I wouldn't be found?

I saw a shadow in the back yard. I saw it move from tree to tree, coming closer to the garage. It was a human. A very large human.

It was Brother Reggie.

I took aim and fired again. Nothing happened. The trigger wouldn't move.

I had been carrying this gun through the whole damn case, and when I finally really needed the fucking thing I managed to get one fucking shot off with it before the thing fucking jammed. As Detective Mull would say.

I tried again. Nothing. Nothing worked anymore, I thought—not guns, not cars, not civilization.

Brother Reggie heard me. He saw me. His eyes glittered with hatred and triumph.

Time to run. I broke through the slats in the fence. I crawled through into the next yard. I heard a shot. I crawled through the snow. The yard was surrounded by a chain-link fence. I started to run. I tried to leap over the fence. I caught my new pants on it and crashed down on the other side. I heard another shot.

I waited.

I heard a familiar voice.

"Dammit, Walter, come back here!"

It was Pete. "Where are you?" I called out. "Did you get Brother Reggie?"

"Yeah. I saved your sorry ass."

I got to my feet. I made my way back through the broken slats, out from behind the garage, and into the first back yard. Brother Reggie lay motionless in the snow. Pete was kneeling next to him, checking his pulse. "He's dead," he said. "You're welcome."

I went back to the street and checked on Dobler. He, too, was dead.

Dobler looked, I dunno, surprised. But that was probably just me. I sat in the snow next to him. I don't like people dying.

Pete came up behind me. "I heard what sounded

like gunfire, and I figured, Walter's gotta be involved in this. Sure enough."

Sure enough. I stood up.

"You OK?" he asked.

I checked. "Probably bruised my knee a bit when I slipped in the driveway," I said. "And I ripped my new pants."

"Fuck your pants. And your knee. What's going on?"

"It's a long story. Thank you, by the way."

"Can we go home now, Walter? Don't bother telling me the story. I don't want to know the story. Killing people wasn't part of the plan."

I looked at him. He was upset. I couldn't blame him. "I know," I said. "I know. Sure, we can go home now. Except there's maybe one last thing."

"Oh, sweet Jesus."

I thought I might have to trudge all the way back to the Church for that one last thing. But no. As if summoned by my prayers, the vision appeared to us out of the trees by the side of the road, luminously beautiful in the falling snow.

"Brother Flynn is dead," I said to the vision. "Are you satisfied?"

Sister Marva inclined her head ever so slightly. "Brother Flynn is with God now."

"Brother Reggie is dead, too. Does that bother you? He worshipped you. He wouldn't obey Brother Harold, but he'd obey you. He'd do anything you said. Like go down to New York and threaten Brother Flynn."

"His reward will be in heaven," she replied.

"It all comes down to love," I said. "That's

what Dobler told me just a few minutes ago. He was in love—but not with you. And you couldn't stand that. You tried to make him jealous. Finally you even got pregnant. But Brother Scott didn't rape you, the way Dobler thought—you seduced him. Maybe after a while you even began to believe that it was Brother Flynn's baby. That's what Dobler thought. But he left you and he left the Church, and this has been your revenge."

"You know nothing of God's plan," Sister Marva murmured.

I recalled Marva sitting by herself in her room, knitting something for baby Joshua. Like Madame Defarge in *A Tale of Two Cities*, I thought, knitting the names of people who were to be killed. "Am I the next one to die?" I asked her. "After all, I could tell the world my story, and at least plant some seeds of doubt in the official version."

She smiled serenely. "Walter, you have already done so much for the Church. Truly, you have both been doing the Lord's work. If you want to tell your story—by all means, do so. And we will tell ours."

I thought about that. It had been my failure to find Dobler that lent plausibility to Sister Lucy's miracle. It had been my visit to the Hamptons with Angelique that convinced Dobler to make his final miraculous appearance at the Church. If I tried to tell my version of the truth, people would pity me or, more likely, despise me. On the other hand, Brother Harold's biography of Dobler was going to sit by everyone's bed.

Scholars would write learned treatises on it. Children would memorize it in school. Old women would clutch it for solace as they lay dying.

Or, perhaps, Harold would be the next one to go. And then there would be only Sister Marva. And her baby.

"Does it bother you that your religion won't be based on the truth?" I asked her.

Sister Marva looked puzzled. "What is 'truth,' Walter? You have yours, and I have mine. The world will judge between them."

I didn't bother arguing with her. If there was no truth, what was the point? "You better take care of those bodies back there," I said. "They died for your truth."

"My Church buries its dead," Sister Marva replied. "Thank you for everything, Walter."

And then the vision seemed to disappear in the snow and the fog, leaving Pete and me behind, standing in silence on the empty road.

CHAPTER 37

Finally we made our way back to the cruiser, which Pete had parked just off the highway.

"Sorry," I repeated when we were back on the road. It was still snowing. The driving seemed a bit worse. Pete was hunched over the steering wheel the way Angelique had been on the trip to the Hamptons.

"Sister Marva is...not what I thought," he replied.

"Yeah, I know."

We drove a bit further, and I thought about everything that had happened—the clues I had missed, the wrong conclusions I had drawn. And then I noticed that Pete's cheeks were wet. From melted snow? No, that wasn't right. He was crying—like Angelique on the way back from the Hamptons.

"Listen, Pete," I said, "it's OK about Brother Reggie. You had to kill the guy, right? You saved my life."

Pete wiped the tears off his cheeks. "Fuck Brother Reggie," he replied. "Fuck Sister Marva. Fuck 'em all."

And then, absurdly, I solved the case—at least, the one little part of this whole misadventure that had been a real case.

"You have both been doing the Lord's work," I quoted softly. "What work of the Lord have you been doing, Pete?"

Pete shook his head. "How should I know? I killed Brother Reggie. Made him a martyr, according to Sister Marva. Isn't that great?"

"But she couldn't have known you were the one who killed Brother Reggie," I pointed out. "She was too far away. It happened behind a house. No, it's something else. Brother Harold went to the Food Market with Sister Marva the morning after Brother Scott ran away. Brother Reggie had to drive me back to Boston, and he was pissed off that Harold had taken his place."

Pete looked over at me. "Yeah? So what?"

"They were worried about Brother Scott—his disappearance wasn't in the plan. They hadn't set everything up yct. Ken Hendrikson hadn't run his stories in the *Globe*. The famous private eye hadn't admitted defeat. Scott had secrets to tell. Maybe people would believe him."

"Shut up, Walter."

"Sister Marva is so understanding, so sympathetic, isn't she? The night before, she took such wonderful care of me after Scott hit me on the head with a rock. You probably talked to her about Mary Beth at some point. You probably told her how you were working extra shifts so Mary Beth could quit her job and you could afford her medicine. Maybe Marva even slipped you some money once in a while—she's that kind of woman."

Pete said nothing.

"I thought at first that Hendrikson might have killed Scott," I went on, "but that didn't really make any sense—they needed Hendrikson to be a true believer, so he could write his stories. They didn't care about you, though. So what happened, Pete? Did Brother Harold take you aside that morning and tell you about Scott and the money he stole? Did he give you the address where you could find him? That's the sort of thing that Harold would know. Did he maybe mention that Scott had raped Sister Marva? Or did Sister Marva tell you, in that way of hers that makes you want to brush the tears from her cheeks? Did Harold tell you to take whatever money you found, so long as you got rid of Brother Scott? There was no money, Pete—Dobler took the money. Scott only had the five dollars I left him because I'm a nice guy."

Tears were leaking out of Pete's eyes again. Finally he spoke. "I used to look at Sister Marva at the Food Market," he said, "so healthy, showing up every day even though she's pregnant, and of course she has her baby, and he's perfect. Why wouldn't he be? And my Mary Beth—I think she's going to die, Walter. Our money was gone, the pregnancy was difficult, and we were starting to get desperate. This guy

Scott was a creep, and he was supposed to have all this money. I really didn't intend to kill him. I went to that rooming house and found him, and there was nothing. A few dollars—like you said. So…I snapped. I snapped. And now I'm going to lose everything."

"You put those signs up at my house and Chris Mull's?"

"Yeah, I did. Trying to scare you away. I should have known better."

"You really need to learn how to punctuate, Pete."

I noticed that my knee was throbbing from where I had slipped in the snow. Fuck my knee, as Pete had said. Being a private eye is a tough business. Physically and, it seemed, ethically. Who was I to sit in judgment of Pete Callahan? Well, there was the law. There was Chris Mull, trying desperately to keep us civilized. Was turning in Pete the price we paid for civilization?

I thought of the two of us in the youth camp, afraid and lonely, sobbing at night in our beds when we thought no one could hear.

If turning in Pete was the price we paid for civilization, someone else would have to pay it. "Look," I said. "I actually can pay you more than the seventy dollars I offered you. This rich lady down in New York gave me way more than I deserved for doing something that turned out to be completely useless. You can have all of it. Also, America's new ambassador to New England is probably at my house with Mary Beth right now, and he owes me a big favor. Not to mention Governor Bolton. I'm sure that between them they can get Mary Beth the care she needs. So accept some help from your friends and kindly quit murdering people."

Pete looked at me in disbelief. "Walter, I can't, I—"

"Jesus, Pete, you just saved my worthless life. Merry Christmas. And watch the road."

"Thank you, Walter," he said, reaching out and touching my arm. "Thank you. And I'm sorry about everything."

"Me too. And kindly keep both hands on the steering wheel, for fuck's sake."

Somehow we made it safely back to Louisburg Square. Back to, you know, where all my own ladders start. Pete parked the cruiser, and we went inside. Everyone was in the parlor, singing Christmas carols while Gwen played the piano. Everyone included Stretch and Abby and Fenwick and Mrs. Fitz.

And, it turned out, Angelique Osborne, sitting timidly in the corner. She had, I noticed, a black eye.

"Welcome home," Gwen said to me when she had finished *Good King Wenceslas*.

"Great to be home."

"How was your evening?"

"Well, it was OK. Probably could have been better."

"Did you see that baby, Walter?" Mrs. Fitz asked.

"Yes, I did. It's the cutest baby ever, Mrs. Fitz."

She nodded with satisfaction. "I knew it."

I turned to Gwen. "Um, could I have a moment with, er—" I gestured to Angelique.

Gwen smiled. "Sure. We'll be here."

Pete took his coat off and sat down next to Mary Beth, who looked tired but happy. Angelique got up and followed me out to the kitchen.

"How did you find me?" I asked when we were alone.

"I went to the *Globe*'s office in Boston and asked. Everyone knew where Walter Sands lives."

"Well, hi."

"I guess going back to my husband wasn't such a great idea," she said. "He beat me up—just to teach me a lesson, you know—and when he left for work the next day I packed a bag and left. If this was my security, if this was my protection from being abandoned, I decided that I didn't want any part of it. I was pretty sure I wasn't going to be safe in New York with him there, so I thought I'd give Boston a try."

"I'm glad," I replied. "Letting you go back to that husband of yours was not the kind of thing a private eye should do. I felt awful about it."

"Gwen said it was OK if I—"

"Of course it's OK. We've got plenty of room here, although we do seem to be filling up a bit. And now I'm afraid I have some bad news." I gave her a brief report on what happened to Dobler.

She took it better than I expected. "It was

Flynn's choice, I suppose," she said. "For all his brilliance, I think he was a bit of a lost soul. He had his chance to be immortal, and he took it."

"Personally, I prefer staying alive."

Angelique smiled through her tears. "Me too."

We returned to the parlor.

Abby and Fenwick were seated next to each other on the sofa, opposite the piano. Abby smiled at me. I went over and sat down on the other side of her, while Angelique went back to her spot in the corner. Gwen played the intro to *O Little Town of Bethlehem*, and then we all started singing.

And that's when the real miracle of the evening occurred. Because, you see, we *all* started singing. Maybe I was the first to notice—I don't know. But I dropped out to listen, and then Fenwick, and then the rest of us, and finally there was just Abby, her voice cracking and off-key but clear—the first time I had heard that voice since I had known her:

> *The hopes and fears of all the years*
> *Are met in Thee tonight.*

Gwen turned around on the piano bench, tears streaming down her face. Abby looked at us shyly, nervously. She clutched my arm. Fenwick clasped her free hand in both of his.

"Merry Christmas," Abby croaked.

"Welcome home," Gwen said again.

Turn the page for an

excerpt from

REPLICA
A Techno-Thriller

Richard Bowker

It was the last day of his life, and the man in the blue nylon jacket was getting nervous.

He stood on the common, hands stuffed in his pockets. It was a little after two by the town-hall clock. He would be dead by a quarter to three.

The crowd was growing now. Lots of Norman Rockwell families: pink-cheeked grandmas, kids in snowsuits clutching balloons, strong-boned women pushing strollers. Plenty of bored, burly policemen. And the occasional gimlet-eyed man in a gray overcoat, watching.

The high school band was playing next to the temporary stage; a young woman was testing the sound system; the hot-chocolate vendors were doing terrific business. What better way to spend a Sunday afternoon?

He hadn't expected to be nervous. But everything was real now, and nothing can prepare you for the reality of death.

He had parked his car in a supermarket lot at the edge of town. It occurred to him that he could turn around, walk back to it, and drive away. Life would go on.

This struck him with the force of great insight. He had been anticipating this day for so long now that the idea of living it like any other day was strange and compelling.

Which would be harder: dying, or living with the knowledge that he had failed?

A helicopter swooped by, and then returned to hover overhead. The band played "From the Halls of Montezuma."

He remembered sitting in the bleak apartment and listening to the others spin their crazy schemes. They were dreamers; worse than dreamers, because they thought they were doing something wonderful and dangerous, when all they were really doing was wasting their lives. "You're trying to get something for nothing," he told them, "and you're not clever enough for that. If you want to do this, then you've got to be willing to risk everything—and then it becomes easy."

But they weren't willing. And he was. So he had left them behind, to end up here and take the risk.

He had been on the road for days. The distance to be traveled was hardly great, but he felt a need to disappear, to find some anonymity in the grimy motels and the self-service gas stations and the fast-food restaurants. Family, lovers, friends, work—it would be easier, he had thought, if he left them all far behind.

But here he was, and it was hard.

Distant sirens. Little boys had climbed the bare trees; infants were perched on parents' shoulders, necks craned, placards waved. Flashing lights, the roar of motorcycle engines, the cheering of the crowd…

…and there he was! Yes, look, in person— something to tell your grandchildren. Reach out and maybe he'll touch your hand!

The man in the blue nylon jacket stood in the crush and gaped like all the rest. The reality of his prey was paralyzing. The high forehead gleaming in the sunlight as if polished, the sharklike smile, the large nose red from the cold…Look, it's him!

We're both going to die.

He was on the stage now, waving. A local politician stood at the microphone and gestured for quiet. "It is my great privilege…"

Hard to breathe. The anger was returning before the man had spoken a word. How could they cheer him? Why couldn't they *see?*

Would one of the gimlet-eyed men notice that *he* wasn't cheering?

The introduction was finished; the cheers continued.

The man on the stage waited for silence, then began. Bad joke, gratitude to the crowd for coming out on such a cold January day. Then on to the substance.

"Four years ago, when I came to New Hampshire, I asked a simple question: do you think your lives are as good as those of your grandparents? As meaningful. As rich in the things that make life worth living. Now as you know, in a couple of years we will be celebrating America's two hundred and fiftieth birthday as a nation. So today I want to ask you fine people a slightly different question: do you think your lives are as good as those of the men and women who brought this great nation into existence? They had no jets to take them across the country, no robots to do their work, no nuclear weapons to wipe out their enemies. But I think you'll agree they had a better chance at happiness than many of us have today, a better chance to attain the dignity and self-respect that go with having a purpose in this life, even if the purpose is as basic as providing food for your family."

How could he say that stuff—and how could the crowd listen to it? Inoculated, anesthetized, sanitized, with twice the life-span of their ancestors and half the pain, they didn't know how good they had it. Maybe they wouldn't know until they destroyed what they had.

"For years we have been fooling ourselves that technological progress must inevitably produce happiness. But now we have come to realize that it produces merely complexity, and tension, and fear. The technologists say: machines make life easier. I say: I don't want my life easy; I want it real. The technologists say: you can't pick and choose your progress. I say: why not? I'll be happy to let them cure cancer, but I'll be damned if they'll force me to own a robot. The technologists say: you can't stand in the way of the future. I say: wanna see me?"

The crowd roared. Someone slapped him on the back. He jammed his hands deeper into his pockets. He should be past trying to understand or to argue now. He should just get ready to do what had to be done.

"And now they are going beyond even robots; they are putting robot brains into living human flesh. They call these creatures androids. I call them the work of the devil, and if I do nothing else during my second administration, I am going to see that their manufacture and sale is made illegal in this great nation."

As he watched and listened, the speaker's head seemed to grow until it filled his field of vision. He imagined it exploding, like a ripe melon dropped on concrete. He imagined the screams and the terror, the hands pointing at him, grappling with him; imagined everything as he had imagined it a hundred times before. But he had run out of time for imagining now; reality was here, ready. He had only to seize it.

He didn't move, and the speech continued.

"I know many of you have been put out of work by robots and similar machines. And in trying to get the jobs that remain, you find yourself competing with immigrants who are willing to work for pennies. Now, contrary to what my opponents are always saying, I have nothing against immigrants. When the wars of the millennium broke out, it was right and fitting that we extended our generosity to their victims. But over twenty years have passed, and we are still paying the price for our good deeds. I say:

enough is enough! Let's put a stop to immigration! Let's call a halt to the incursions of technology on the quality of our lives! Let's regain control of our nation!"

Cindy Skerritt. He hadn't thought about her in years. He wondered how she was doing. Still living in Montpelier? Still fooling around with those stupid Tarot cards? Geez, they had had some good times together. Why did they ever break up? He could be in Montpelier by nightfall.

He could turn around, walk back to his car, and drive away.

He didn't want to die.

Maybe he could kill the man and still escape. Why not? He wouldn't miss. He knew he wouldn't miss.

The common was overrun with Secret Service agents. He had even seen one with a robot scanner; they were convinced a techie was going to send out a robot to do the deed. But they couldn't be everywhere, couldn't watch everything. He just needed a little distance.

He made his way through the crowd out onto the sidewalk. It was full of cops standing next to their cycles, waiting for the motorcade to resume. He crossed the street. A few people were perched on the steps of town hall. He looked around. There was nobody by the Methodist church. He sauntered over to it and turned. He was almost directly behind the stage now, and he no longer had a clear shot.

But he wouldn't miss.

He climbed the stairs and stood in front of the

white double doors. He casually tried them. They were unlocked. He opened one a little and stepped back inside. The stage was still visible, his target still there, head bobbing slightly as he reached the climax of his oration.

His dying words.

"I truly believe that for the first time in generations we are headed in the right direction—toward an America that is more concerned with its people than with its machines, more concerned with its spiritual well-being than with its physical comfort, more concerned with life than with progress. If you will give me your help once again—"

He imagined walking through the streets, unnoticed in the turmoil, getting into his car, driving away. No one would even know he had been in town. *Montpelier by nightfall.*

And a lifetime to enjoy the memory.

He took the gun out of his pocket and lifted it into firing position. The crowd was cheering.

And the people on the stage were on their feet, applauding, surrounding the man, shaking his hand. The speech was over.

"Hey, what are you doing?"

He fired and fired and fired. Felt the arm clutching at him, heard the cheers turn to screams, saw the jumble of bodies on the stage, the pointing fingers. Then he turned and faced his attacker.

It was a minister, overweight, jowls trembling with fright. Doing his duty even though it meant he was going to die. He knew that feeling. He shrugged off the minister's feeble grip and shot him in the face.

Blood everywhere. Had to get out of here. He raced down the center aisle of the church, taking off his bloody jacket as he ran. The place smelled of furniture polish and flowers. *Had to get out.* Past the pulpit, through a door, into darkness. His knee banged into something sharp. He cursed and limped ahead. He found a knob, turned it, and saw sunlight. He forced himself to run down the stairs and along the side street. Which way to his car? If he could only get to his car, everything would be all right.

He heard sirens, squealing tires. He veered onto the sidewalk and dived into a shop.

It was a drugstore, brightly lit, antiseptic. No customers—just a pharmacist, bald, skinny, terrified. He realized he still had his gun in his hand.

The clock over the counter said quarter to three.

"Rear door," he gasped.

The pharmacist pointed past the shelves of pills. The man hurdled the counter and made his way through a storage room piled high with empty cartons. The door was bolted. He slid the bolt back and wrenched the door open. A dumpster, a car, a chain-link fence with houses beyond. He headed for the fence.

The wire ripped his pants, cut into his hands. He didn't feel it. A Doberman was running toward him. He shot it, then noticed it was on a leash. A woman stared at him from her kitchen window.

He ran.

Had to find his car. The parking lot couldn't be far. *Montpelier by nightfall.* Sirens everywhere.

Cindy, will you tell me my fortune?

His knee was on fire. Couldn't run much farther.

Just around the corner. I'm sure it's—

The first shot hit him in the shoulder as he reached the corner. The car wasn't there. All he saw was flashing blue and red. He stopped and breathed the pure cold air.

The car wasn't there.

He wanted to apologize to that woman for killing her Doberman. Reflex. Unavoidable.

The second shot hit him in the left buttock.

And a lifetime to enjoy the memory.

The third and fourth shots hit him in the spinal column and the right kneecap, respectively, and he fell to the ground. The fifth shot smashed through the rib cage and lodged in his heart.

The thing of it was, he didn't know if he had succeeded. And now he would never know.

<hr>

REPLICA

available in print and ebook

THE LAST P.I. SERIES

Dover Beach

The Distance Beacons

Where All The Ladders Start

Richard Bowker is the author of *Replica*, *Senator*, and other novels. He lives near Boston with his wife and two sons.

You can contact Richard through his website: www.richardbowker.com